THERE WERE THREE GUYS WALKING ON AIR—

all of them in old-time armor. As they started throwing thunderbolts, I headed for the safety of the manor. I hit the doorway and skidded to a halt. Something far worse than three guys in armor was tearing its way in through the roof, going at it like the place was made of paper. A big, shiny, ugly, purplish-black face like that of a fangy gorilla glared through the hole. Then it started ripping the hole bigger.

It dropped through the hole, landed at the far end of the pool room, fifty feet away. It was twelve feet tall, had six arms, and might have been a monster straight off one of those temple coins that had suddenly been appearing around town. It wavered as though I was seeing it through an intense heat shimmer. Or as if it didn't know if it wanted to be a six-armed gorilla or something even uglier.

And then my time for peaceful observing ran out, as the thing suddenly roared and charged straight for me. . . .

COLD COPPER TEARS

Glen Cook

A SIGNET BOOK

NEW AMERICAN LIBRARY

SIGNET, SIGNET CLASSIC, MENTOR, ONYX, PLUME,
MERIDIAN and NAL BOOKS are published by NAL PEN-
GUIN INC., 1633 Broadway, New York, New York 10019

First Printing, October, 1988

3 4 5 6 7 8 9

PRINTED IN THE UNITED STATES OF AMERICA

1

Maybe it was time. I was restless. We were getting on toward the dog days, when my body gets terminally lazy but my nerves shriek that it's time to do something—a cruel combination. So far sloth was ahead by a nose.

I'm Garrett—low thirties, six-feet-two, two hundred pounds, ginger hair, ex-Marine—all-around fun guy. For a price I'll find things or get the boogies off your back. I'm no genius. I get the job done by being too stubborn to quit. My favorite sport is female and my favorite food is beer. I work out of the house I own on Macunado Street, halfway between the Hill and waterfront in TunFaire's midtown.

I was sharing a liquid lunch with my friend Playmate, talking religion, when a visitor wakened my sporting nature.

She was blonde and tall with skin like the finest satin I'd ever seen. She wore a hint of unusual scent and a smile that said she saw through everything and Garrett was one big piece of crystal. She looked scared but she wasn't spooked.

"I think I'm in love," I told Playmate as old Dean showed her into my coffin of an office.

"Third time this week." He drained his mug. "Don't mention it to Tinnie." He stood up. And stood up. And stood up. He's nine feet tall. "Some of us got to work." He waltzed with Dean and the blonde, trying to get to the hall.

"Later." We'd had a good time snickering about the scandals sweeping TunFaire's religion industry. Playmate had considered a flyer in that racket once but

I had managed to collect a debt owed him, and the cash had kept him alive in the stable business.

I looked at the blonde. She looked at me. I liked what I saw. She had mixed feelings. The horses don't shy when I pass, but over the years I've been pounded around enough for my face to develop a certain amount of character.

She kept smiling that secret smile. It made me want to look over my shoulder to see what was gaining on me.

Dean avoided my eye and did a fast fade, pretending he had to make sure Playmate didn't forget to close the front door behind him. Dean wasn't supposed to let anybody in. They might want me to work. The blonde must have charmed his socks off.

"I'm Garrett. Sit." She wouldn't have to work to charm the wardrobe off me. She had that something that goes beyond beauty, beyond style—an aura, a presence. She was the kind of woman who leaves eunuchs weeping and priests cursing their vows.

She planted herself in Playmate's chair but didn't offer a name. The impact was wearing off. I began to see the chill behind the gorgeous mask. I wondered if anybody was home.

"Tea? Brandy? Miss? . . . Or Dean might find a spot of TunFaire Gold if we sweet-talk him."

"You don't remember me, do you?"

"No. Should I?"

The man who could forget her was already dead. But I left the remark unspoken. A chill had dropped over me, and the chill had no sense of humor.

"It's been a while, Garrett. Last time I saw you I was nine and you were going off to the Marines."

My memory for nines isn't what it is for twenties. No bells rang, though that was more years ago than I want to remember; I've tried to forget the five in the Marines ever since.

"We lived next door, third floor. I had a crush on you. You hardly noticed me. I'd have died if you did."

"Sorry."

She shrugged. "My name is Jill Craight."

She looked like a Jill, complete with amber eyes that

ought to smolder but looked out of arctic wastes instead. But she wasn't any Jill I ever knew, nine years old or not.

Any other Jill, and I would have come back with a suggestion about making up for lost time. But the cold over there was getting to me. My restraint will get me a pat on the head next time I go to confession. If I ever go. Last time was when *I* was about nine. "You got over me while I was gone. I didn't see you on the pier when I came home."

I'd made up my mind about her. She had stoked the fire to get past Dean, but it was out now. She was a user. It was time she stopped decorating that chair and distracting its owner from his lunch. "You didn't just drop by to talk about the old days on Peach Street."

"Pyme Street," she corrected. "I may be in trouble. I may need help."

"People who come here usually do." Something told me not to shove her out the door yet. I looked her over again. That was no chore.

She wasn't a flashy dresser. Her clothes were conservative but costly, tailored with an eye to wear. That implied money but didn't guarantee it. In my part of town some people wear their whole estate. "Tell me about it."

"Our place burned when I was twelve." That should have rung a bell, but didn't till later. "My parents were killed. I tried staying with an uncle. We didn't get along. I ran away. The streets aren't kind to a girl without a family."

They aren't. That would be when the iceberg formed. Nothing would touch her, or get close to her, or hurt her, ever again. But what did yesterday have to do with why she was here today?

People come to me because they feel disaster breathing down their necks. Maybe just getting through the door makes them feel safe. Maybe they don't want to go back out again. Whatever the reason, they stall, talking about anything but what's bothering them. "I imagine."

"I was lucky. I had looks and half a brain. I used

them to make connections. Things worked out. These days I'm an actress."

That could mean anything or nothing, a catchall behind which women pursue uncomfortable ways of keeping body and soul together.

I grunted encouragement. Garrett is nothing if not encouraging.

Dean peeked in to make sure I hadn't gone rabid. I tapped my mug. "More lunch." It looked like a long siege.

"I've made some important friends, Mr. Garrett. They like me because I know how to listen and I know how to keep my mouth shut."

I had a notion she was the kind of actress who gives the same service as a street girl but gets paid better because she smiles and sighs while she's working.

We do what we have to do. I know some good people in that line. Not many, but some. There aren't that many good people in any line.

Dean brought my beer and a whistle-wetter for my guest. He'd been eavesdropping and had begun to suspect he'd made a mistake. She turned on the heat when she thanked him. He went out glowing. I took a drink and said, "So what are we sneaking up on here?"

The glaciers reformed behind her eyes. "One of my friends left me with something for safekeeping. It was a small casket." She made hand gestures indicating a box a foot deep, as wide, and eighteen inches long. "I have no idea what's in it. I don't want to know. Now he's disappeared. And since I've had that casket there have been three attempts to break into my apartment." Bam. Like a candle snuffed, she stopped. She had said something she shouldn't have. She had to think before she went on.

I smelled a herd of rats. "Got any idea what you want?"

"Someone is watching me. I want it stopped. I don't have to put up with that kind of thing anymore." There was some passion there, some heat, but all for some other guy.

"Then you think it could happen again. You think

somebody's after that casket? Or could they be after you?''

What she thought was that she shouldn't have mentioned the casket. She ran it around inside her head before she said, ''Either one.''

''And you want me to stop it?''

She gave me a regal nod. The snow queen was back in charge. ''Do you know what it's like to come home and find out that someone's been tearing through your stuff?''

A minute ago they were just trying to get in.

''A little like you've been raped, only it doesn't hurt as much when you sit down,'' I replied. ''Give me a retainer. Tell me where you live. I'll see what I can do.''

She handed me a small coin purse while she told me how to find her place. It was only six blocks away. I looked in the purse. I don't think my eyes bugged, but she had that little smile on again when I looked up.

She'd decided she could run me around like a trained mutt.

She got up. ''Thank you.'' She headed for the front door. I got up and stumbled over myself trying to get there to see her out, but Dean had been lying in ambush to make sure he got the honors. I left him to them.

2

Dean shut the door. He faced it for a moment before he turned to face me, wearing a foolish look.

I asked, "You fall in love? At your age?" He knew I wasn't looking for clients. He was supposed to discourage them at the door. And this sweet ice with the tall tales and long legs and nonsense problem and sack of gold that was ten times what a retainer ought to be looked like a client I especially didn't want. "That one is trouble on the hoof."

"I'm sorry, Mr. Garrett." He gave me feeble excuses that only proved a man is never too old.

"Dean, go to Mr. Pigotta's. Tell him he's invited to supper. You'll be fixing his favorites if he gets balky." Pokey Pigotta never turned down a free meal in his life. I gave Dean my best glower, which struck him like rain off a turtle.

You just can't get good help.

I retired to my desk to think.

Life was good.

I'd had a couple of rough ones recently and I'd not only gotten out alive, but also managed to turn a fat profit. I didn't owe anybody. I didn't need to work. I've always thought it sensible not to work if you're not hungry. You don't see wild animals working when they're not hungry, so why not just fiddle around and put away a few beers and worry about getting ready for winter when winter comes?

My trouble was that word was out that Garrett could handle the tough ones. Lately every fool with an imaginary twitch has been knocking on my door. And when they look like Jill Craight and know how to turn on the heat, they have no trouble getting past my first line of defense. My second line is more feeble than my first. That's me. And I'm a born sucker.

I've been poor and I've been poorer, and the practical side of me has learned one truth: money runs out. No matter how well I did yesterday, the money will run out tomorrow.

What do you do when you don't want to work and you don't want to go hungry? When you were born you didn't have the sense to pick rich parents.

Some guys become priests.

Me, I'm trying to get into subcontracting, the wave of the future.

When they get past Dean and they fish me with their tales of woe, I figure I ought to be able to give the work to somebody else and scrape twenty percent off the top. That should keep the wolf away for a while, save me exercise, and put some money in the hands of my friends.

For tail and trace jobs I could call on Pokey Pigotta. He's good at that. For bodyguard stuff there was Saucerhead Tharpe, half the size of a mammoth and twice as stubborn. If something hairy turned up I could yell for Morley Dotes. Morley is a bonebreaker and lifetaker.

This Craight thing smelled. Damn it, it reeked! Why give me that business about being a neighbor when she was a kid? Why drop it at the first sign I doubted her? Why back off so fast on the high heat and shift to the ice maiden?

There was one answer I didn't like at all.

She might be a psycho.

People who get into a fix where they think I'm their only out are unpredictable. Add weird. But when you've been at the game awhile you think you get a feel for types.

Jill Craight didn't fit.

For a second I wondered if that wasn't because she *was* an actress who had done her homework and had decided to grab my curiosities with both hands. I can be had that way sometimes.

The clever, cutesy ones are the worst.

I could go two ways here: lie back and forget Jill

Craight until I gave her to Pokey, or walk across the hall and consult my live-in charity case.

That woman had given me the jimjams. I was restless. The Dead Man it was, then. After all, he's a self-proclaimed genius.

They call him the Dead Man. He's dead, but he's not a man. He's a Loghyr, and somebody stuck him with a knife about four hundred years ago. He weighs almost five hundred pounds, and his four-century fast hasn't helped him lose an ounce.

Loghyr flesh dies as easily as yours or mine, but the Loghyr spirit is more reluctant. It can hang around for a thousand years, hoping for a cure, getting more ill-tempered by the minute. If Loghyr flesh corrupts it may do so faster than granite, but not much.

My dead Loghyr's hobby is sleeping. He's so dedicated he'll do nothing else for months.

He's supposed to earn his keep by applying his genius to my cases. He does, sometimes, but he has a deeper philosophical aversion to gainful employment than I do. He'll bust his butt to shirk the smallest chore. Sometimes I wonder why I bother.

He was asleep when I dropped in—much to my chagrin, but little to my surprise. He'd been at it for three weeks, taking up the biggest room in the house.

"Hey, Old Bones! Wake up! I need the benefit of your lightning intelligence." The best way to get anything out of him is to appeal to his vanity. But the first task is waking him, and the second is getting him to pay attention.

He wasn't having any today.

"That's all right," I told the mountain of cheesy flesh. "I love you despite yourself."

The place was a mess. Dean hates cleaning the Dead Man's room, and I hadn't kept after him so he'd let it slide.

If I didn't watch it the bugs and mice got in. They liked to snack on the Dead Man. He could handle them when he was awake, but he wouldn't stay awake anymore.

He was ugly enough on his own, without getting eaten.

I puttered around, sweeping and dusting and stomping, singing a medley of bawdy hymns I learned in the Marines. He didn't wake up, the stubborn hunk of lard.

If he wasn't going to play, neither was I. I packed it up. I reloaded my mug with beer and went out to the stoop to watch the endless and ever-changing panorama of TunFaire life.

Macunado Street was busy. People and dwarfs and elves hurried to arcane destinations, to clandestine rendezvous. A troll couple strolled past, kids so infatuated they had eyes for nothing but one another's warts and carbuncles. Ogres and leprechauns hastened to assignations. More dwarfs scurried by, dependably industrious. A fairy messenger more beautiful than my recent visitor cussed like a sailor as she battled a stubborn head wind. A brownie youth gang, chukos, way off their turf, played whistle past the graveyard, probably praying the local Travellers would not come out. A giant, obviously an up-country rube, gawked at everything. He had fantastic peripheral vision. He almost batted the head off a pixie who tried to pick his pocket.

I saw half-breeds of every sort. TunFaire is a cosmopolitan, sometimes tolerant, always venturesome city. For those with that turn of mind, it's interesting to speculate on the mechanics of how some of their parents managed to conceive them. If you're of a scientific mind and want to take your data from direct observation, you can visit the Tenderloin. They'll show you anything down there as long as you come across with the money.

My street was always a carnival, like TunFaire itself. But it's all darkness grinning behind a party mask.

TunFaire and I have a ferocious love-hate relationship that comes of us both being too damned stubborn to change.

3

When they built Pokey Pigotta they used only leftover angles and extralong parts, then forgot to give him a coat of paint. He was so pallid that, after dark, people sometimes took him for one of the undead. He had no meat on him and his gangly limbs were everywhere, but he was tough and smart and one of the best at what he did. And he had an appetite like a whale-shark. Whenever we have him over he eats everything but the woodwork. Maybe it's the only time he gets to eat real cooking.

Dean is good for that. Sometimes I claim it's the only reason I keep him on. Sometimes I believe what I say.

We hadn't had a strange face in for a while, which spurred Dean to one of his better efforts. That and the fact that Pokey can lay it on with a shovel when he wants and Dean is addicted to everybody's flattery but mine.

Pokey leaned back and patted his stomach, drenched Dean with a bucket of bullhooly, belched, and looked at me. "So let's have it, Garrett."

I lifted an eyebrow. It's one of my best tricks. I'm working on my ear-wiggling. I know the ladies will love that.

"You took on a client you want to farm out," Pokey went on without waiting. "Good-looking woman with style, I'd guess, or she wouldn't have gotten past Dean. And if she had, you wouldn't have listened to her."

Had he been listening at the keyhole? "Regular deductive genius isn't he, Dean?"

"If you say so, sir."

"I don't. He was probably hanging around trying to beg crumbs from our castoffs." I told Pokey the story. All I left out was the size of the retainer. He didn't need to know that.

"Sounds like she's running a game," Pokey agreed. "You said Jill Craight?"

"That's the name she gave. You know it?"

"Seems like I should. Can't put a finger on why." He used his pinkie to scratch the inside of his ear. "Couldn't have been important."

Dean produced a peach cobbler, something he'd never do without company present. It was hot. He buried it in whipped cream. Then he served tea. Pokey went to work like he wanted to store up fat for the next ice age.

Afterwards we leaned back, and Pokey lighted one of those savage little black stink sticks he favors, then went to catching me up on the news. I hadn't been out of the house for days. Dean hadn't kept me posted. He hoped silence would drive me out. He never says so but he worries when I'm not working.

"The big news is Glory Mooncalled did it again."

"What now?" Glory Mooncalled and the war in the Cantard are special interests around my house. When he's awake the Dead Man makes a hobby of trying to predict the unpredictable, the mercenary Mooncalled.

"He ambushed Firelord Sedge at Rapistan Sands. Ever heard of it?"

"No." That was no surprise. Glory Mooncalled was operating farther into the Venageti Cantard than any Karentine before him. "He took Sedge out?" It was a safe guess; his ambushes had yet to fail.

"Thoroughly. How many left on his list?"

"Not many. Maybe three." Mooncalled had begun his war on the Venageti side. The Venageti War Council had managed to tick him off so bad he'd come over to Karenta vowing to collect their heads. He'd been picking them off ever since.

He's become a folk hero for us ordinary slobs and a big pain in the patoot for the ruling class, though he's winning their war. His easy victories have shown them to be the incompetents we've always known they are.

Pokey said, "What happens when he's done and all of a sudden we don't have a war for the first time since before any of us were born?"

The Dead Man had an answer. I didn't think it would go over with Pokey. I changed the subject. "What's the latest on the temple scandals?" Playmate had tried to give me the scoop but his heart hadn't been in it. The scandals weren't the circus for him they were for me. His religious side was embarrassed by the antics of our self-annointed spiritual shepherds.

"Nothing new. Plenty of finger-pointing. Lot of 'I was framed.' On the retail level it's still at the swinging-drunks-in the-tavern stage."

For now. It would turn grim if Prester Legate Warden Agire and his Terrell Relics didn't turn up.

Agire was one of the top ten priests of the squabbling family of sects we lump together as Orthodox. His title Prester indicated his standing in the hierarchy, at about the level of a duke. Legate was an imperial appointment, supposedly plenipotentiary, in reality powerless. The imperial court persists and postures at Costain but has had no power for two hundred years. It survives as a useful political fiction. Warden is the title that matters. It means he's the one man in the world entrusted with guardianship of the Terrell Relics.

Agire and the Relics had disappeared.

I don't know what the Relics are. Maybe nobody but the Warden does anymore. He's the only one who ever sees them. Whatever, they're holy and precious not only to the Orthodox factions but to the Church, the Eremitics, the Scottites, the Canonics, the Cynics, the Ascetics, the Renunciates, and several Hanite creeds for whom Terrell is only a minor prophet or even an emissary of the archenemy. The bottom line is that they're important to almost all the thousand and one cults with followings in TunFaire.

Agire and the Relics had vanished. Everyone assumed the worst. But something was wrong. Nobody claimed responsibility. Nobody crowed over having gotten hold of the Relics. That baffled everybody. Possession of the Relics is a clear claim for the favor of the gods.

In the meantime, the whispering war of revelation had intensified. Priests of various rites had begun whittling away at rivals by betraying their venalities, corruptions, and sins. It had begun as border-incident stuff, little priests excoriating one another for drunkenness, for selling indulgences, for letting their hands roam during the confessional.

The fun had spread like fire in a tenement block. Now a day was incomplete without its disclosure about this or that bishop or prester or whatnot having fathered a child on his sister, having poisoned his predecessor, or having embezzled a fortune to buy his male mistress a forty-eight-room cabin in the country.

Most of the stories were true. There was so much real dirt, fabrication wasn't necessary—which satisfied my cynical side right down to its bunions. Reputations were getting reaped in windrows, and it couldn't happen to a nicer bunch of guys.

Pokey was bored by the whole business. If he had a weakness it was his narrowness. His work was his life. He could talk technique or case histories forever. Otherwise, only food held his attention.

I wondered what he did with his money. He lived in a scruffy one-room walk-up although he worked all the time, sometimes on several projects at once. When clients didn't find him, he went looking. He even went after things—deadly things—just to satisfy his own curiosity.

Whatever, he didn't feel like yakking up old news. His belly was full. I'd tantalized him with a wicked aroma. He wanted to get hunting.

I helped him puff Dean's ego, then walked him to the door. I sat down on the stoop to watch him out of sight.

4

The descending sun played arsonist among high, distant clouds. There was a light breeze. The temperature was perfect. It was a time to just lean back and feel content. Not many of those times fell my way.

I yelled for beer, then settled in to watch Nature redecorate the ceiling of the world. I didn't pay attention to the street. The little man was there on the stoop, making himself at home, passing me the big copper bucket of beer he'd brought, before I noticed him.

Up to no good? What else? But the beer was Weider's best lager. I don't get it that often.

He was a teeny dink, all wrinkled and gray, with a cant to his eyes and a yellow of tooth that suggested a big dollop of nonhuman blood. I didn't know him. That was all right. There are a lot of people I don't know, but I wondered if he was one of the ones I wanted to keep on not knowing.

"Thanks. Good beer."

"Mr. Weider said you'd appreciate it."

I'd done a job for Weider, rooting out an in-house theft ring without getting his guilty children too dirty. To discourage a relapse the old man kept me on retainer. I wander around the brewery when I have nothing better to do. I make people nervous there. Considering what he'd been losing, I'm cheap insurance. The retainer isn't much.

"He tell you to see me?"

The dink took the bucket back, sipped like an expert. "I'm unfamiliar with many facets of the secular world, Mr. Garrett. Mr. Weider is face-to-face with it every day. He said you were the man I need. Provided, as he put it, I can pry you off your dead ass."

That sounded like Weider. "He's more achievement oriented than I am." And how. He started out with nothing; now he's TunFaire's biggest brewer and has fingers in twenty other pies.

"So I gather."

We passed the bucket back and forth.

He said, "I looked you over. You seem perfect for my needs. But the factors that make you right make it hard to recruit you. I have no way to appeal to you."

It was a mellow evening. I was too lazy to move. I had nothing else on my mind but a couple of oddballs down the way who were dead ringers for a couple of oddballs who were hanging around last time I came out. "You bought the beer, friend. Speak your piece."

"I'd expected that courtesy. Trouble is, once I tell you the cat will be out of the bag."

"I don't gossip about business. That's bad for business."

"Mr. Weider did praise your discretion."

"He's got reason."

We went back and forth with the beer. The sun ambled on. The little guy held a conference with himself to see if his trouble was really that bad.

It was worse, probably. Usually they're going down for the third time when they ask for help—and then they want to sneak up on it like a virgin.

"My name is Magnus Peridont."

I didn't wilt. I didn't gasp or faint. He was disappointed. I said, "Magnus? Nobody in real life is named Magnus. That's a handle they stick on some guy who's been dead so long everybody's forgotten what a horse's ass he was."

"You've never heard of me?"

It was one of those names you ought to know. It had turned up on a loo wall somewhere, or something. "Doesn't ring any bells."

"My father thought I was destined for greatness. I'm sure I was a disappointment. I'm also known as Magister Peridont and Peridontu, Altodeoria Princeps."

"I hear a distant campanile." A Magister is that rarest of all fabulous beasts, a sorcerer sanctioned by the Church. The other title was a relic of antiquity. It meant something like he was a Prince of the City of God. There was a bunk in heaven with his name on it, guaranteed. The bosses of the Church had made him a saint before he croaked.

A thousand years ago that would have made his a dyed-in-the-wool, hair-shirt-wearing, pillar-sitting holy man. These days it probably meant he scared the crap out of everybody and they wanted to buy him off with baubles.

I asked, "Would Grand Inquisitor and Malevechea fit in there somewhere?"

"I have been called those things."

"I'm getting a fix on you." *That* Peridont was one scary son-of-a-bitch. Luckily, we live in a world where the Church is always one gasp short of being a dead issue. It claims maybe ten percent of Karenta's human population and none of the nonhuman. It says only humans have souls and other races are just clever animals capable of aping human speech and manners. That makes the Church real popular with the clever animals.

"You're dismayed," he said.

"Not exactly. Say I have philosophical problems with some of the Church's tenets." Elvish civilization antedates ours by millenia. "I didn't know Mr. Weider was a member."

"Not in good standing. Call him lapsed. He was born to the faith. He spoke to me as a favor to his wife. She's one of our lay sisters."

I remembered her, a fat old woman with a mustache, always in black, with a face like she had a mouth full of lemons. "I see."

Now that I knew who he was, we were on equal ground. Now he needed leading around to the point. "You're out of uniform."

"I'm not making an official representation."

"Under the table? Or personal?"

"Some of both. With permission."

Permission? Him? I waited.

"My reputation is greatly exaggerated, Mr. Garrett. I've encouraged that for its psychological impact."

I grunted and waited. He didn't look old enough to have done all the evil laid at his doorstep.

He said, "Are you aware of the tribulations besetting our Orthodox cousins?"

"I haven't been so entertained since my mother took me to the circus."

"You've put a finger on the crux, Mr. Garrett. The mess has become a popular entertainment. There are no heretics more deserving of Hano's justice than the Orthodox. But no one views these events as a scourging. And that fills me with dread."

"Uhm?"

"Already the rabble have begun to step forward with revelations just to keep the pot boiling. I fear the day when the Orthodox vein plays out and they seek new lodes."

Ah. "You think the church might be next?" That wouldn't break my heart.

"Possibly. Despite my vigilance, some will stumble into sin. But no, my concern isn't for the Church, it's for Faith itself. Every revelation slashes Belief with a brutal razor. Already some who never questioned have begun to wonder if all religion isn't just a shell game perpetrated by societies of con men who milk the gullible."

He looked me in the eye and smiled, then passed the beer. That could have been a quote. And he knew it. He had done his homework.

"You have my attention." I suddenly knew how Pokey felt when he took a job just to satisfy his own curiosity.

He smiled again. "I'm convinced there's more here than a scandal gone brushfire. This is being orchestrated. There's a malign force bent on savaging Faith. I think a rock needs to be lifted and that social scorpion revealed."

"Interesting and interestinger. I'm surprised by your secular way of stating it."

He smiled again. The Grand Inquisitor was a happy runt. "The diabolical provenance of the attack is beyond question. What interests me are the identities, resources, goals, and whatnot of the Adversary's mundane adjuncts. All that can be defined in secular terms, like a street robbery.''

And a robbery could, no doubt, be defined in sectarian cant.

The runt seemed awfully reasonable for a supposed raving fanatic. I guess the first talent a priest develops is acting ability. "So you want to hire me to root out the jokers putting the wood to the Orthodox priesthoods.''

"Not exactly. Though I have hopes that their unmasking will be a by-product.''

"You just zigged when I zagged.''

"Subtlety and credibility, Mr. Garrett. If I hire you to find conspirators and you unearth them, even I couldn't be completely sure you hadn't cooked the evidence. On the other hand, if I hire a known skeptic to search for Warden Agire and the Terrell Relics and in the course of the hunt he kicks some villains out of the weeds. . . .''

I took a long drink of his beer. "I admire your thinking.''

"You'll take it on, then?''

"No. I can't see getting in a mess just for money. But you know how to pique a guy's curiosity. And you know how to scheme a scheme.''

"I'm prepared to pay well. With an outstanding bonus for recovery of the Relics.''

"I'll bet.''

The Great Schism between Orthodoxy and its main offshoot happened a thousand years ago. The Ecumenical Council of Pyme tried to patch things up. The marriage didn't last. The Orthodox snatched the Relics in the settlement. The Church has been trying to snatch them back ever since.

"I won't press you, Mr. Garrett. You were the best man for the job, but for that reason the least likely to take it. I have other options. Thank you for your time. Have a nice evening. Should you have a change of heart, contact me at the Chattaree.'' He and his bucket marched off into the dusk.

I was impressed with the little guy. He could be a

gentleman when he wanted. You don't see that much in people accustomed to power. And he was one of the most feared men in TunFaire, within his sphere. A holy terror.

5

Dean stepped outside. "I've finished up, Mr. Garrett. I'll be going home if there's nothing else."

He always talks like that when he wants something. Right now he hoped I'd have that something else. He lives with a platoon of spinster nieces who make him crazy.

One of the legacies of the war in the Cantard is a surplus of women. For decades Karenta's youth have gone south to capture the silver mines and for decades half of them haven't come back. It makes it nice for us unattached survivor types, but hell on parents with daughters to support.

"I was sitting here thinking it would be a nice evening for a walk."

"That it would be, Mr. Garrett." When the Dead Man is sleeping somebody always stays in to bolt the door and wait for whoever is out. When the Dead Man is awake we have no security problems.

"You think it's too early to see Tinnie?" Tinnie Tate and I have a tempestuous friendship. She's the one they had in mind when they set the specs for redhead stereotypes, only they toned them down because nobody would believe the truth.

You might call Tinnie changeable. One week I can't run her off with a stick, the next I'm tops on her hate list. I haven't figured out the whys and wherefores.

I was listed this week. Past the peak and dropping but still in the top ten.

"It's too early."

I thought so, too.

Dean is in a bind where Tinnie is concerned. He likes her. She's beautiful, smart, quick, more square with the world than I'll ever be. He thinks she's good for me. (I don't dare risk his opinion on the flip-flop issue.) But he has all those nieces in desperate need of husbands and half a dozen have standards low enough to covet a prince like me, squeaky armor and all.

"I could go see how the girls are."

He brightened, checked to see if I was teasing, and was set to call my bluff when he realized that would put me there while he was here, unable to defend their supposed virtues. He imagined me in there like a bull shoulder-deep in clover, like they couldn't possibly have sense enough to look out for themselves. "I wouldn't recommend that, Mr. Garrett. They've been especially troublesome lately."

It was all a matter of perspective. They hadn't troubled me. When I first took Dean on, they did. They kept me up to my ears in cookery, trying to fatten me up for the kill.

"Perhaps I should just go, Mr. Garrett. Perhaps you should wait another day or two, then go apologize to Miss Tate."

"I got no philosophical problem with apologizing, Dean, but I like to know why I'm doing it."

He chuckled, pulled on the mantle of worldly-wise old warrior passing his wisdom along. "Apologize for being a man. That always works."

He had a point. Except I have a flair for getting sarcastic.

"I'll just stroll over to Morley's, quaff me a few celery tonics."

Dean pruned up. His opinion of Morley Dotes is so low it has to look up at snakes' bellies.

We all have rogues in our circles, maybe just so we can tell ourselves, "What a good boy am I."

Actually, I like Morley. Despite himself. He takes some getting used to but he's all right, in his way. I just keep reminding myself that he's part dark elf and has different values. Sometimes, very different values. Always malleable values. Everything is situational for Morley.

"I won't be out long," I promised. "I just need to work off some restlessness."

Dean grinned. He figured I was getting bored with loafing and we'd see some excitement pretty soon.

I hoped not.

6

It isn't a long walk to Morley's place, but it is a walk over the border into another world. The neighborhood hasn't acquired a name like so many others, but it is a distinct region. Maybe call it the Safety Zone. Members of all species mix there without much friction—though humans have to put in overtime to be acceptable.

There was a little light still in the air. The clouds out west hadn't quite burned out. It wasn't yet time for the predators to hit the streets. I was no more than normally wary.

But when the kid stepped into my path I knew I had trouble. Big trouble. It was something about the way he moved.

I didn't think. I reacted.

I gave him a high kick he wasn't expecting. My toe snapped in under his chin. I felt a bone break. He squealed and ran backwards, arms flapping as he tried to keep his balance. A hitching post jumped in his way and gored him from behind. He spun around and went down, losing his knife as he fell.

I slid toward the nearest building.

Another came at me from what had been behind. He was an odd one, kid-sized but clad in a cast-off army work uniform. He was an albino. He had a nasty big knife. He stopped eight feet away, awaiting reinforcements.

There were at least three more, two across the street and one back up the way, standing lookout.

I took off my belt and snapped it at the albino's eyes. That didn't scare him but did give me time to frisk the building.

The buildings around there were a week short of falling down. I had no trouble finding a loose, broken brick. I pulled it out and let fly. I guessed right and he ducked into it. I got him square in the forehead, then jumped him while his knees were watery, took his knife, grabbed him by the hair, and flung him toward the two coming across the street. They dodged. He sprawled.

I screeched like a banshee. That stopped the two. I feinted left, right, came back to fake a cut at the knife hand of the guy with the blade I'd taken, then snapped my belt at his eyes. He saved himself by jumping back.

He fell over the albino. I shrieked again and flung myself through the air. It never hurts to have them think you're crazy. I landed with both knees on the guy's chest, heard ribs crack. He squealed. I bounced away as the other came at me.

He stopped when he saw I was ready. I sidestepped and kicked the albino in the head. That's me, Fairplay Garrett. At least I was going to get out alive. I looked around. Broken Jaw had taken a hike, leaving his knife. The lookout had opted for discretion.

"Just you and me now, Shorty." He was no kid. None of them were, really. I should have seen it sooner. Kids that size aren't out roaming the streets of TunFaire, they're in the army. They keep taking them younger and younger.

They were dark-elf breeds, half elf, half human, outcasts from both tribes. The mix is volatile: amoral, asocial, unpredictable, sometimes crazy. Bad.

Like Morley, who'd managed to live long enough to learn to fake it.

My short friend wasn't impressed by the fact that he was alone against somebody bigger. That's another problem with darko breeds. Some don't have sense enough to be scared.

I went back for my brick.

He shifted stance, held his knife like it was a two-handed sword. I teased him with the belt and tried to guess what he'd do when I let the brick fly. He was deciding to come at me when I did.

I went around and head-kicked the others to make sure they stayed down.

That got Shorty pissed. He came. I threw the brick. He dodged. But I hadn't gone for the head or body. I'd gone for the foot I'd hoped he'd push off from. The part of him that would be last to move.

I got his toes. He yelped. I went in after him, belt, knife and feet.

He held me off.

Hell, we could dance all night. I'd done what I needed to do. How fast could he chase me on a bad foot?

I looked at the two guys down and heard my Marine sergeants: "You don't leave a live enemy behind you."

No doubt cutting their throats would have been a boon to civilization. But that wasn't my style.

I collected dropped knives.

Shorty figured I was going to pull out. "Next time you're dead."

"Better not be a next time, chuko. Because I don't give second chances."

He laughed.

One of us was crazy.

I went away with a chill between my shoulders. What the hell was all that? They hadn't been out to rob me. They'd been out to bust me up. Or kill me.

Why? I didn't know them.

There are people who don't have much use for me, but I couldn't think of any who would go that far. Not all of a sudden, now. It was lightning out of a clear blue sky.

7

It never fails. When I step through the doorway into Morley's place, the joint goes dead and everybody stares. They ought to be used to me by now. But I have this reputation for thinking I'm on the side of the angels and a lot of those guys are anything but.

I saw Saucerhead Tharpe at his usual table, so I headed that way. He was alone and had a spare chair.

Before the noise level rose, a voice said, "I'll be damned! Garrett!" Whip crack with the name.

What do you know? Morley himself was working the bar, helping dispense the carrot, celery, and turnip juice. I'd never seen that before. I wondered if he watered their drinks after they'd had three or four.

Dotes jerked his head toward the stairs. I said, "How you doing?" to Saucerhead and sailed on by. He grunted and went on massacring a salad big enough to founder three ponies. But he was the size of three ponies and their mothers, too.

Morley hit the stairs behind me. "Office?" I asked. "Yes."

I went up and in. "Things have changed." It looked less like the waiting room in a bordello, maybe because the inevitable lovely was absent. Morley, relaxing at home, always had something handy.

"I'm trying to change myself by changing my environment." That was Morley sounding like Morley the vegetarian crackpot and devotee of obscure gurus. "What the hell are you up to, Garrett?" That was Morley the thug.

"Hey! How come the ice? I get antsy and walk down here to maybe tip a rhubarb brew with Saucerhead and I—"

"Right. You just decide to show up looking like the losing mutt at a dogfight." He shoved me in front of a mirror.

The left side of my face was pancaked with blood. "Hell! I thought I ducked." The short guy had gotten me while we were dancing, somehow. I still didn't feel the cut. Some sharp knife.

"What happened?"

"Some of your crazy cousins jumped me. Chukos." I showed him the three knives. They were identical, with eight-inch blades and yellowed ivory grips into which small black stylized bats had been inset.

"Custom," he said.

"Custom," I agreed.

He picked up the speaking tube connecting with his barmen. "Send me Puddle and Slade. And invite Tharpe if he's interested." He smothered the tube, looked at me. "What are you into now, Garrett?"

"Nothing. I'm on vacation. Why? You looking for another chance to kite me and get out from under your gambling debts?" I realized it was the wrong thing to say before I finished saying it. Morley was worried. When Morley Dotes worries about me it's time to shut my yap and listen.

"Maybe I deserve that." His cohorts Puddle and Slade came in. Puddle I'd met before. He was a big, sloppy fat guy with flesh sagging in gross rolls. He was as strong as a mammoth, smart as a rock, cruel as a cat, quick as a cobra, and completely loyal to Morley. Slade was new. He could have been Morley's brother. Short by human standards, he had the same slim, darkly handsome looks, was graceful in motion, and was totally self-confident. He, like Morley, was a flashy dresser, though Morley had toned it down considerably tonight.

Morley said, "I've managed not to put a bet down for a month, Garrett. With my willpower and a little help from my friends."

Morley had a bad problem with gambling. Twice he's used me to get out from under debts of lethal scale, which has been a cause of friction.

Morley's vegetarian bar and restaurant and thug

hangout is more hobby and cover than career. What he really does is bust kneecaps and break heads, free-lance. Which is why he has his Puddles and Slades around.

Saucerhead came in. He nodded to everybody and dropped into a chair. It creaked. He didn't say anything. He doesn't talk much.

Saucerhead's line splits the difference between mine and Morley's. He'll pound somebody for a fee but he won't kill for money. He does mostly bodyguard and escort work. If he's really short he'll do collections. But never assassinations.

"Right, then," Morley said, with the players in place. "Garrett, you've saved me a trip. I was going to drop by your place after we closed."

"Why?" They looked at me like I was a freak-show exhibit instead of a broken-down, self-employed ex-Marine.

"You sure you don't have something going?"

"Nothing. Come on. What gives?"

"Sadler dropped by. He had a message for the trade from the kingpin." The kingpin is Chodo Contague, emperor of TunFaire's underworld. He is a very bad man. Sadler is one of his lieutenants and a worse man. "Someone wants your head, Garrett. The kingpin is putting out word that whoever tries for it will answer to him."

"Come on, Morley."

"Sure. He's as drifty as a fairy girl on weed. He's obsessed with honor and favors and debts and bal-ances. He thinks he owes you big and he's by damned going to keep you alive to collect. If I was you I'd never do it, so I'd always have him behind me like my own pet banshee."

I didn't want a guardian angel. "That's only good for as long as he stays alive." Kingpins have a way of dying almost as frequently as Karenta's kings.

"Gives you a vested interest in his health, don't it?"

"One hand washes the other," Saucerhead rumbled. "You really don't got nothing shaking?"

"Nothing. Zero. Zip. I've only had two prospects

in the last ten days. I turned them both down. I'm not working. I don't want to work. It's too much like work. I'm perfectly happy just sitting around watching everybody else work.''

Morley and Saucerhead made faces. Morley worked as much as he could because he thought it was good for him. Saucerhead worked all the time because he had to feed his huge body.

Morley asked, "What about those prospects?"

"Good-looking blonde this afternoon. Probably a class hooker. Had somebody harassing her and wanted it stopped. I gave it to Pokey Pigotta. Just before I came down here, an old guy who wanted me to find something he thought was lost. Now he's looking for somebody else."

Morley frowned. He looked at the others and found no inspiration there. He picked up the three chuko knives, handed one to Puddle, one to Slade, and tossed the other to Saucerhead, who said, "Chuko knife."

Morley said, "Garrett had an encounter on his way down here. We don't usually see gangs in the neighborhood. They know better. Tell us about it, Garrett."

My feelings were hurt. Nobody was impressed by the fact that I'd taken away three knives.

I told it all.

Saucerhead said, "I gotta remember that brick-on-the-toes trick."

Morley looked at Puddle. Puddle said, "Snowball."

Morley nodded. "That's the albino, Garrett. A total crazy. Boss of a gang called the Vampires. He halfway thinks he's a vampire. The one you left standing sounds like Doc, the brains of the gang. He's crazier than Snowball. Won't back down from anything. And him a bleeder. I hope you had sense enough to finish it while you could."

He looked at me and knew I hadn't.

"They're crazies, Garrett. A big gang. As long as Snowball is alive they'll keep coming. You embarrassed him." He got out pen, ink, paper, and started writing. "Puddle. Take two men and see if there's still anyone around out there."

"Sure, boss." A real genius, Puddle. I wondered who tied his shoes.

Morley scribbled. "The Vampires were way off their turf, Garrett. They come from North Reservoir Hill. Priam Street. West Bacon. Around there."

I understood. They hadn't come south on a lark. I hadn't been a target of opportunity.

I got that chill between my shoulders again.

Morley sanded what he'd written, folded it, dashed something on the outside, then handed it to Slade. Slade looked at it, nodded, and walked out. Morley said, "If I was you, Garrett, I'd go home and bar my doors and sit tight with the Dead Man."

"Probably a good idea."

We both knew I wouldn't. What if word got around that Garrett could be pushed?

Morley said, "I don't keep up with street gangs. There're too many of them. But the Vampires have been making a name. Getting ambitious. Snowball wants to be top chuko, captain of captains . . . Excuse me."

His speaking tube was making noises. He picked it up. "I'm listening." He held it to his ear. Then, "Send him up." He looked at me. "You leave a broad trail. Pokey Pigotta is here looking for you."

8

Pokey wandered in looking like a living skeleton. Morley said, "Plant yourself, Pokey," and gave him that look he gives when he's planning a new diet for someone. Part of Morley believes there's no problem that can't be solved by upping your intake of green leafies and fiber. He was certain we could achieve peace in our time if we could just get everybody to stop eating red meat.

I asked, "You looking for me?"

"Yes. I have to give you your money back. I can't do the job."

Pokey refusing work? "How come?"

"Got a better offer to do something that's more interesting, and I can't handle both jobs. You want to farm it out to Saucerhead? I'll give you what I got. For nothing."

"You're a prince. You doing anything, Saucerhead?" He wasn't the best man for the job but what could I do? Pokey had set me up.

"Give me the skinny," Saucerhead said. "I ain't buying no pig in a poke." He was suspicious because Pokey wanted out.

I gave him what I'd given Pokey, word for word.

Pokey gave me my retainer, said, "I cased the area but didn't make contact with the principal. The building is being watched, front and rear, by nonprofessionals. I assume the principal is their target, though the building contains nine other apartments. There's a caretaker who lives in the basement. The tenants are all single women. The watchers left when it got dark. They went to the Blue Bottle, where they share a third-floor room as Smith and Smith. Once it was apparent they were off duty and were not going to be replaced, I went home. I found my new client waiting."

Pokey described Smith and Smith, who sounded like your basic nondescript working stiffs.

"I can handle it, Garrett," Saucerhead said. "If you don't want to keep it for yourself."

I handed him the retainer. "Take care of the woman."

Pokey said, "That takes care of my business. I'd better go. I want to get an early start."

Morley grunted a farewell. He *was* changing. He ached to give Pokey some wholesome dietary advice, for his own good, but he bit his tongue.

What the hell? The world wouldn't be half as interesting if Morley changed that much.

When just the two of us were left, he looked at me. "You're *really* not into anything?"

"Promise. Cross my heart."

"I never saw anyone like you, Garrett. I don't know anybody else who could have chukos come all the way from the North End to whack him for taking a walk."

That bothered me, too. It looked like I'd have to go to work whether I liked it or not. And it would be a double not. I make a lousy client. "Maybe they heard where I was headed."

"What?"

"They might have gotten carried away by compassion for my stomach."

"Stuff it, Garrett. I don't need the aggravation."

"Testy, eh? Maybe cold turkey on everything isn't the way to go."

"Maybe not."

Puddle lurched in before we got going good. "Nothing but blood spots, Morley."

"Didn't think there would be. Thanks for going." Morley looked at me. "When are you going to learn? Now Snowball has his ego tied up in it."

"Maybe if I'd known who he was and his reputation—"

"Crap! That hasn't got anything to do with giving him a second chance. You going to ask for references? Even Snowball probably has a mother who loves him.

That won't keep him from setting your balls on fire if he gets the chance. I'm amazed that you've stayed alive as long as you have.''

He had a point. The world sure as hell doesn't care about one man's moral parameters. But I have to live with myself, too. "Might be because I have friends who look out for me. Come on downstairs. My treat."

"I'll pass. Buy yourself one. Carrot juice. Carrots are good for your eyes. You could stand to be a little more clear-sighted. Eat some fish, too. It's supposed to be brain food.''

9

I got a drink, but I did it after I got home, after I sent Dean off and got the place locked up. I drew a pitcher off the keg in the cold well, took it to the office, put my feet up and tried to brainstorm.

I had a tempest in a beer mug.

I came up with no angles at all.

I considered a connection with Jill Craight's visit. I considered one with the holy terror. If the connection was there, nothing betrayed it.

In any case, Snowball's bunch would have started from the North End before Peridont reached my place.

I reflected on old cases, trying to recall individuals who might be vindictive enough to want me smoked. There could be some out there, but I couldn't come up with any names.

What if Snowball had simply picked the wrong target? Suppose he was after somebody else?

Pure reason liked that hypothesis. Intuition screamed, "Bullshit!"

Somebody wanted me dead. And I didn't have a notion why, let alone who.

Maybe the Dead Man could spot a fact I'd overlooked. I wandered across the hall. No good. He was out of it. I worked off some nervous energy cleaning, then went back to the office to settle down and think it all through again.

I was still there when Dean pounded on the door in the morning. I was so stiff it was a task getting down the hall to the door. Morley wasn't all wrong when he talked about me abusing myself. I'm not seventeen anymore. The body won't stay in tune by itself. I pinched a few pounds of muscle that had drifted south. I needed to get more selective about my loafing.

I would start exercising first thing tomorrow. I didn't feel up to it today. My schedule was full, anyway.

I went upstairs and napped in a real bed while Dean started in the kitchen. He woke me when he had breakfast ready.

"You sure you're all right?" he asked when he brought my hotcakes. I hadn't told him much. "You look like hell."

"Thanks. You're one of Nature's great beauties yourself." I knew what he meant. But I have to ride him or he thinks I don't appreciate him. "You should've seen the other guys."

"I expect it's just as well I didn't." Someone rapped at the door. "I'll get it."

I grunted around a mouthful of hotcakes smothered in blueberry preserves.

Our visitor was Jill Craight. Dean brought her into the kitchen. Remarkable. She really had him whammied.

She didn't have as much impact this morning. She hadn't fixed herself up for it. She looked like she'd had a bad night. And she was spoiling for a fight.

"Good morning, Miss Craight. Won't you join me?"

She sat. She took tea when Dean offered it but declined anything more substantial. She had fire in her eyes. Too bad it wasn't for me. "I had a visit from a man named Waldo Tharpe."

"Saucerhead? Good man. Though sometimes his manners lack polish."

"His manners were adequate. He told me he was supposed to find out who was giving me trouble. He told me you sent him."

"I did. Anybody ever tell you you're beautiful when you're mad?"

"Men tell me I'm beautiful whatever my mood. It's bullshit. Why did you send that man? I hired you."

"You brought me a situation you didn't like. I sent somebody to take care of it. Where's your problem?"

"I hired you."

"And only I will do?"

She nodded.

"That's great for the ego, but—"

"I didn't pay for some second-rate unknown."

"Interesting. Considering Saucerhead is probably better known than I am." I looked her hard in the eye for a dozen seconds, until she shifted her attention to Dean. "I wonder what your real game is," I said softly.

She jerked her attention back to me.

"First you tried to con me. Then you gave me way too much money. If you wanted to buy a man to impress somebody, anybody who knows me will know Saucerhead. And be more intimidated by him. I'm a pussycat. Finally, and dearest to my heart, not five hours after you saw me, somebody tried to kill me."

Her eyes got big. I had to remind myself she'd said she was an actress.

"It was a cold-blooded ambush, Jill. Five men, plus whoever did the watching and running messages. A major effort."

Her eyes got bigger.

"You know an albino half-breed chuko called Snowball?"

She shook her head. It was a very impressive head. She was beautiful when she was frightened.

"How about a street gang called the Vampires?"

She shook her pretty head.

I had obviously recovered from my unpleasant night, because I was starting to pant. I slapped myself down. "What *do* you know? Anything? How about why you want to play me for a sucker. Or has that slipped your mind, too?"

She got mad again. But she swallowed her anger. She'd decided to clam.

I got up. "Come with me." Sometimes a good surprise loosens them up.

I took her into the Dead Man's room. Her response was cliché. "Yuk! That's gross!" But that was it.

I fished her retainer out from under the Dead Man's chair, which is the safest place in TunFaire. "I'll hang onto some of this, for Saucerhead's time and my aggravation." I took a couple coins in a gesture mainly symbolic, and handed the rest to her.

She eyed that purse like it was a snake. "What are you doing?"

"You're unhappy. I'm giving your money back and getting out of your life."

"But . . ." She went into a huddle with herself. While the committee was in conference I sneered at the Dead Man. Brought one right in here with you, Chuckles.

I was trying to get two birds with one big hunk of alum.

There's no prod more effective than bringing a woman into the house. The prettier the gal the more heated the reaction. Jill Craight could set the house afire. If he was sandbagging he wouldn't be able to keep it up.

Damn him. He didn't do a thing. And I'd been half-way sure he was hiding out from the rent collector.

"Mr. Garrett?"

"Yeah?"

"I'm scared. I made a promise. I can't tell you any more till I know who I have to be afraid of. Take this back. I want you. But if you can't do the job I'll take what I can get."

She *was* scared. If she'd been five feet tall and baby-faced, my protective instincts would have been inflamed. But she was damned near tall enough to look me in the eye and had no knack for playing helpless. You looked at her and you wanted to get into mischief with her, but you didn't have much inclination to take care of her. You knew she could take care of herself.

"If it wasn't for last night I'd give in about now, Jill. But somebody tried to whack me. Finding out who and why and talking him out of trying again is going to occupy my time. So Saucerhead is what you get."

"If I must, I must."

"You must." I put her retainer back under the Dead Man. "Now that we're done yelling at each other and we're all friends again, why don't you come by for dinner? Dean's culinary skills don't get much exercise.''

She opened her mouth to turn me down, but inclination ran head-on into her instinct for self-preservation.

She didn't have to be nice to me. That wasn't a condition here. But I'm not so nice a guy I wouldn't let her find that out for herself. ''It would have to be late,'' she said. ''I do have to work.''

''Pick your time. Tell Dean. Give him an idea what you'd like. It'll be better than anything you've had for a while.''

She smiled. ''All right.'' I think that was the first genuine smile she'd shown me. She marched off to the kitchen.

I paused, leaned against the door frame, and sneered at the Dead Man. I had my ulterior motives for wining and dining Jill Craight—beyond those I'd been born with. She still might stir old Chuckles up. I'm also a great believer in synchronicity.

It was a lead-pipe cinch that, because I'd made a date, Tinnie would suffer a miraculous remission from the sulks. Somebody from the Tate place would come to let me know before Jill went home.

Jill came back. ''Dean is a nice man.''

Was the implication that I was not? ''Tricky, too. You got to watch him. Especially if you're not married. A great ambassador for the institution of marriage, Dean is.''

''But he's not married himself.''

A quick vixen, friend Jill. How much had she pried out of him? ''Not married and never has been. But that doesn't slow him down. Come on. I'll walk you home.''

''You sure you can spare the time?''

''It's on my way,'' I lied. I figured I could use a chat with Saucerhead.

10

Tharpe fell in on Jill's far side before we'd walked a hundred yards. She was startled. I chuckled. "Get used to it."

That didn't excite her. It was one more hint that things were going on that she didn't want known.

I still had her pegged for a working girl, if a class model of same.

"Anything interesting going on?" I asked Saucerhead.

"Nope."

"Smith and Smith watching the place again?"

"Yeah. Pokey was right. They're amateurs. They look like a couple of farmers. Want me to grab one and tie him in knots till he talks?"

"Not yet. Just keep an eye on them. See who they report to."

Saucerhead grunted. "There's somebody watching your place, too. I spotted them while I was waiting."

I wasn't surprised. "Chukos?"

He shrugged. "Could be. They was young. But they wasn't showing colors."

"They wouldn't be if they were Vampires." I live in Travellers' territory, just inside their frontier with the Sisters of Doom.

We walked on. As we approached Jill's place I tried to talk us inside for a look around. She wouldn't have it. In fact, she didn't want to be seen with us in her own neighborhood. She probably thought we'd lower property values.

Saucerhead and I wandered around so I could get a look at Smith and Smith. They did look like farmers. They certainly didn't look dangerous, but I didn't spend much time worrying about them. That was Saucerhead's job.

I jogged a block out of my way going home, stopping at a tenement so decayed derelicts shunned it. I went around the side, down to a cellar door. Standing a foot deep in trash, I knocked. The door almost collapsed.

It opened an inch. An eye looked at me from brisket level. "Garrett," I said. "I want to talk to Maya." I flashed a piece of silver. The door shut.

Now a little game, a stall just to show me who ran things here.

The door opened. A girl of thirteen wearing nothing but a potato sack—probably stolen with the potatoes still inside—and a lot of dirt stood there. The sack was so frayed one ripening rosebud peeked out. She caught my glance and sneered.

"Love your hair, kid." It might have been blonde. Who could tell? It hadn't been washed in recent generations.

From inside I heard, "Cut the comedy, Garrett. You want to talk to me get your butt in here."

I stepped into the citadel of the Sisters of Doom, TunFaire's only all-human, all-female street gang.

There were five girls there, the oldest sneaking up on eighteen. Four of the five shared the urchin's hairdresser and tailor. Maya wore real clothing and was better groomed, but not much. She was eighteen going on forty, war chief of a gang claiming two hundred "soldiers." She was so emotionally sliced up you never knew which way she would jump.

Most of the Sisters were emotional casualties. They'd all suffered severe abuse, and a murmur of defiance had driven them into the Doom's never-never land. That hung, precariously and eternally, at right angles to reality, between childhood as it should have been and the adulthood of the untormented. They'd never recover from their wounds. Most of the girls would die of them. But the Doom gave them a fortress into which they could retreat and from which they could strike back, which left them better off than the tortured thousands who went through the hell without support.

Maya had suffered more than most. I met her when she was nine, when her stepfather offered to share her if I'd buy him some wine. I'd declined to the crackle of his breaking bones.

She was a lot better now. She was normal most of the time. She could talk to me. Sometimes she came to the house to cadge a meal. She liked Dean. Old Dean was every girl's ideal uncle.

"Well, Garrett? What the hell you want?" She had an audience. "Let's see the color of your money."

I tossed her a coin. "Faith offering," I told her. "I want to swap information."

"Come ahead. I'll tell you to go to hell when you get on my nerves."

If she took a fit, I could go out looking like chopped meat. Those girls could be vicious. Castration was a favorite sport.

"You know the Vampires? Run by an albino darko called Snowball and a crazy bleeder named Doc? North End."

"I've heard of them. They're all crazy, not just Doc. I don't know them. Word is, Doc and Snowball are getting ambitious, trying to rent muscle and recruit soldiers from other gangs."

"Somebody might take exception."

"I know. Snowball and Doc are too old for the street but not old enough to know they can't trespass."

It's a classic cycle. And sometimes the young ones pull it off. About once a century.

Today's kingpin was a street kid. But that organization recruited him from a gang and promoted him from within.

"The Doom have any relationship with the Vampires?" The girls prefer being called the Doom. They think it has a nicer ring than the Sisters or the Sisterhood.

"All take and no give, Garrett. I don't like that."

"If you're running with the Vampires I don't have anything to give you."

She gave me the fish eye.

"Snowball and Doc tried to take me out," I said.

"What the hell were you doing in the North End?"

"I wasn't, sweetie. I was on Warhawks' turf. War-hawks have a treaty with the Vampires?"

"No need. No contact. Same with the Doom." She shifted. "You're sneaking up on something, Garrett. Get to the point."

"There are a couple guys watching my house. I'd guess chukos. Probably Vampires, considering last night."

She thought about that. "A genuine hit? You're sure?"

"I'm sure, Maya."

"Your place is on Travellers' ground."

"You're starting to get it. Trouble is, I don't have any friends with the Travellers since Mick and Slick got caught in the sweep."

The relationships between the races have become terribly complex, them being all mixed together but each owning its own princes and chiefs and quirky root cultures. TunFaire is a human city. Human law prevails in all civil matters. A plethora of treaties have established that entering a city voluntarily constitutes acceptance of the prevailing law. In TunFaire a crime in human law remains a crime when committed by anyone else, even when the behavior is acceptable among the perpetrator's people.

Treaties deny Karenta the power to conscript persons of nonhuman blood, nonhuman being defined as anybody of quarter blood or more who wants to revoke his human rights and privileges forever. Lately, though, the press gangs had been grabbing anybody who couldn't produce a parent or grandparent on the spot. That's what happened to the captains of the Travellers, though they were breeds.

Maya said, "So you want a couple of chukos off your back."

"No. I want you to know they're there. If they bother me I'll just knock their heads together."

She looked at me hard.

Maya has a byzantine mind. Whatever she does she has a motive behind her surface motive. She isn't yet wise enough to know that not everyone thinks that way.

"There're a couple of farmer types staying at the Blue Bottle, using the names Smith and Smith. If somebody was to run a Murphy on them and it was to turn out that they had documents, I'd be interested in buying them." That was spur of the moment but would satisfy Maya's need for a hidden motive.

It couldn't be that I just wanted to see how she was doing. That would mean somebody cared. She couldn't handle that.

I paused at the door. "Dean says he's whomping up something special for supper. And a lot of it." Then I got out.

I hit the street and stopped to count my limbs. They were all there, but they were shaky. Maybe they have more sense than my head does. They know every time I go in there I run the chance of becoming fish bait.

11

Dean was waiting to open the door. He looked rattled.
"What happened?"

"That man Crask came."

Oh. Crask was a professional killer. "What did he
want? What did he say?"

"He didn't say anything. He doesn't have to."

He doesn't. Crask radiates menace like a skunk radiates a bad smell.

"He brought this."

Dean gave me a piece of heavy paper folded into an
envelope. It was a quarter-inch thick. I bounced it on
my hand. "Something metal. Draw me a pitcher." As
he headed for the kitchen I told him, "Maya might
turn up tonight. See that she eats something and slip
her a bar of soap. Don't let her steal anything you're
going to miss."

I went into the office, sat, placed Crask's envelope
on the desk, my name facing me, and left it alone until
Dean brought that golden draft from the fountain of
youth. He poured me a mug. I drained it.

He poured again and said, "You're going to get
more than you bargained for if you keep trying to do
something for those kids."

"They need a friend in the grown-up world, Dean.
They need to see there's somebody decent out there,
that the world isn't all shadow-eat-shadow and the
prizes go to the guys who're the hardest and nastiest."

He faked surprise. "It isn't that way?"

"Not yet. Not completely. A few of us are trying
to fight a rearguard action by doing a good deed here
and there."

He gave me one of his rare sincere smiles and headed for the kitchen.

Maya would eat better than Jill and I if she bothered to show.

Dean approved of my efforts. He just wanted to remind me that my most likely reward would be a broken head and a broken heart.

I wasn't going to get into heaven or hell letting Crask's present lie there. I broke the kingpin's wax seal.

Someone had wrapped two pieces of card stock tied together with string. I cut the string. Inside I found a tuft of colorless hair and four coins. The coins were glued to one card. One coin was gold, one was copper, and two were silver. They were of identical size, about half an inch in diameter, and looked alike except for the metal. Three were shiny new. One of the silver pieces was so worn its designs were barely perceptible. All four were temple coinage.

Old style characters, a language not Karentine, a date not Royal, apparent religious symbology, lack of the King's bust on the obverse, were all giveaways. Crown coinage always shows the King and brags on him. Commercial coinage shouts the wonders of the coiner's goods or services.

Karentine law lets anyone coin money. Every other kingdom makes minting a state monopoly because seigniorage—the difference between the intrinsic metal value of a coin and its monetary value—is a profit that accrues to the state. The Karentine Crown, though, gets its cuts. It requires private minters to buy their planchets, or blanks, from the Royal Mint, costs payable in fine metal of a weight equal to that of the alloy planchets. There's more state profit in not having to make dies and pay workmen to do the striking.

The system works most of the time and when it doesn't, people get roasted alive, even if they're Princes of the Church or officials of the Mint who are cousins of the King. The foundation of Karentine prosperity is the reliability of Karenta's coinage. Karenta is corrupt to the bone but will permit no tampering with the instrument of corruption.

I gave the gold piece the most attention. I'd never seen private gold. It was too expensive just to puff an organizational ego.

I picked up the top piece of card stock and read the terse note, "See the man," followed by a fish symbol, a bear symbol, and a street name that constituted an address. Few people can read so they figure out where they are by reference to commonly understood symbols.

Crask wanted me to see somebody. This provocative little package was supposed to provide useful hints.

If Crask was dishing out hints, that meant Chodo Contague was serving up suggestions. Crask didn't take a deep breath without Chodo telling him. I decided to check it out. There was no point getting Chodo miffed.

The address would be way up north. Of course. I needed a long hike.

I didn't have anything going until Jill arrived. And I'd been telling myself I needed exercise.

North End, eh?

I went upstairs and rummaged through my tool locker, selected brass knucks, a couple of knives, and my favorite eighteen-inch, lead-weighted head-knocker. I tucked everything out of sight, then went down and told Dean I'd be out for a few hours.

12

Most of us are in worse physical shape than we like to think, let alone admit. I'm used to that being more the other guy's problem than mine. But by the time I covered the six miles to the North End, I felt it in my calves and the fronts of my thighs. This was the body that had carried me through weeks of full-pack marches when I was a Marine?

It wasn't. This body was older and it had been beaten up and banged around more than its share since.

The neighborhood was elfin and elfin-breed, which means it was tidy and orderly in an obsessive fashion. This was a neighborhood where elvish wives whitened stonework with acids and reddened brickwork with dyes once a week. When it rained the gutters ran with color. Here the men tended trees as though they were minor deities and trimmed their tiny patches of lawn with scissors, one blade of grass at a time. You had to wonder if their private lives were as ordered and passionless and sterile.

How had this environment, with its rigid rectitude, produced Snowball and the Vampires?

I turned into Black Cross Lane, a narrow two-blocker in the shadow of Reservoir Hill. I looked for the fish and bear and stray Vampires.

It was quiet. Way too quiet. Elvish women should have been out sweeping the streets or walks or doing something to stave off the entropy devouring the rest of the city. Worse, the silence smelled like an old one, in place because something unimaginably awful had happened and the street remained paralyzed by shock. My advent had not caused it. Even in this neighborhood there would have been folks getting out of the way if I was headed into an ambush.

I have such comforting thoughts.

I found the place, a four-story gray tenement in fine repair. The front door stood open. I went up the stoop. The silence within was deeper than that which haunted the street.

This was the heart of it, the headwater from which the treacle of dread flowed.

What was I supposed to do?

Do what I do, I guessed. Snoop.

I stepped inside figuring I'd work my way to the top floor. I didn't need to. The first apartment door stood open a crack. I knocked. Nobody answered but I heard a thud inside. I gave the door a push. "Yo! Anybody home?"

Frantic thumping sounded from another room. I proceeded with extreme caution. Others had been there before me. The room had been stripped by locusts.

There was a smell in the air, faint yet, but one you never mistake. I knew what I'd find in the next room.

It was worse than I thought it could be.

There were five of them, expertly tied into wooden chairs. One had tipped himself over. He was doing the thumping, trying to attract attention. The others would attract nothing but flies ever again.

Someone had placed a loop of copper wire, attached to a stick, around each of their necks, then had twisted the loops tight. The killers had taken their time.

I recognized everybody—Snowball, Doc, the other two who had tried to whack me. The live one was the kid who had stood lookout. They were efficient that way, Crask and Sadler.

It was a little gift for Garrett from Chodo Contague, an interest installment on his debt. The vig, against the day I called in the nut.

What do you think at a moment like that, surrounded by people snuffed as casually as you would stomp a roach, without anger, malice, or remorse? It's scary because it's death without fire behind it, as impersonal as accidental drowning.

Squish! Game's over.

The wire loop is Sadler's signature.

I could see Slade giving Sadler the message Morley had written. I could see Sadler telling Chodo. I could see Chodo getting so worked up he might adjust the blanket covering his lap. "So take care of it," Chodo might say, like he'd say, "Throw out that fish that's starting to smell." And Sadler would take care of it. And Crask would bring me a few coins and a lock of a dead man's hair.

That was death in the big city.

Did Doc and Snowball and the others have anyone to mourn them?

I was getting nowhere standing around feeling sorry for guys who'd had it coming. Crask wouldn't have made a trip across town if he hadn't thought I'd find something interesting here.

I guessed I'd get it from the one they'd left alive.

I sat him up facing the wall. I hadn't let him see me yet. I walked around and leaned against the wall, looked him in the eye.

He remembered me.

I said, "Been your lucky day so far, hasn't it?" He'd survived Crask and Sadler and those opportunists who had taken everything that wasn't nailed down. I waited until his eyes told me he knew his luck had run out. Then I abandoned him.

I scrounged around until I found a water jug in a second-floor apartment. The locusts hadn't gone that high, fearing they'd get cut off. I checked the street before going back to my man. It was still quiet out there.

I showed the chuko the jug. "Water. Thought you might be dry."

He wasted a little moisture on tears.

I cut his gag off, gave him a sip, then backed off to prop up the wall. "I think you have things to tell me. Tell me right, tell me straight, tell me everything, maybe I'll let you go. They make sure you heard everything during the interviews?" Clever euphemism, Garrett.

He nodded. He was about as terrified as he could get.

"Start at the beginning."

His idea of the beginning antedated mine. He started with Snowball taking over the building by dumping his human mother in the street. She had inherited it from his father, whose family had owned it since the first elvish migrated to TunFaire. The entire neighborhood had been elvish for generations, which was why it was in such good shape.

"I'm more interested in the part of history where the Vampires got interested in me."

"Can I have another drink?"

"As soon as you've earned it."

He sighed. "A man came yesterday morning. A priest. Said his name was Brother Jercé. He wanted Snow to do some work. He was a front guy, like, you know? He wouldn't say who sent him. But he brought enough money so Snow's eyes bugged and he said the Vampires would do whatever he wanted. Even when Doc tried to talk him out of it. He never went against Doc's advice before. And look what that got him."

"Yeah, look." I knew what it got him. I wanted to know what he did to get it.

The priest wanted the Vampires to keep tabs on me and a priest called Magister Peridont. If Peridont came to see me, the Vampires were supposed to make me disappear. Permanently. For which they would get a fat bonus.

Snowball took it because it made him feel big-time. He didn't care that much about the money. He wanted to be more than a prince of the streets.

"Doc kept trying to tell him that takes time. That you can't go making a name without the big organization noticing you. But Snow wouldn't back down even after word hit the streets that the kingpin was saying lay off a guy named Garrett. He was so crazy he wasn't scared of nothing. Hell. None of us was scared enough."

He had that right. They were too young. You have to put a little age on before you really understand when to be afraid. I gave him a small drink. "Better? Good. Tell me about the priest. Brother Jercé. What religion was he?"

"I don't know. He didn't say. And you know how priests are. They all dress the same in those brown things."

He had that right, too. You had to get close and know what to look for to tell Orthodox from Church from Redemptionist from several dozen so-called heretical splinter cults. Not to mention that Brother Jercé's whole show could have been cover.

I asked myself if any man could have been dumb enough—or confident enough—to have given these punks his right name and have paid them in the private coin of his own temple. Maybe it was just my dim opinion of priests, but I decided it was possible. Especially if Brother Jercé was new to all this. After all, how often does a job get botched up as thoroughly as the Vampires had done? I should have been dead and nobody the wiser.

I asked many more questions. I didn't get anything useful until I took out the coins Crask brought me. "Was all the payoff money like this?"

"The money I seen was. Temple stuff. Even gold. But Snow didn't make a show. I bet he lied about how much he got paid."

No doubt. I hit him with the big question. "*Why* did this priest want me hit?"

"I don't know, man."

"Nobody asked?"

"Nobody cared. What difference did it make?"

Apparently no difference if smoking somebody is just business. "I guess that's it, then, kid." I took out a knife.

"No, man! Don't! I gave it to you straight! Come on!"

He thought I was going to kill him.

Morley would say he had the right idea. Morley would tell me the guy would haunt me if I didn't, and that damned Morley is right more often than not. But you have to do what you think is right.

I wondered if surviving this mess would scare the kid off the road to hell. Probably not. The type can't see danger until it's gnawing their legs.

I moved toward him. He started crying. I swear, if

he'd called for his mother . . . I cut the cord holding his right arm and walked out. It would be up to him whether he got loose or stayed and died.

I stepped out into another gorgeous evening.

I marvelled at my surroundings. Once I got out of Black Cross Lane I saw elvish women sweeping and washing their stoops and walks and the streets in front of their buildings. I saw their menfolk manicuring greenery. It was the evening ritual.

The elvish do have their dark underside. They have little tolerance for breed offspring. Poor kids.

13

It was thoroughly dark before I got home. I spotted several shooting stars, supposed by some diviners to be good omens and by others the opposite. One gaudy show-off broke up into lesser streaks.

Dean let me in. "Damn, that smells good," I said.

"It will be," he promised. He smiled. "I'll bring you a beer. Did you learn anything useful?"

"I don't know." What was this? He wasn't himself. "What are you up to?"

He gave me his kicked-puppy look. I think he practices it. "Nothing."

"What happened while I was gone?"

"Nothing. Except Maya came. In fact, she just left. When you knocked."

I grunted. She had obviously been working on Dean. "You'd better count the silver."

"Mr. Garrett!"

"Right. Any sign of Miss Craight?" Walking home I'd decided she wouldn't show. What was in it for her? I was pretty sure she was a gal who didn't take a deep breath without calculating her return on investment. Such a shame; all that beauty wasted.

"Not yet. She did say it would be a late dinner."

How late was late? "I'm going to freshen up." I went upstairs. A wash would help clean the body, but it couldn't do anything for the stains on my soul.

Jill was there when I came back down. She had charmed old Dean again. He was letting her set the table. Unprecedented.

They were gossiping like old friends.

I said, "I hope that's not me you're ripping."

Jill turned. "Hi, Garrett. Nope. You aren't that

lucky.'' She smiled. There wasn't any more heat in it than in a forest fire.

"Had a good day?"

"The best. Business was marvelous. And I talked to my friend. He apologized for the trouble he'd caused me. He hadn't expected it. He's taken care of it. I won't be bothered again."

"That's nice." I checked her over. I tried not to be too obvious. She could set dead men panting. Her fear had gone. "I'm glad for you. But poor Saucerhead will be brokenhearted."

Dean gave me a disappointed scowl. Couldn't I get my mind off *that* for five minutes?

Are you kidding? I'm not dead yet. But I took his hint. It wouldn't be worth the trouble, anyway, just to get turned down. Sour grapes.

She got along with him better than she did with me. For us it was one of those things where nobody could think of anything to say.

Garrett tongue-tied around a gorgeous blonde? That did wonders for my self-esteem. But Dean's ducks were so good they made up for the lack of crisp repartee.

The main trouble was that Jill Craight wasn't about to tell me anything about Jill Craight. Not about her now, not about her then. She was slick, changing the subject or just sliding away from it so smoothly I didn't realize what she was doing until she'd done it several times.

Giving up on her left me only one area of expertise where I could talk extensively: Garrett. And a little bit of Garrett goes a long way.

I guess the high point was the wine she'd brought. It was an import. It was almost good.

To me wine is just so much spoiled fruit juice. It all tastes the same, with rare exceptions. This was the rarest. It was as good as the famous TunFaire Gold, which meant I drank most of my gobletful without sneaking off to wash the taste out of my mouth with a slug of beer.

The ice maiden was on holiday, but this thing wasn't

going anywhere. I figured as soon as dessert was over we ought to put it out of its misery.

Jill was more a lady than I thought. She got us through the difficulties. We helped Dean clear the dead soldiers, then I walked her home.

We'd gone less than a block when I missed something you can't miss if he's in the neighborhood. "What's happened to Saucerhead?" It wasn't like him to wander off.

"I let him go. I don't need him now. My friend straightened things out."

"I see." Especially why she was willing to let me walk her home.

I didn't say much after that. I watched for shooting stars but the gods had closed the show. We said good night outside her apartment building, a refurbished tenement. Jill did not ask me in for a nightcap and I made no attempt to fish an invite. She gave me a sisterly peck on the cheek. "Thanks, Garrett." She marched inside. She never looked back.

I considered the newly risen moon with misdirected animosity. I muttered, "Sometimes you have nothing at all in common." Not even a language where the words mean the same things.

I turned toward home and almost fell over Maya.

14

She'd come out of nowhere. I hadn't heard a sound. She laughed.

"What were you doing with that woman, Garrett?" She sounded like Tinnie asking the same question. What was this?

"We had dinner. You object?"

"I might. You never took me to dinner."

I grinned. "I didn't take her, either. She came to the house." I'd call her bluff. "You want me to take you someplace classy? The Iron Liar? You got it. But get yourself a bath, comb your hair, put on something a little more formal." I chuckled. I could just picture the Liar if Maya walked in. They'd scatter like roaches in sudden light.

"You're making fun of me."

"No. Maybe going at it the long way around, telling you to think about growing up." I hoped she wouldn't be one chuko who fought that.

She sat down on somebody's steps. The moonlight was in her face. She was pretty under the grime. She could even be a heart stopper if she wanted to be. First she'd have to come to terms with her past and decide she wanted to attack the future. If she kept drifting she'd be another burned-out whore living off garbage in fifteen years, brutalized by anyone who wanted to bother, protected by no one.

I sat down beside her. She seemed to want to talk. I didn't say anything. I'd said enough to make her defensive.

"Nobody watching your place anymore, Garrett. Vampires or anybody else."

"Probably pulled out when they heard about Snowball and Doc."

"Uhm?"

"The kingpin had them put to sleep."

She didn't say anything while that sank in. Then, "Why?"

"Chodo doesn't like people who don't listen. He put it out to lay off me and they didn't."

"Why would he look out for you?"

"He thinks he owes me."

"You get to meet a lot of people, don't you?"

"Sometimes. Usually they turn out to be the kind I wish I didn't know. There are some bad people in this world."

She was quiet for a while. She had something on her mind. "I met some of those today, Garrett."

"Oh?"

"Those guys you said to run a Murphy on. I used Clea because she can get a statue excited. They almost killed her." She got graphic with her account of the torture of a thirteen-year-old.

"I'm sorry, Maya. I had no idea they were . . . What can I do?"

"Nothing. We take care of our own."

I had a bad feeling. "And the two Smiths?" The Doom wouldn't have been kind.

She mulled over how much to admit. "We were going to cut them, Garrett." That was a mark of the Doom. "Only somebody already did it."

"What?"

"Both of them. Somebody took all their business off. They'll have to squat like women."

This was getting weird. They don't make eunuchs anymore, even as a criminal punishment.

"So we just broke their legs."

"Remind me not to get on the bad side of the Doom. Did you find out anything?"

"Garrett, if those guys weren't walking around they wouldn't exist. They didn't have anything but their clothes. You should see the woman at the Blue Bottle. A cow."

"Weirder and weirder, Maya. What do you think?"

"I don't, Garrett. You do that."

"Eh?"

"You said do a Murphy on two guys watching that place. Tonight you go strolling over there with Tawny Dawn Gill, she gives you a peck on the cheek, I figure you're working for her and you know what's doing."

"I didn't even know that name. She told me it was Jill Craight. You know her?"

"She was in the Doom when they took me in. Never told the truth when a lie would do. Had a different name every week. Toni Baccarat. Willi Gold. Brandy Diamond. Cinnamon Steele. Hester Podegill. That's the only one that sounded dumb enough to be real. She lied all the time about who her family was and the famous people she knew and all the stuff she'd done. She mostly hung out with the younger girls because everybody else had her figured out and wouldn't listen to her shit."

"Hold on. Hester Podegill?"

"Yeah. One of her thousand and one names." She looked at me odd.

There were Podegills off in a back room of my mind. Neighbors in the old days. Bunch of daughters. A couple of them turned up pregnant at thirteen. I began to recall the talk and the way people had shunned the parents . . . Third floor, that's where they'd lived. And the little one, a blonde named Hester, would have been about ten when I left for the Marines.

But the Podegills were dead.

The only letter my brother wrote in his life he wrote to tell me how the Podegills died in a fire. The tragedy really broke him up. He'd had it bad for one of the girls.

That letter had taken two years to catch up to me. By the time it did my brother had been in the Cantard a year himself. He's still down there. Like a lot of others, he won't be coming home.

Maya asked, "That name mean something to you, Garrett?"

"It reminded me of my brother. I haven't thought about him for a long time."

"I didn't know you had one."

"I don't now. He was killed at Flat Hat Mesa. Ask me sometime and I'll show you the medal they gave my mother. She put it in a box with the ones for her father, her two brothers, and my father. My father got it when I was four and Mikey was two. I used to be able to remember Dad's face if I tried hard. I can't anymore."

She was quiet for a few seconds. "I never thought about you having a family. Where's your mom now?"

"Gone. After they gave her Mikey's medal she just gave up. Nothing to live for anymore."

"But you—"

"There's another medal in that box. It has my name on it. The Marines delivered it four days before the Army delivered Mikey's."

"Why? You weren't dead."

"They thought I was. My outfit was on an island the Venageti invaded. They claimed they killed us all. Actually, we were out in a swamp, living on cattails and bugs and crocodile eggs while we picked them off. Mom was gone before the news got back after Karenta recaptured the island."

"That's sad. I'm sorry. It isn't fair."

"Life isn't fair, Maya. I've learned to live with it. Mostly, I don't think about it. I don't let it shape me or drive me."

She grunted. I was getting preachy and she was getting ready to respond the way kids always do. We'd been sitting there no more than ten minutes but it seemed a lot longer.

"Somebody's coming," she said coldly.

15

Somebody was Jill Craight looking like she'd seen a zombie and his seven brothers. She would have run past us if I hadn't said, "Jill?"

She squeaked and jumped. Then she recognized me. "Garrett. I was coming to see you. I didn't know where else to turn." Her voice squeaked. She looked at Maya but didn't recognize her.

"What's the trouble?"

Jill gulped air. "There's . . . There are dead men in my apartment. Three of them. What should I do?"

I got up. "Let's go look."

Maya bounced up and invited herself along. Jill was too rattled to care. I figured she'd be safer tagging along than wandering around alone.

Near the door to Jill's building I spied something I'd missed when the light was poorer—blood. The women didn't notice.

I found more spots inside, small, nothing to grab the attention if you weren't looking. I noted that the building was in better shape than its contemporaries.

Lamps on the landings lighted the stairs. I caught sounds of life as we stole to the second-floor landing, first a woman's laughter sudden as the shattering of a glass, then sounds of a woman either having one heck of a good time or fighting a bad bellyache.

There were four doors down the second-floor hall from which the sounds came. There had been four on the first. The apartments couldn't be big, sound not much retarded. How come the place wasn't an over-turned anthill if three guys had gotten killed?

Because Jill lived higher on the hog. Her floor was

class, only two larger apartments. "Who lives across the way?"

Jill pushed her door open. "Nobody right now. It's empty."

"Wait." I wanted to go in first just to be sure. I checked the door. The lock was designed to keep the honest folks out. Anyone with a little know-how could get past it.

So somebody with no knowledge had used a wrecking bar for a key. And nobody had heard that?

People do tend to mind their own business.

The room appeared untouched. It was a lot classier than a Jill Craight could afford. I'd seen less luxury in places on the Hill.

Jill Craight had a sugar daddy. Or she had something heavy on somebody with a lot to lose, which could be an explanation for somebody watching and trying to get in. Maybe she had a piece of deadly physical evidence.

A trail of blood led to a door standing two inches ajar. It opened on a room eight-feet by eight, jammed with stuff. That's all you could call it. Stuff. Jill was a pack rat.

Sprawled amid the plunder was a body, blond, middle twenties, still marked by that weathered look you pick up in the Cantard. He might have been handsome. Now he just looked surprised and uncomfortable. And very dead.

"Know who he was?" I asked.

Jill said, "No." Maya shook her head. I frowned. Maya let go of the silver doohickey she was about to pocket.

"I'd guess he walked in on somebody who was digging through your stuff and both of them were surprised." I stepped over the dead man to a door.

The room beyond was where Jill slept and maybe paid her rent. It had that look.

There were two more stiffs in there, and blood all over, like somebody lugged in buckets and threw it around. It looked like several men had chased the guy from the walk-in while more had headed him off at the bedroom door, which opened on a hallway. Both bodies were near the door.

Maybe if you're a Crask, or Sadler, or even Morley Dotes, you get so the red messes don't touch you. It took me a minute to get my brain moving, judging the splash patterns and the way things were kicked around. I went over to eyeball the dead men.

I don't know how long it was. A while. Jill touched my arm. "Garret? Are you all right?" There wasn't any ice in her eyes. For a moment the woman behind the masks looked out, humanly concerned.

"I'm all right." As all right as I could be looking at a guy I'd had over to supper less than thirty hours ago.

What the hell was Pokey doing in Jill's apartment in the first place, let alone getting himself killed there? He'd given the job to Saucerhead and Jill had fired Tharpe before he'd gotten started.

I went to the bed, picked a clean spot, and sat down. I had some thinking to do.

Pokey had been less of a close friend than a professional acquaintance I respected. And he hadn't been working for me when he'd gotten it. I didn't owe him. But something got me on a level where there isn't any common sense.

I wanted whoever had done it.

Maya spoke for the first time. "Garrett," was all she said but her tone told me it was important.

She was in the walk-in, squatting by the dead man. I joined her. Jill stayed in the doorway, paying attention to Maya for the first time. She did not look happy.

"What?"

"Pull his pants down."

"Say what?"

"Just do it, Garrett."

Maya was too serious to answer with a wisecrack. I did it, turning a pretty shade of pink. "Hunh?"

He'd been surgically and thoroughly desexed. He'd healed but the scar tissue was still a virulent purple. It had been done since his return from the Cantard.

I scrunched up like I had spiders stomping on my naked skin.

Jill said, "That's sick."

I agreed. I agreed just a whole hell of a lot. That mess of scars gave me the heebie-jeebies.

I didn't want to, but I went and checked the other one.

He was older. His scars had lost their color long ago.

I went back to my place on the bed. After a while, I told Jill, "You can't stay here. Somebody will come to clean up."

"You think I could stay here with this? Are you crazy?"

"You got anywhere to go?"

"No."

I sighed. It figured. "What about your friend?"

"I don't know how to get ahold of him. He finds me."

Of course he would. Nobody's husband wanted his mistress turning up on his doorstep. Had he given her his real name? "Put together what you'll need for a few days." Now I had to make a choice. I wanted to track the guys who had gotten away. They'd left a bloody trail. But somebody ought to walk Jill over to my place.

I glanced at Maya, looking bad in her colors. She said, "No way, Garrett. I'm sticking with you."

Hell, it was bad enough having the ones my own age read my mind. Now kids were going to start, too?

Jill said, "I can make it from here to your place, Garrett."

I didn't argue. She wasn't high on my list of favorite people. "You have a lantern around here?"

She told me where to find one.

16

It was quiet out, but it wasn't trouble quiet. There just wasn't anybody around.

It was after midnight but that doesn't make much difference most places. The day people go to bed, then the goblins and kobolds and ratmen and whatnot come out to do the night work. I guess it just wasn't their kind of neighborhood.

I opened the lantern's shutter and looked for blood spots. They got harder to see as they dried.

Maya asked, "How come all the lights in her place, Garrett? She must have had twenty lamps burning."

"You got me." It had been bright in there. I hadn't paid attention, though. "Guess they wanted to see what they were doing."

"She done pretty good since she left the Doom."

"If you say so." Was she going to chatter at me all night?

"You don't think so?"

"Is that your goal in life? To have some guy keep you in an apartment full of dead men? Those guys came with whatever is going on in her life."

She had to think about that. I finally got some quiet.

It didn't last. "You notice she had real glass windows in that fancy sitting room?"

"Yeah." That I'd noticed. Real glass is expensive. I know. I've had to replace a few panes. Those had impressed me.

"The other apartment had them, too."

"Yeah. So?"

"So somebody was watching us from there when we left."

"Oh?" Interesting. "What did he look like?"

"I couldn't even tell if it was a he. All I saw was a face. It was only there for a second. Plain luck I saw it."

I grunted, not giving her my complete attention. The trail was getting harder to follow, like maybe the guy doing the bleeding had had most of the juice squeezed out. The going was getting slower.

The trail led into an alley so narrow a horseman would lose his knees if he tried to get through. It was not an inviting place. I shone the light in but couldn't see anything.

"You're not gong in there, are you?"

"Sure I am." I fished out my brass knuckles. I hadn't brought my favorite head-knocker. It hadn't seemed appropriate dress for a dinner date.

"Is that smart?"

"No. Smart would be to throw you in first and see what eats you." Either Maya had begun to wear or I was getting crabby. "How come you're following me around, anyway?"

"So I can learn the trade. So I can find out what kind of man you are. You put on a good show but nobody is that decent. There's something weird about you. I want to find out what it is."

Maya was wearing real thin. Weird! No woman had called me that before. "Why's that?"

"I'm thinking about marrying you."

"Hoo!" I went into that alley without throwing rocks first. There was nothing in there that scared me now.

I found the dead guy ten paces into the darkness. Somebody had set him down with his back against a building, had made him comfortable, then had gone on, presumably to get help. He'd bled to death there.

I squatted, checked him out. Maya held the lantern.

He was still dead. He didn't have anything to tell me. I figured he was even less happy about the situation than I was. But he wasn't complaining.

I took the lantern and moved on.

There was more blood, but not much.

Poke had put him up a hell of a fight.

The trail petered out in the next street. I gave it my best look but couldn't take it any farther.

Maya asked, "What're you going to do now?"

"Hire a specialist." I started walking. She caught up. I asked, "Doesn't any of this bother you?" She'd stayed cooler than Jill Craight.

"I've been on the street five years, Garrett. Only things that bother me are the ones people try to do to me."

She wasn't that tough, but she was getting there. And that was a shame.

17

Sometimes it seems Morley's place never closes. It does, but only during those hours of the dawn and morning when only the most twisted are up and about. Noon to first light the place serves its strange clientele.

It had thinned out, but forty pairs of eyes watched us from the entrance to the serving counter, eyes more puzzled than hostile.

Wedge was behind the counter. Of all Morley's henchmen he's the most courteous. "Evening, Garrett." He nodded to Maya. "Miss." Just as though she didn't look like death on a stick and smell like it, too.

"Morley still up?"

"He's got company." The way he said it told me the company wasn't business.

"That resolution didn't last long."

Wedge flashed me a smile. "Were you in the pool?"

"No." They would, that bunch.

Wedge went to the speaking tube, talked and listened, talked and listened, then came back. "He'll be a while. Said have dinner while you wait. On the house."

Ugh.

Maya said, "That sounds great," before I could turn him down. "I could eat a horse."

I grumbled, "You won't eat one here. Horseweed, horse fennel, horseradish, horse clover, yeah, but . . ."

Wedge yelled into the back for two specials, then leaned on the counter. "What you need, Garrett? Maybe I can save you some time."

I glanced at Maya. She smiled. She knew damned

well Wedge was being nice because I had a woman along.

How do they get that way so young?

"I need a stalker, Wedge. A good one. I'm trying to track a guy."

"Cold trail?"

"Not very. And he was bleeding. But it's getting colder."

"Back in a few. I know what you need." He went into the kitchen. Another human-elf breed took his place. He was younger. He plunked a couple of platters on the counter, tossed up some utensils, looked at Maya like he wondered if it was catching, and went to the end of the counter to take somebody's order.

"That one's no prince," Maya told me. "But the old guy was all right." She eyed her platter.

The special looked like fried grass on a bed of blanched maggots, covered in a slime sauce filled with toadstool chunks and tiny bits of black fur. I muttered, "No wonder vegetarians are so nasty."

Maya assaulted her meal. When she stopped to catch her breath she said, "This ain't bad, Garrett."

I'd begun nibbling the mushrooms out of mine. She was right. But I wasn't going to admit it out loud, in front of witnesses. I muttered, "Wedge is no prince, either. He takes people out on the river, ties rocks to their feet, dumps them in, and tells them he'll race them back to shore. Tells them he'll turn them loose if they beat him. I hear some of them paddle like hell all the way to the bottom."

She checked to see if I was joking. She saw I wasn't. Well, maybe I'd exaggerated a little, but Wedge wasn't nice people. Morley Dotes didn't have nice people working for him.

She was reading my mind again. "Aren't there any decent people anymore?"

"Sure. We just don't run into many."

"Name two," she challenged.

"Dean. Friend of mine named Tinnie Tate. Her uncle Willard. Friend of mine called Playmate."

"All right."

"Not to mention I have a fair opinion of myself."

"You would. I said all right, Garrett. Forget I asked. You going to finish that? I'll take it."

I pushed my platter over. Where was she putting it?

Wedge came back with the sleaziest ratman I'd ever seen. He had a lot of the old blood: long whiskers, a long snoot, patches of fur, a four-foot tail. He'd be a descendant of one of the less successful experimental strains of two centuries back, when the life magics were the rage and anybody who could diddle up a spell was trying to create new forms. None of those sorcerers are remembered today but their creations are with us still. They'd been inordinately fond of messing with rats.

I pride myself on my open mind and freedom from prejudice, but I've always found room to exclude rat-people. I can't help it. I don't like them and none of them have done anything to improve my opinion.

Wedge told me, "This is Shote, Garrett. As good a stalker as you'll find. And he's available."

I nodded to Shote and tried to shelve the prejudice. "Wedge tell you what I need?"

Shote nodded. "Forrow sssomebody whosss breeding."

I grinned. None of those guys were going to do any breeding. "Basically, I've got a solid starting point. Shouldn't be hard."

"Two marks frat fee, I take you to the end of the track. Arr I do is track. No fighting. No portering. No nothing erse."

"That's fine with me." I dug out two marks silver.

Morley arrived. He leaned on the counter beside me. He looked at Maya. "Picking them a little young, aren't you?"

"This is Maya, my self-appointed assistant and understudy. Maya, the famous Morley Dotes."

"Charmed." She eyed him. "He a friend of yours, Garrett?" She'd know the name.

"Sometimes."

"You going to invite him to the wedding?"

She had set me up and cut me off at the knees.

Morley had to ask. "What wedding?"

''Him and me,'' Maya said. ''I decided I'm going to marry him.''

Morley grinned. ''I'll be there. Wouldn't miss it for a barge loaded with gold.'' I've seen toads with straighter faces than he had on.

I bet they heard my teeth grind all the way to the waterfront.

''Maya Garrett?'' Morley said. ''It does have a ring.'' He looked at the ratman. ''Shote. How you doing? I thought you didn't have anything going, Garrett.'' He was having a hell of a time keeping from laughing.

''I didn't. Now I do. Somebody offed Pokey Pigotta. I want to ask them why.''

That took the grin off his clock. ''You taking it personal?'' He thinks I take everything personal.

''I don't know. Pokey was all right, but he wasn't really a friend. I just want to know why he turned up dead where he did.''

Morley waited for me to tell him where and when. I disappointed him. I asked Shote, ''Are you ready? Let's go.''

Maya downed the rest of my celery drink and pushed away from the counter. She grinned at me.

Morley asked, ''Mind if I tag along?''

''Not at all.'' He'd be useful if we walked into something.

18

I expected the dead man's friends would have collected him, but when we reached that death-trap alley, there he was, taking it easy, like a drunk sleeping it off.

"They left this one where he croaked," I said. "At least one more was bleeding when they left."

The ratman grunted and started sniffing around.

"Morley, I want to show you something." I had Maya hold the lantern while I pantsed the dead guy.

"What are you, some kind of pervert?" Morley asked.

"Just take a look. Ever seen anything like this?"

Morley looked for a long time. Then he shuddered and shook his head. "No. I've never seen anything like that. That's sick. Crazy sick. How did you know? What have you gotten yourself into?"

"This is the fifth one today. All cut bald." I didn't go into detail.

Morley said, "Why would anybody let somebody do that?"

"There are a lot of crazies in this world, old buddy."

"I didn't think there was anybody that çrazy."

"That's because you think with yours."

"Ha! The pot calling the kettle black."

"If you're ready?" The ratman sounded offended.

"Whenever you are," I told him.

"One man went on from here. He was wounded, as you surmised." Put me in my place. He led off, dropping to all fours so his legs folded up like a grasshopper's hind legs. That hurt just to see but didn't bother him. He snuffled and muttered and scooted along, growling at Maya to douse the damned light.

The trail turned south, headed across town a mile, a mile and a half into a better part of the city, not wealthy like the Hill and the neighborhoods clinging to its skirts, but definitely middle-class.

I began to get the feeling I'd missed something important. I suspected I knew something I didn't know I knew. I tried going over everything.

I should know better than to force it. That never works. Thinking just confuses me.

The stalk turned out to be a giant anticlimax. We caught our quarry in another alleyway. "Dead as a wedge," Shote announced. "Been gone a couple of hours."

"He was alone?" Morley asked.

"Did I tell you he was alone? I told you he was alone. He was alone."

"Touchy, touchy."

Maya searched the body. I hadn't done that with the others, except cursorily. I expect it would have been a waste of time. Maya didn't find anything.

Morley said, "I didn't know old Pokey had it in him. He was always a talker. He could bullshit his way out of anything."

"I don't think he had time to talk."

Maya asked, "What do we do now, Garrett?"

"I don't know." My inclination was to go home and sleep. We'd hit a dead end here. "We could keep going the way we were headed, see if we run into anything that bites."

Morley said, "There's nothing ahead but the Dead Zone, the Dream Quarter, and the Slough of Despond." Those were vulgar names for the diplomatic community, the area where TunFaire's religions maintain their principal temples, and the tight island where the city maintains two workhouses and a jail, a madhouse, and a branch of the Bledsoe charity hospital. The Slough is surrounded by a high curtain wall, not to keep anyone in or out but to mask the interior so as not to offend the eyes of passersby headed for the Dead Zone or the Dream Quarter.

There was a lot more to the South End, including industry, fairgrounds, shipyards, acres and acres of graveyards, and most of the Karentine Army's city facilities. But I thought I caught what Morley meant.

There was a chance our dead madmen had originated in one of those three areas. I'd be hard put to decide which was the craziest.

I said, "Whoever sent those guys might be wondering what happened to them. I'm going back where Pokey got it and see if anybody turns up."

Maya thought that was a good idea. Morley shrugged. "I've had a long day. I'm going to get some sleep. I'd be interested in hearing if you find something, Garrett. Want to head back, Shote?"

The ratman grunted.

I had a thought. That happens. So do lunar eclipses. "Wait up. I want you to look at something. Everybody." I took out my coin card. "Shine the light on this, Maya."

"Temple coinage," Morley said. "Can't tell what temple."

Maya and Shote couldn't tell me anything, either.

Morley asked, "It have anything to do with this?"

"No. These have to do with who sicced Snowball on me. Whoever hired him paid him in these."

Morley pruned his lips. "Check the Royal Assay. They're supposed to keep samples of private coinages."

That was a good idea. I wished I'd thought of it. I thanked him and said good night.

19

Maya and I had a quiet walk back. Maybe she was as worn out as I was. I didn't try to make conversation.

I tried to stay alert. It was late for chukos but I was crossing town with the warchief of the Doom, showing her colors, asking for trouble if she was spotted.

Trouble didn't find us. We saw mostly ratpeople sweeping streets, clearing trash, scrounging, stealing whatever wasn't nailed down. I have to admit they contribute, mainly by doing work no one else wants. They are industrious.

I went back to the steps where Maya and I had been sitting when Jill brought the bad news. The moon had moved along. The place was no longer in the light. Jill's building was. I watched.

Maya helped. She seemed disinclined to head for her lair. After a while, she said, "The Vampires were really trying to kill you?"

"Sure seemed like it." I shrugged. "Doesn't matter now."

"Huh? That Snowball is crazy. He'll try again."

Was she kidding? "No he won't. He really is dead, Maya."

The look she gave me.

After that we didn't talk much.

I ran out of patience. Weariness will do that. "I'm going over there. See what happened while we were roaming."

Maya followed me. She moved like she was worn out. At eighteen? After only these few hours? Hell, I was the old-timer here.

We had no trouble getting in the street door, same as before. That implied the place had heavyweight

protection, something to check on, though it would
lead back to Chodo if the women were what I thought.
If the place was his and he found out who sent those
men, somebody was in for hard times. Chodo's en-
forcers go after their jobs with the gusto and arrogance
of tax collectors. They don't stop coming and they
don't leave you anywhere to hide.

The place was quiet. The keepers had gone home to
less winsome company. The kept were asleep, visions
of presents prancing in their pretty heads.

We went up slowly, carefully. Earlier there had been
lamps to light the way, but now they were dark. I
figured the caretaker had extinguished them but I
wasn't going to dance into an ambush because it
seemed unlikely.

We reached Jill's door. I listened. Nothing. I pushed
the door. It swung inward, as it should, quietly. I stuck
my head inside.

All but two lamps had burned out, and those
wouldn't be with us long. I saw no evidence that we
weren't alone. "See if you can find some oil." While
she looked I checked the corpses. They hadn't walked
away.

I came back to find Maya filling lamps. "Long as
we're here I'm going to toss the place. Those guys
were looking for something and they didn't find it."

"How do you figure?" She got a couple of refills
burning.

"They didn't have anything when we found them.
And we accounted for all of them. So whatever it was
it's here or wasn't here to begin with." I thought. I
hoped.

"Oh."

"I'll do this room first so we can get the lights out.
Keep an eye on the street. Anyone comes, holler."

I ripped the room apart. Jill would be pissed if she
found out. I wouldn't tell her. Let her think the bad
boys did it.

I demolished furnishings. I looked for secret hiding
places. I didn't find doodly squat. And Maya didn't
see anything in the street.

"Darken the room so nobody will see the lights and

wonder. Stay back a few feet so the moonlight doesn't hit your face." I recalled the face she'd seen in the window of a supposedly empty apartment. Maybe we'd take a look in there, too.

"All right."

"Getting tired?" She sounded it.

"Yes."

"I'll hurry."

"If you're going to do it, do it right. I'll stay awake."

I hoped so. I didn't need a surprise like the one Pokey got.

I did the walk-in next. All I found out was that Jill couldn't get rid of anything. There are two kinds— sentimentalists who keep everything for what it meant, and the ex-poor, who keep everything as a hedge against revenant poverty. I pegged Jill for the latter.

I hit the kitchen next. All I learned there was that Jill didn't eat at home. In fact, as I went along, despite the heap of stuff in the walk-in, I began to suspect that Jill didn't really *live* there, but just kept stuff there and met someone there.

I stalled doing the bedroom until I'd drawn blanks everywhere else. I didn't want to keep climbing over Pokey, reminded that life is chancy for guys like us. It might be enough to rattle me into getting a job.

I didn't like it but I went at it, doing a fast round first, in case something turned up the easy way.

It didn't. I hadn't counted on it, anyway. The only thing that comes easy is trouble.

I went after it the hard way.

Still nothing.

Well, Jill hadn't struck me as stupid. She'd had plenty of storm warnings.

I wondered if she'd carried whatever it was over to my place. I hadn't watched her pack. Sure she had, if it had been here and was portable.

Had I just wasted a couple of hours I could have spent sleeping?

I made only one find of more than passing interest.

A small chest of drawers stood beside the bed. It was an expensive piece. The top drawer was just two

inches deep. Jill had used it to dump small change.
There had to be a pound of copper in there. Junk
money to her, probably, though there were characters
on the street who would take her head off for less.

I sat on the bed, pulled the drawer into my lap, and
stirred its contents. The coins weren't all copper.
Maybe one in twenty was a silver tenth mark.

The mix was eclectic, new and old, royal and private, as you'd expect of general change. Should I let
Maya know the rainbow ended here?

Whoa! A perfect, mint-condition brother of the copper coin on the card in my pocket. A gem of the min-
ter's art. I fished it out.

It meant nothing, of course. . . .

"Garrett!" Maya called.

I shoved the drawer into the chest and headed for
the front room. "What you got?"

"Take a look."

I looked. Six men moved around the street below,
furtive, studiously ignoring the building while they
talked.

Maya asked, "How do we get out?"

"We don't. Keep watching. I'll be across the hall.
Let me know when they come inside." I got a lamp,
scurried across the hall, knelt, and got to work with a
skinny knife.

I had the door open when Maya arrived. "Four are
coming in."

I doused the lamp and moved forward into darkness,
assuming the layout to reflect that of Jill's apartment,
going slowly so I wouldn't get bushwhacked by rogue
furniture.

I'd gone about eight feet when somebody knocked
me ass over appetite. I never saw him, just heard his
feet and Maya's squeak as he pushed past her. I fought
off a man-eating chair with fourteen arms and legs.
"Close the door. Quietly."

She did. "What do we do now?"

"Sit tight and hope they don't break in here. You
carrying?"

"My knife."

They always have that. For chukos the knife is who they are. Without it they're just civilians.

"You get a look at that guy?"

"Not really. He was bald. He was carrying something. A corner of it hit me in the tit. I thought I'd scream."

"Don't talk like that."

"What'd I say?"

"You know . . . Ssh!" They were in the hall. They were trying to be quiet but had invaded unfamiliar territory in the dark.

Maya whispered, "He had a funny nose, too."

"Funny how?"

"Big and bent. Like it was broken or something."

"Sshh."

We waited. After a while I sent Maya to watch from the window, in case they left without us hearing them. I got into ambush near the door in case they decided to drop in. I wondered what had become of the guy who had run out. If he'd been one of them we'd have had company by now. And if he'd run into them there would have been some kind of uproar.

It was a long wait. The sky had begun to show some color when Maya said, "They're leaving."

I went and watched. The two biggest men each carried one of the lighter corpses. The other two carried the heavier corpse. The whole bunch got out of there fast.

I figured the smart thing would be to follow their example. So of course I took my dead lamp across the hall to see if I couldn't get it lit.

I was so long Maya was in a panic when I got back. "They cleaned the place up so it looks like nothing happened."

"Why would they do that?"

"You tell me and we'll both know."

"You going to follow those guys?"

"No."

"But—"

"There are six of them and one of me and they're going to be looking for trouble. They're real nervous right now, I guarantee you. I've been there. If they've got the sense the gods gave a duck they'll get rid of those bodies fast, then scatter. And anyway, I'm so tired I couldn't not walk into something. The best thing we can do is get some sleep.''

''You're just going to drop it?'' There was a peculiar edge to her voice.

''What's it matter to you?''

''How am I going to learn?''

''You don't have an audience here, Maya.'' That proved how tired I was.

She took it like a slap in the face. She didn't have anything to say after that.

I glanced around a minute later. Maya wasn't with me anymore.

I suffered a twinge of self-disgust. I hadn't needed to stomp all over her. She'd had enough of that from the rest of the world.

20

I slept past noon. When I stumbled into the kitchen I found Jill Craight with Dean, the two of them chattering like old girlfriends who'd been out of touch for years.

Jill asked brightly, "What did you find out last night?"

Dean looked expectant. I hadn't told him anything when he'd let me in. I'd growled and snorted and stamped hooves some and gone to bed. Anything he knew he'd gotten from Jill.

"A whole bunch of nothing," I grumbled. I plopped into a chair. It barked back at me. "That damned Pokey put up too damned good a fight. Both guys that got out croaked before they got wherever they were headed."

Dean filled my teacup. "Mr. Garrett is a little ragged before he's had breakfast."

I folded my lips back in a snarl.

"Don't work so hard at it, Garrett," Jill said. "I know you're a wolf."

"Ouch."

She laughed. That surprised me. Snow queens can't have a sense of humor. That's in the rule book somewhere.

She said, "So they're all dead. That mean it's over?"

"No. They didn't find what they were after. But you deal with that however you want. It's your problem."

Dean brought me a platter piled with rewarmed biscuits, a pot of honey, butter, apple juice, and more tea. Just a morning snack for the boss. But the boss's houseguest had eaten better than the king had this morning.

Jill looked at me. "You said Pokey did too well. Who is Pokey?"

I had stepped right in that time. I would have to be more careful not to put that foot in my mouth. "Pokey Pigotta. The skinny dead man in your apartment. He was in the same business as me, more or less. You paid him, he found things out, took care of things for you. He was the best at what he did, but his luck ran out."

"You knew him?"

"There aren't a lot of us in this racket. We know each other."

Dean looked at me weird. He didn't give me away.

She thought a bit. "You couldn't guess who might have sent him, could you?"

I did have a notion and planned to check it out. "No."

"Looks like I'll have to try to hire you again. I can't live like this."

"You ever tried running through the woods in the dark?"

"No. Why?"

"You do, you keep smashing your face against things you can't see. Running in the dark can shorten your life. I don't run in the dark."

She got the message. There was no way I'd work for her if she wouldn't tell me what was going on. "I have a prior commitment, anyway."

"What's that?"

"Somebody tried to kill me. I want to find out who."

She didn't try to con me out of that.

I told her, "Get Saucerhead Tharpe. He's no investigative genius but he'll keep you safe. You thought about what might've happened if you'd been home when those guys dropped in?"

I could see that she had. She was worried.

"Get ahold of Saucerhead." I got up. I told her how to find Tharpe. "Dean, on the off chance Maya turns up, tell her I apologize for running my mouth. For a minute I forgot she wasn't a civilian.''

Dean's face pruned up and I knew he was going to say something I didn't want to hear. "Mr. Garrett?" There it was. Hard proof. Bad news, bad news. "Miss Tate was here this morning."

"Yes?"

He wilted. "I . . . Uh . . ."

"What did she say?"

"Well, I . . . Uh . . . Actually, Jill . . . Miss Craight answered the door. Miss Tate left before I could explain."

That was my gal Tinnie. She kept her gorgeous figure through vigorous exercise jumping to conclusions.

"Thanks." I wasted a raised eyebrow on him. "I'm going out." I did. I stood on the front stoop and wondered what else could go wrong.

I figured I had two choices. I could go to the Royal Assay Office to check the provenance of the temple coinage or I could go to the Dream Quarter after Magister Peridont and the answer to a question that had nagged me since I'd found Pokey.

Or I could find Tinnie. But right now hunting thunder lizards held more appeal.

The Assay Office seemed of more immediate interest, yet . . . I took out the coin I'd swiped from Jill's drawer. I flipped it. Well. The Grand Inquisitor it was.

I started walking. Though I shuffled along and might have looked preoccupied, I was reasonably alert. I noticed, for example, that the sky was overcast and a chill breeze was as busy as a litter of kittens tumbling leaves and trash. There wasn't much else to notice as far as I could see.

21

Chattaree, the Church's citadel-cum-cathedral, sits at the hub of the Dream Quarter. I looked it over from across the avenue. How many millions of marks did it take to erect that limestone monstrosity? How many more to keep it up?

In a city where you see uglies as a matter of course, artisans had had to stretch to make Chattaree hideous. Ten thousand fabulous beasties snarl and roar from the cathedral's exterior—supposedly to keep Sin at bay. The Church has that neatly personified in a platoon of nasty minor demons. Maybe the uglies work. They gave me the creeps as I started across to the cathedral steps.

There are forty of those. Each has a name and they surround the cathedral completely. It looks like somebody started to build a pyramid and suffered a change of heart a third of the way through the project. The cathedral itself starts thirty feet above street level, all soaring spires covered with curlicues and ugly boys. The steps are uneven in width and height to make running difficult for unfriendly people in a hurry to drop in. There was a time when rivalries between sects were less restrained.

The dungeons where Magister Peridont reputedly had his fun were supposed to exist as catacombs wormholed into the foundations beneath the steps.

Halfway up I met an old priest. He smiled and nodded benevolently, one of those guys who are what priests are supposed to be, and as a consequence, remain at the foot of the episcopal ladder throughout their lives.

"Excuse me, Father," I said. "Can you tell me how to find Magister Peridont?"

He seemed disappointed. He studied me and saw I wasn't one of the faithful. That left him perplexed. "Are you sure, my son?"

"I'm sure. He invited me over, but I've never been here before. I don't know my way around."

He looked at me funny again. I guess people don't come prancing in looking for Malevechea every day. He gave me a lot of near-gibberish Church cant. Boiled down, it told me I should ask the guy on guard duty inside the cathedral door.

"Thanks, Father."

"For nothing, my son. Have a pleasant day."

I clambered to door level and surveyed the Dream Quarter. The Church's nearest neighbor was also its most bitter competitor. The sprawling grounds of the Orthodox basilica and bastion began a hundred yards to the west. Its domes and towers looked somber behind surrounding trees. People came and went at the minority temple but nothing moved over there. It was as silent as a place under siege. I guess the scandals were bad for business.

I stepped in out of the gloom, found the guard and woke him up. He didn't like that. He liked it even less when I told him what I wanted.

"What do you want him for?"

"About twenty minutes."

He didn't get it, which was why he had a guard's job. He wasn't smart enough for anything else. He wasn't your everyday parish priest. He was a no-neck kind of guy who probably should have been a wrestler. His frown threatened to fold a mountain range in the center of his forehead. He deduced that I was poking fun and didn't like it.

I told him, "Me and the Magister are old war buddies. Tell him Garrett is here."

A second mountain range rose atop the first. An old buddy of Malevechea? He knew he'd better be careful until he got the go-ahead to stomp me. "I'll tell him you're here. You keep an eye out. Don't let nobody carry nothing off.'' He looked at me like he wondered if maybe I might plunder the altars.

It was not a bad idea if you could get away with it. You'd need a train of wagons to haul the goodies away.

He was gone a while. I hung around beaming at passersby. The regulars did a double take and frowned, but went about their business when I told them, ''New on the job. Don't mind me.'' A dumb smiled helped.

The guard came back looking perplexed. His world was tilting. He'd expected Peridont to tell him to bounce me down all forty steps. ''You're supposed to come with me.''

I followed him, surprised that it had been so simple. I trod warily. When it's easy you don't go barefoot because there's always a snake in the grass.

I didn't see any prisoners. I didn't hear any wails of despair. But the ways we followed were narrow and dark and damp and rat-haunted and sure would have made nice dungeons. Hell, I was disappointed.

No-Neck brought me to a cadaverous, bald, hook-nosed character about fifty years old. ''This is the guy. Garrett.''

Hawknose gave me the fish eye. ''Very well. I'll take charge. Return to your post.'' His voice was a heavy, breathy rasp, like somebody had smashed his voice box for him. It's hard to describe how creepy it was, but it gave me the feeling he was the guy who had all the fun tightening the thumbscrews.

He gave me the evil eye. ''Why do you want to see the Magister?''

''Why do you want to know?''

That caught him off balance, like what I wanted *really* wasn't any of his business.

He looked away, got himself under control, grabbed papers off his escritoire. ''Come with me, please.''

He led me through a maze of passages. I tried to picture him as the guy who'd run over me and Maya last night. He had no hair and a weird nose but was about a foot too tall. He tapped on a door. ''Sampson, Magister. I've brought the man Garrett.''

''Show him in.''

He did. Behind the door lay a chamber twenty feet

by twenty and cheerful for a place that was buried. Magister Peridont didn't have ascetic tastes, either. "Doing all right for yourself, I see."

Hawknose pursed his lips, handed over his papers, bowed toward Peridont, and hurried out, closing up behind me.

I waited. Peridont didn't say anything. I told him, "That Sampson is a creep."

Peridont put the papers on a table twelve feet long and four wide. They vanished in the litter already there. "Sampson has social disabilities. But he makes up for that. So. You've reconsidered?"

"Possibly. I'll need some information before I make up my mind. It may have become personal."

That puzzled him. He studied me. I was doing a boggle on everybody today. It's all in knowing how, I guess. "Let's have the questions, then. I want you on the team."

I never trust guys who want to be my pal. They always want something I don't want to give.

I showed him the coins. "You recognize these?"

He placed the card on his table, put on bifocals as he sat down. He stared for half a minute and took his cheaters off. "No, I don't. Sorry. Do these have a bearing on our business?"

"Not that I know of. I thought you might know who put them out. They're temple coinage."

"Sorry. That's strange, isn't it? I should." He perched those bifocals on the tip of his nose and eyed the coins again. He handed me the card. "Curious."

I'd tried. "More to the point. Did you hire somebody else when I turned you down?"

He poked at that question before he admitted he had.

"It wouldn't have been Pokey Pigotta, would it? Wesley Pigotta?"

He wouldn't answer that one.

"It's a small field. I know everybody. They know me. Pokey would have suited your requirements. And he took on a new client right after I turned you down."

"Is this important?"

"If you did hire Pokey, you're short a hired hand. He got himself killed last night."

His start and pallor answered my question.

"So. A big setback?"

"Yes. Tell me about it. When, where, how, who. And why you know about it."

"When: last night after dark sometime. Where: an apartment on Shindlow Street. I can't tell you who. Four men were involved. None survived. I know about it because the person who found the bodies asked me what to do about them."

He grunted, thought. I waited. He asked, "That's why you came? Pigotta's death?"

"Yes." That was partly true.

"He was a friend?"

"An acquaintance. We respected each other but kept our distance. We knew we might butt heads someday."

"I don't quite see your interest."

"Somebody tried to kill me, too. Me and Pokey both doesn't read coincidence to me. I talk to you and somebody tries to off me. You hire Pokey, he gets it. I wonder why but even more I wonder who. I want to cool him down. If that helps you, so be it."

"Excellent. By all means, if the people responsible for Pigotta's death tried to kill you too."

"So who did it?"

"I don't follow you, Mr. Garrett."

"Come on. If somebody wants in your way bad enough to kill anybody you talk to, you ought to know who. There can't be so many you can't pick somebody out of the crowd."

"Unfortunately, I can't. When I tried to hire you I told you I think there's a concerted effort to discredit Faith, but I don't have one iota of evidence that points in any particular direction."

I gave him my eyebrow trick in its sarcastic mode. He wasn't impressed. I'll have to learn to wiggle my ears. "If you want me to find somebody or something—like the Warden and his Relics—you'll have to give me somewhere to start. I can't just yell 'Where the hell are you?' Finding somebody is like picking apart an old sweater. You just keep pulling loose threads till everything comes apart. But you have to have the loose threads. What did you give Pokey? Why was he where he was when he got killed?''

Peridont got up. He prowled. He lived on another plane. He was deaf to anything he didn't want to hear. Or was he? "I'm disturbed, Mr. Garrett. Being outside this you miss the more troublesome implications. And they, I regret, tie my hands and seal my lips. For the moment.''

"Oh?'' I gave my talented eyebrow one last chance.

He missed it again. "I want your help, Mr. Garrett. Very much. But what you've told me puts matters into a new perspective. Contrary to popular imagining I'm not a law unto myself. I'm one tree in a forest of hierarchy.''

"A tall tree.''

He smiled. "Yes. A tall one. But only one. I'll have to consult my peers and ask for a policy decision. Bear with me a few hours. If they want to pursue this I'll give you the information at my disposal. Whatever the decision, I'll be in touch. I'll see you're compensated for what you've already done.''

How very thoughtful of him. How did such a nice guy get such a nasty reputation?

He was being nice because he wanted something he couldn't get by tossing me into a cell and pulling my nails. I said, "I have to get moving on my own hunt.''

"I'll get in touch at your home. Before you go—''

I interrupted. "The name Jill Craight mean anything to you?''

"No. Should it?''

"I don't know. Pokey died in an apartment occupied by a Jill Craight.''

"I see. Would you hold on a minute?'' He opened a cabinet. "I don't want to lose another man. I want you to take something as a hedge against the kind of surprises that got Pigotta.'' He pawed around amongst several hundred small bottles and phials, selected three.

He placed those on the table, three colorful soldiers all in a row: royal blue, ruby, and emerald. Each bottle was two inches tall. Each had a cork stopper. He said, "The ultimate product of my art. Use the blue where maximum confusion would benefit you. Use the green where death is your only other out. Break the bottles or just unstop them. That doesn't matter.''

He took a deep breath, lifted the red bottle carefully. "This is the heavyweight. Be careful. It's deadly. Throw it against a hard surface at least fifty feet away. You don't want to be any closer. Run if you have the chance. Got that?''

I nodded.

"Be careful. Twenty years from now I want to tip one with you and reminisce about the bad old days.''

"Careful is my middle name, Magister.'' I put the bottles away gingerly, where I could grab them in a hurry. Garrett never argues with a gift horse. I can always deal it to the glue works.

I sneaked a peek at his cabinet. What could those other bottles do? They came in every color. "Thanks. I can find my way out.'' I shot my final question as I neared the door. "You ever hear of a cult that cuts its members? Takes all their equipment, not just their testicles?''

He blanched. I mean, he really turned white. For a second I thought his hair would change. But he showed no other reaction. He lied, "No. That's grisly. Is it important?''

Lie to me, I'll lie to you. "No. It came up in a bull session the other night. The weather was pretty drunk out. Somebody heard something like that from somebody who heard something about it from somebody else. You know how that goes. You can't trace the source.''

"Yes. Good day, Mr. Garrett.'' Suddenly he wanted me out of there.

"Good day, Magister.''

I closed the door behind me. Smiling Sampson was right there to make sure I had no trouble finding the street.

22

A drizzle had started. The breeze had freshened. I put my head down and walked into it, grumbling. I wouldn't be out in this if the world would learn to leave me alone. How thoughtless of it.

Head down with not much going on inside—some would say that's the normal state of my bean—I trudged toward that small district beyond the Hill where both city and Crown maintain their civil offices. I hoped the Royal Assay people could tell me what Peridont wouldn't.

He had recognized the coins.

I didn't believe much of what he'd told me—though some of it might have been true. I disbelieved only selectively. I took nothing at face. Everywhere I turned religion popped up, and that's a game of masks and deceits and illusions if ever there was one.

My course took me within a block of the Blue Bottle, where curiosities Smith and Smith had holed up. Wouldn't hurt to stop by, see what Maya had missed.

The place didn't look promising. There'd been no upkeep done in my lifetime. But it was a cut above places where all you got for your copper was a place on a rope that would support you while you slept standing up.

It was the sort of place frequented by the poor and the lowest-order bad boys. The people who operated it wouldn't be eager to talk. I'd have to use my wits to get anything.

Not always the best hope with me.

The interior delivered the promise of the outside. I stepped into a dingy common room inhabited only by a flock of three winebirds hard at their trade. Some invisible force had pushed them to the extremities of the room. One was educating himself in a continuous muttered monotone. I couldn't make out one word in five but he seemed to be engaged in a furious debate on social issues. His opponent wasn't apparent and seemed to have a hard time making himself heard.

I didn't see anybody who looked like a proprietor. Nobody responded to the bell over the door. "Yo! Anybody home?"

That didn't bring any customer-conscious landlord charging in from his toils in the kitchen. But one of the silent drunks detached himself from his chair and reeled toward me. "Wha'cha need? Room?"

"Looking for a couple of my pals, Smith and Smith, supposed to be staying here."

He leaned against the serving counter, bathed me in fumes and knotted his face into a ruddy prune. "Uh. Oh. Third floor. Door at the end." He didn't work up much disappointment over the fact that I wasn't going to put money in his pocket.

"Thanks, pal." I gave him a couple of coppers. "Have one on me."

He looked at the coins like he couldn't figure out what they were. While he pondered the mystery I went upstairs. Carefully. The way those steps creaked and sagged it was only a matter of hours until one collapsed.

I wasn't disappointed by the third floor, either. It was more like a half story—five rooms under the eaves, two to either side of a claustrophobically narrow hall and one at the end. Two of the side rooms didn't have a hanging to ensure privacy. One still had a door that hung on one hinge, immobile. My destination was a door that wouldn't close because of a warp in the floor.

The Smiths weren't home. Surprise, surprise. I hadn't expected them to be after their encounter with the Doom. I pushed inside.

Whatever plot or conspiracy or outfit the Smiths were with, it was miserly. They'd slept on blankets on the floor. And they hadn't had a change of clothing to leave behind.

I started going over the room anyway. You never

know when something minute will make everything fall together.

I was on my knees looking into the canyons between floorboards when the hallway floor creaked. I looked over my shoulder.

The woman looked like the Dead Man's wife. There was enough of her to make four women with some to spare. How had she gotten that close without raising a roar? How had the stairway survived? Why was the building standing? It was top-heavy enough to tip over.

"What the hell you doing, boy?"

She was spoiling for a fight and there wouldn't be any getting around it. "Why do you ask?"

"Because I want to know, shithead."

So it don't always work.

She was carrying a club, a real man-sized head-buster. I pitied the guy who got hit when she got her weight behind it.

It looked like I might get a chance to practice my self-pity if I didn't use those wits I'd been daydreaming about. "Who the hell are you? What the hell are you doing sticking your face in my room?"

When you don't have space to dazzle them with your footwork you try baffling them with bullshit.

"*Your* room? What the hell you yelling, boy? This room belongs to two guys named Smith."

"The guy I paid said take this room. I did what he told me. You got a problem with that you take it up with the management."

She glared at me. "That goddamned Blake up to his old tricks, eh?" Then she yelled, "I *am* the management, shithead! You been conned by a wino. Now get your ass out of here. And don't come whining to me for your money back."

What a dreamboat.

She turned around and stomped away. I held onto the floor. If the building went I could ride it down. She kept grumbling. "I'm going to kill that sonofabitch this time."

What a sweetheart. It was a good thing she didn't get physical, because I don't think I could have taken her.

I did some more quick looking, but when the yelling started downstairs I figured it was time I made my getaway.

Then I spotted something.

It was a copper coin all the way down in a crack. I whipped out a knife and started digging.

There was no reason to believe the coin had been lost by the Smiths. It could have been there for a hundred years.

It could have been. But I never believed that for a second.

Maybe I wished hard enough. That scrungy little hunk of copper was the brother of those I'd collected already.

Click. Click. Click. Pieces started falling together. Everything was part of the same puzzle, except, improbably, Magister Peridont. Improbably because he'd lied. He knew something about what was going on even if he wasn't involved himself.

It was time to go.

23

Big Momma was in full cry when I hit the bottom of the stairs. She was after the drunk I'd tipped. He dodged her with the nimbleness of long practice. She took a mighty swing as I arrived, but missed him. Her club smashed a bite out of a table. She yowled and cursed the day she'd married him.

The muttering drunk paid no attention. Maybe he was a regular and had seen it all before. The other drunk had disappeared. I thought he'd set a good example.

I slid toward the door.

Big Momma spotted me. She whooped. "You sonofabitch! You lying sonofabitch!" She headed my way like a galleon under full sail.

I'm not a fool every time. I got the hell out of there. The drunken husband must have zigged when he should have zagged. He came flying through the doorway, ass over appetite, and lay panting and puking in the drizzle. The woman did some yelling but didn't come out for the kill. When she quieted down I went to see how the guy was.

He had scrapes and a bloody nose and needed throwing into a river but he'd survive. "Come on." I offered him a hand up.

He took it, got up, teetered, looked at me with eyes that wouldn't focus. "You really done it to me, man."

"Yeah. Sorry about that. I didn't know your personal situation was so bad."

He shrugged. "Once she calms down she'll beg me to come back. A lot of women don't got any husband at all."

"That's true."

"And I don't cheat on her or beat her."

Somehow I couldn't picture him as a wife-beater. Not with that wife.

He asked, "What the hell were you trying to do, anyway?"

"Find out something about those guys Smith and Smith. Some friends of theirs killed a buddy of mine. Come on. Let's go somewhere out of the wet."

"Why should I believe anything you tell me after the stories you told already?" His speech wasn't that clear but that's what he wanted to say.

He was unhappy with me but that didn't keep him from tagging along. He muttered, "I need to get cleaned up."

So he wasn't all the way gone to wine. Yet. There's a point beyond which they just don't care.

I led him to a place a couple blocks away, as seedy as his own. It was a little more densely populated—five guys had gotten there ahead of us—but the ambience was the same: gloom laden with despair.

The operator was more businesslike. A frail ancient slattern, she was on us before we got through the doorway. She made faces at my newfound friend.

"We need something to eat," I told her. "Beer for me and tea for my buddy. You got someplace he can clean himself up?" A flash of silver stilled her protests.

"Follow me," she told him. To me, "Take that table there."

"Sure. Thanks." I let them get out of the room before I went to the door for a peek outside. I hadn't imagined anything. Mumbles had followed us. He was doing his routine against a wall down the street. I suppose he was talking about the weather.

If he'd taken a notion to keep an eye on me he wouldn't be going anywhere. I could handle him when I wanted. I planted myself at the appointed table and waited for my beer. The prospect of the kind of food such places served depressed me.

My pal didn't look much better when he came back but he did smell sweeter. That was improvement enough for me. "You look better," I lied.

"Bullshit." He dropped into a chair, slouched way down. The old woman brought beer and tea. He gripped his mug with both hands and looked at me. "So what do you want, pal?"

"I want to know about Smith and Smith."

"Not much to tell. Them wasn't their real names."

"No! Do tell. How long did they stay there?"

"They first come two weeks ago. Some old guy come with them. Paid for them to stay, room and board, for a month. He was a cold fish. Eyes like a basilisk. They wasn't none of them from TunFaire."

That got my attention. "How do you figure?"

"Their accents, mán. More like KroenStat or CyderBen, somewhere out there, only not quite. Wasn't one I ever heard before. But it was like some. You get what I'm saying?"

"Yeah." I got it. Sometimes I catch on real fast. "That man who came with them. Did he have a name? What was he like?"

"I told you what he was like. Cold, man. Like a lifetaker. He didn't exactly encourage you to ask questions. One of the Smiths called him Brother Jersey."

"Jercé?"

"Yeah. That's it."

Well, well. The very boy who hired Snowball and Doc. That coin from up there maybe didn't prove anything but this did. "Any idea how I could find him? He's got to be the guy who had my friend killed."

"Nope. He said he'd come around again if Smith and Smith had to stay more than a month."

"What about them? Anything on them?"

"You kidding? They never said three words. Didn't socialize. Ate in their room. Mostly they was out."

I nibbled at him this way and that while we ate a chicken and dumpling mess that wasn't half bad. I couldn't get anything else until I showed him my coin collection.

He barely glanced at them. "Sure. That's the kind that Brother Jersey used to pay the rent. I noticed on account of most all of them was new. You don't see a bunch of new all together at once."

You don't. It was a dumb move, calling attention

that way. Except Jercé probably figured Smith and
Smith would never get made.

"Thanks." I paid up.

"Been a help?"

"Some." I gave him a silver tenth mark for his trouble. "Don't spend it all in one place."

He ordered wine before I got to the door.

I went out thinking I had to bone up on my geog-
raphy. KroenStat and CyderBen are out west and
west-northwest, good Karentine cities but a far piece
overland. I'd never been out that way. I didn't know
much about the region.

I also thought about asking Jill Craight a few more
questions. She was in the center of the action. She
knew a lot more than she'd admitted.

Mumbles was on the job. I'd make it easy for him
to. stick if he wanted—if he wasn't following my
drunken buddy or wasn't there by absurd coincidence.
I didn't care if I was followed.

24

I was followed.

The drizzle tapered off to nothing most of my walk. But as I neared the Royal Assay Office the sky opened up. I ducked inside grinning, leaving Mumbles to deal with it.

Considering the size of Karenta as a kingdom and considering TunFaire's significance as largest city and chief commercial center, the Assay Office was a shabby little disappointment. It was about nine feet wide, with no windows. A service counter stood athwart it six feet inside. There was no one behind that. The walls were hidden behind glass plates fronting cases that contained samples of coins both current and obsolete. Two antique chairs and a lot of dust completed the decor.

No one came out though a bell had rung as I entered. I studied the specimens.

After a while somebody decided I wouldn't go away.

The guy who came out was a scarecrow, in his seventies or eighties, as tall as me but weighing half as much. He was thoroughly put out by my insistence on being served. He wheezed, "We close in half an hour."

"I shouldn't need ten minutes. I need information on an unfamiliar coinage."

"What? What do you think this is?"

"The Royal Assay Office. The place you go when you wonder if somebody is slipping you bad money." I figured I could develop a dislike for that old man fast. I restrained myself. You can't get a lot of leverage on minions of the state. I showed him my card. "These look like temple coinage but I don't recognize them. Nobody I know does, either. And I can't find them in the samples here."

He'd been primed to give me a hard time but the gold coin caught his eye. "Temple emission, eh? Gold?" He took the card, gave the coins a once-over. "Temple, all right. And I've never seen anything like them. And I been here sixty years." He came around the counter and eyeballed the coins on one section of wall, shook his head, snorted, and muttered, "I know better than to think I'd forget." He hobbled around the counter again to get a scale and some weights then took the gold coin off the card and weighed it. He grunted, took it off the scale, gouged it to make sure it was gold all the way through. Then he fiddled with a couple other tests I figured were meant to check the alloy.

I studied the specimens quietly, careful not to attract attention. Nowhere did I spy a design akin to the eight-legged fabulous beasties on those coins. Real creepies, they looked like.

"The coins appear to be genuine," the old man said. He shook his head. "It's been a while since I was stumped. Are there many circulating?"

"Those are all I've seen but I hear there's a lot more." I recalled my drunk's remark about accents. "Could they be from out of town?"

He examined the gold piece's edge. "This has a TunFaire reeding pattern." He thought a moment. "But if they're old, say from a treasure, that wouldn't mean anything. Reeding patterns and city marks weren't standardized until a hundred fifty years ago."

Hell, practically the night before last. But I didn't say that out loud. The old boy was caught up in the mystery. He'd already worked past his half hour. I decided not to break his concentration.

"There'll be something in the records in back."

I bet on his professional curiosity and followed him. He didn't object though I'm sure I broke all kinds of rules by passing the counter.

He said, "You'd think the specimens out there would be enough to cover every inquiry, wouldn't you? But at least once a week I get somebody who has coins that aren't on display. Usually it's just new coinage from out of town and I haven't gotten my specimens mounted. For the rest we have records which cover every emission since the empire adopted the Karentine mark.''

Hostility certainly fades when you get somebody cranked up on their favorite thing.

''I've been at this so long that most of the time I can take one look and tell you what you need to know. Hell. It's been five years since I had to look anything up.''

So, he was excited by the challenge. I'd brought novelty into his life.

The room we entered was twenty feet deep. Both side walls, to brisket level, boasted cabinets containing drawers three-quarters of an inch high. They contained older and less common specimens, I presumed. Above the cabinets, to the ten-foot ceiling, were bookshelves filled with the biggest books I've ever seen. Each was eighteen inches tall and six inches thick, bound in brown leather, with embossed gold lettering.

The back wall, except for a doorway into another room, was covered with shelves bearing the tools and chemicals an assayer needed. I hadn't realized there was so much to the business.

A narrow table and reading stand occupied the middle of the room.

The old man said, ''I suppose we should start with the simple and work toward the obscure.'' He hauled out a book entitled *Karentine Mark Standard Coinages: Common Reeding Patterns: TunFaire Types I, II, III.*

I said, ''I'm impressed. I didn't realize there was so much to know.''

''The Karentine mark has a five-hundred-year history, as commercial league coinage, as city standard, then as the imperial standard, and now as the Royal. From the beginning it's been permissible for anyone to mint his own coins because it began as a private standard meant to guarantee value.''

''Why not start with my coins?''

''Because they don't tell us much.'' He snagged a shiny new five-mark silver piece. ''Just in. One of one thousand struck to commemorate Karentine victories during the summer campaign. The obverse. We have a bust of the King. We have a date below. We have an inscription across the top which gives us the King's name and titles. At the toe of the bust we have a mark which tells us who designed and executed the engraving for the die, in this case Claddio Winsch. Here, behind the bust, we have a bunch of grapes, which is the TunFaire city mark.''

He placed my gold coin beside the five-mark piece. "Instead of a bust we have squiggles that might be a spider or octopus. We have a date, but this is temple coinage so we don't know its referent. There are no designer's or engraver's marks. The city mark looks like a fish and probably isn't a city mark at all but an identifier for the temple where the coin was struck. The top inscription isn't Karentine, it's Faharhan. It reads, 'And He Shall Reign Triumphant.' ''

"Who?''

He shrugged. "It doesn't say. Temple coinage is meant for use by the faithful. They already know who.'' He stood the coins on edge. "TunFaire Type Three reeding on the five-mark piece. Used by the Royal Mint since the turn of the century. Type One on the gold. All Type One means is that the reeding device was manufactured before marking standards were fixed. Minting equipment is expensive. The standardization law lets coiners use their equipment until it wears out. Some of the old stuff is still around.''

I was intrigued but also beginning to feel out of my depth. "Why city identification by marks and reeding both?''

"Because the same dies are used to strike copper, silver, and gold but copper coins and small fractional silver aren't reeded. Only the more valuable coins get clipped, shaved, or filed.''

I got that part. The little lines on the edge of coins are added so alterations will be obvious. Without them the smart guys can take a little weight off every coin they touch, then sell the accumulated scrap.

The human capacity for mischief is boundless. I once knew a guy with a touch so fine he could drill into the edge of a gold coin, hollow out a quarter of it, fill the hollow with lead, then plug the drill hole undetectably.

They executed him for a rape he didn't commit. I guess you'd call that karma.

The old man turned the coins face down and went on about the markings on their reverses. They told us nothing about the provenance of my coins either.

"Do you read?" he asked.

"Yes." Most people don't.

"Good. Those books over there all have to do with temple coinage. Use your own judgment. See if you can luck onto something. We'll start from the ends and see what we can uncover."

"All right." I took down a book on Orthodox emissions just to see how it was organized.

The top of each page had an illustration of both sides of a coin from a rubbing of the original, lovingly and delicately inked. Below was everything anyone could possibly want to know about the coin: number of dies in the designs, the date each went into service, the date each was taken out and destroyed, dates of repairs and reengravings on each, quantities of each kind of coin struck. There was even a statement about whether or not there were known counterfeits.

I had a plethora of information available to me for which I could see little practical use. But the purpose of the Assay operation is partly symbolic. It is the visible avatar of Karenta's commitment to sound, reliable money, a commitment which has persisted since before the establishment of a Karentine state. Our philosophical forebears were merchants. Our coinage is the most trusted in our end of the world, despite the absurdities of its production.

I spent an hour dipping into books and finding nothing useful. The old man, who knew what he was doing, moved from the general to the particular, one reference after another, narrowing the hunt by process of elimination. He came to the wall I was working, scanned titles, brought a ladder from a corner, went up, and brushed a century's worth of dust off the spines of some books on the top shelf. He brought one down, placed it in his work table, flipped pages.

"And here we are." He grinned, revealing bad teeth.

And there we were, yes. There were only two examples listed, one of which matched the coins I had except for the date. "Check the date," I said.

It had to be important. Because according to the book these coins had last been struck a hundred seventy-seven years ago. And if you added one hundred seventy-six to the date pictured you got the date on the gold piece I'd brought in.

"Curious." The old man compared coin to picture while I tried to read around his hands.

My type of coin had been minted in TunFaire for only a few years. The other, older type had been minted in Carathca . . . Ah! Carathca! The stuff of legend. Dark legend. Carathca, the last nonhuman city destroyed in these parts, and the only one to have been brought low since the Karentine kings had displaced the emperors.

Those old kings must have had good reason to reduce Carathca but I couldn't recall what it was, only that it had been a bitter struggle.

Here was one more good reason to waken the Dead Man. He remembered those days. For the rest of us they're an echo, the substance of stories poorly recalled and seldom understood.

The old man grunted, turned away from the table, pulled down another book. When he moved away I got my first clear look at the name of the outfit that had produced the coins. The Temple of Hammon.

Never heard of it.

The TunFaire branch was down as a charitable order. There was no other information except the location of the order's temple. Nothing else was of interest to the Assay Office.

I hadn't found the gold at the end of the rainbow but it had given me leads enough to keep me busy— particularly if I could smoke the Dead Man out.

I said, "I want to thank you for your trouble. How about I treat you to supper? You have time?"

Frowning, he looked up. "No. No. That's not necessary. Just doing my job. Glad you came in. There aren't many challenges anymore.''

"But?" His tone and stance told me he was going to hit me with something I wouldn't like.

"There's an edict on the books concerning this emission. Still in force. It was ordered pulled from circulation and melted down. Brian the Third. Not to mention that there's no license been given to produce the ones you brought in.''

"Are you sneaking up on telling me I can't keep my money?"

"It's the law.'' He wouldn't meet my eye.

Right. "Me and the law will go round and round, then.''

"I'll provide you with a promissory note you can redeem—''

"How young do I look?"

"What?"

"I wondered if I look young enough to be dumb enough to accept a promissory note from a Crown agent.''

"Sir!''

"You pay out good money when somebody brings you scrap or bullion. You can come up with coins to replace those four.''

He scowled, caught on his own hook.

"Or I can take them and walk out and you won't have anything left to show anybody.'' I had a feeling they'd constitute a professional coup when he showed them to his superiors.

He weighed everything, grunted irritably, then stamped off through the rear door. He came back with one gold mark, two silver marks, and a copper, all new and of the Royal mintage. I told him, "Thank you.''

"Did you notice,'' he asked as I turned to go, "that the worn specimen is an original?''

I paused. He was right. I hadn't noticed. I grunted and headed out, wondering if that, too, had been part of the message I was supposed to get.

I didn't want to go anywhere near the kingpin but I was starting to suspect I'd have to. He might know what was going on.

25

It had turned dark. The rains had gone. My pal Mumbles hadn't. He was right where I'd left him, soggy, and shivering in the breeze. It was cold. A freeze before dawn wouldn't be a surprise.

I passed within two feet of him. ''Miserable weather, isn't it?'' I wish there'd been more light, the better to appreciate his panic.

He decided I was just being friendly, that I hadn't made him. He gave me a head start, then tagged along. He wasn't very good.

I wondered what to do with him. I couldn't see him as a threat. And he couldn't report on me while he was on my trail—if he wasn't just a drunk who liked to follow people.

I thought about going back to the Blue Bottle to check him out but couldn't bring myself to go nose to nose with Big Momma again. I thought about giving him the shake, then reversing our roles. But I was tired and cold and hungry and fed up with walking around alone in a city where some strange people were taking too much interest in me. I needed to go somewhere where I could get warm, get fed, and not have to worry about watching my back.

Home and Morley's place recommended themselves. The food would be better at home. But at Morley's I could work while I loafed. If I played it right I could get my job on Mumbles done for me. The disadvantage was the food.

It was the same old story. The crowd—down a little because of the weather—went silent and stared when I stepped inside. But there was a difference. I got the feeling that this time I wasn't just a wolf from another pack nosing around, I was one of the sheep.

Saucerhead was at his usual table. I invited myself to join him and nodded politely to the cutie with him. He has a way of attracting tiny women who become fervently devoted.

"I take it Jill Craight didn't get in touch."

He wasn't pleased by my intrusion. The story of my life. "Was she supposed to?"

"I recommended it." I had the feeling he was surprised to see me. "She needs protection."

"She didn't."

"Too bad. Excuse me. Morley beckons." I nodded to his lady friend and headed for Dotes, who had come to the foot of the stairs.

Morley looked surprised to see me, too. And he was troubled, which wasn't a good sign. About the only time Morley worries is when he has his ass in a sling. He hissed, "Get your butt upstairs quick."

I went past him. He backed up the stair behind me. Strange.

He slammed his office door and barred it. "You trying to start a riot, coming around here?"

"I thought some supper would be nice."

"Don't be flip."

"I'm not. What gives?"

He gave me the fish eye. "You don't know?"

"No. I don't. I've been busy chasing a two-hundred-year-old phantom charity. Here's your chance. What gives?"

"It's a marvel you survive. It really is." He shook his head.

"Come on. Stop trying to show how cute you are. Tell me what's got your piles aching."

"There's a bounty out on you, Garrett. A thousand marks in gold for the man who hands over your head."

I gave him a hard look. He has the dark-elfin sense of humor.

He meant it.

"You walk into this place, Garrett, you jump into a snakepit where the only two cobras that won't eat you are me and Tharpe."

And I wasn't so sure about Morley Dotes. A thousand in gold can put a hell of a strain on a friendship. That's more than most people can imagine.

"Who?" I asked.

"He calls himself Brother Jercé. Staying at the Rose and Dolphin in the North End, where he'll take delivery anytime."

"That's dumb. Suppose I just waltzed in to take him out first?"

"Want to try? Think about it."

There'd be a platoon of smart boys hanging around figuring I might try that.

"I see what you mean. That old boy must be worried I'll get next to him somehow."

"You still not working on something that's going to get you killed anyway?"

"I'm working now. For myself. Trying to find out who wants to kill me. And why."

"Now you know who." He chuckled.

"Highly amusing, Morley." I dragged one of my copper temple coins out. I hadn't shown them all at the Assay Office. I sketched what I'd learned. Then, "Carathca was a dark-elfin city. Know anything about it? This thing seems to go back there."

"Why should I know anything more about Carathca than you do about FellDorhst? That's ancient times, Garrett. Nobody cares. This thing keeps yelling religion. Find your answers in the Dream Quarter." He studied the coin. "Doesn't say anything to me. Maybe you ought to have a skull session with the Dead Man."

"I'd love to. If I could get him to take a twenty-minute break from his crusade against consciousness."

Someone pounded on the door. Morley looked startled, then concerned. He indicated a corner. "What is it?"

"Puddle, boss."

Morley opened a large cabinet. It was the household arsenal, containing weapons enough to arm a Marine platoon. He tossed me a small crossbow and quarrels, selected a javelin for himself. "Who's with you, Puddle?"

"Just me, boss." Puddle sounded confused. But life itself confuses Puddle.

Morley lifted the bar and jumped back. "Come ahead."

Puddle came in, looked at the waiting death, asked, "What'd I do, boss?"

"Nothing, Puddle. You did fine. Close the door and bar it, then fix yourself a drink." Morley replaced the weapons, closed the cabinet, and settled into his chair. "So what do you have for me, Puddle?"

Puddle gave me the fish eye, but decided it was all right to talk in front of me. "Word just came that Chodo put a two-thousand-mark bounty on that guy who put the thousand on Garrett."

Morley laughed.

Great. "It isn't funny." Here was a chance for the daring to make a truly outrageous hit by selling my head to Brother Jercé, then taking his and selling it to Chodo.

Morley laughed again, said, "It is funny. The auction is on. And this Brother Jercé would have to be awful naive to think he could outbid the kingpin."

TunFaire is full of people who want to do favors for Chodo.

Puddle said, "Chodo says he'll give two hundred a head for anybody who even talks about laying a hand on Garrett. Three if you bring him in alive so he can feed him to his lizards."

My guardian angel. Instead of using guard dogs he has a horde of carnivorous thunder lizards that will attack anything that moves. He favors them because they dispose of bodies, bones and all.

"What a turnaround!" Morley crowed. "Suddenly you've got everybody in TunFaire looking out for you."

Wrong. "Suddenly I've got everyone watching me. Period. And getting underfoot, maybe, while they wait for somebody to take a crack at me so they can snag him and collect on him."

He saw it. "Yeah. Maybe you'd be better off if everybody thought you were dead."

"What I should do, if I had any sense, is say the

hell with it all and go see old man Weider about a full-time job at the brewery.'' I got myself a drink uninvited. Morley doesn't indulge but he keeps a stock for guests. I thought. Then I told Morley about Mumbles and how I'd like to know a little more about him, only I'd had about all I could take for one day and just wanted to go home and get some sleep.

Morley said, ''I'll put a tag on him, see where he goes.'' He seemed a little remote since Puddle's advent, which is how he gets when he's thinking about pulling something slick. I didn't see how he could make things worse so I didn't really care.

''It should be safe now. I'm heading out.'' I no longer wanted what I'd gone there to find. The quiet and loneliness of home had more appeal.

''I understand,'' Morley said. ''Keep Dean over and have him wait up. I'll get word to you. Puddle, send me Slade.''

''Thanks, Morley.''

Things had changed downstairs. Word was out. I didn't like the way they looked at me now any more than I'd liked their looks before.

I went out into the night and stood a few minutes in the cold letting my eyes adjust. Then I headed for home. As I passed Mumbles I said, ''There you are again. Have a nice evening.''

26

I strolled into Macunado Street daydreaming about a pound of rare steak, a gallon of cold beer, a snuggly warm bed, and a respite from mystery. I should have remembered my luck doesn't run that way.

The pill-brain microdeity whose mission is to mess with my life was on the job.

There was a crowd in front of the house. Floating in the air around it were a half-dozen bright globules of fire. What the hell?

I was running slow in the gray matter. It took me a minute to realize what had happened.

Some fans of mine had decided to firebomb my house. The Dead Man had sensed the danger and wakened, catching the bombs on the fly and juggling them now, to the consternation of bombers and witnesses.

I pushed through. The bombers were still there, rigid as statues, faces contorted into shapes as ugly as the gargoyles on Chattaree. They were alive and aware and as frightened as men can be. I stepped in front of one. "How you doing? Not so good, eh? Don't worry. It'll turn out all right."

The bombs began to sputter. "I have to go inside. Wait right here. We'll chat when I get back." I knew he'd be thrilled.

Dean opened the door a crack. "Mr. Garrett!"

Yeah. Right. I shouldn't be playing with these guys. "See you in a couple." I trotted up the steps. Dean let me in, slammed the door, secured all the bolts.

"What's going on, Mr. Garrett?"

"I kind of hoped you'd tell me."

He looked at me like I was off my nut. He probably wasn't far wrong. "So let's see what Chuckles has to

tell us." I wouldn't need to bust my butt and theirs if
I could get the Dead Man to read their minds. It would
save everyone a lot of trouble—except for him.

I went into the room. Dean waited outside. He won't
go in unless he has what *he* considers a compelling
reason. "I'll keep an eye on those brigands, Mr. Garrett."

"You do that." I faced the Dead Man. "So, Old
Bones. You will wake up to save your own skin. Now
I know how to get your attention. Light a fire under
you."

*Garrett, you plague upon my final hours, what have
you brought down upon my house this time?*

"Nothing." It was going to be one of those discus-
sions.

Then why are those maniacs pitching bombs at me?

"Those boys outside? Hell. They don't even know
about you. They're just having fun trying to burn *my*
house."

Garrett!

"I don't have the slightest idea. You want to know,
poke around in their brains."

*I have. And I have found a fog. They did it because
they were told to do it. They believe they need no other
reason than the will of the Master. They were joyful
because they had been entrusted with a task that would
please him.*

"Now we're cooking. The Master? Who is he?
Where do I find him?"

*I can answer neither question. It may not be possi-
ble. I do not exaggerate when I tell you it is their
express and certain belief that the Master they serve
has neither form nor substance and manifests himself
only where and when he chooses, in any of a hundred
forms.*

"He's like a ghost or spirit or something?" I wasn't
going to say the word god.

*He is a bad dream that has been dreamed by so
many so intensely that he has gained a life of his own.
He exists because will and belief compel him to
exist.*

"Woo-oo! We're getting weird here."

Why did you stir these madmen up, Garrett?

"I didn't stir anybody, Chuckles. They stirred me. Out of the blue, for no reason, somebody has been trying to send me off. Crazy stuff has been happening all over. Especially in the Dream Quarter. Maybe I ought to catch you up on the news."

I am supremely uninterested in your squalid little slitherings through the muck and stench of this cesspit city, Garrett. Save it to impress the tarts you drag under my nose to harass me.

So, he was crabbed about Jill. He doesn't like women much. Having one in the house will set him off every time.

Tough.

"So we're going to go straight from the snooze stage to the sulks, eh? Saves us time on courtesy and catching up on the latest adventures of Glory Mooncalled. We'll just wake up and act like a cranky three-year-old."

Don't vex me, Garrett.

"The gods forfend! Me be vexatious? With my angelic disposition?" I didn't like this.

We go at it tooth and claw but it's always a game. There was a dark undercurrent of hostility this time. This wasn't play. I wondered if he was moving into some new and darker phase of being dead. Nobody knows much about dead Loghyrs, or even much about live ones for that matter since both kinds are so damned rare.

You have had the benefit of my wisdom and instruction long enough to stand on your own legs now, Garrett. There is no justification for your incessant pestering.

"There isn't any for your freeloading, either, but you do it." My temper was shorter than I'd thought. "The Stormwarden Raver Styx wanted to buy you a while back. She made a damned good offer. Maybe I shouldn't have been so damned sentimental."

I stepped out then, before the foolishness got out of hand. I looked for Dean.

He was watching the street.

The firebombs had burned out. With no entertain-

ment to be had the crowd had dispersed. But the bombers were still there, rigid as lawn ornaments. "Help
me carry one of those guys in so I can ask him what
he was doing." I opened the door.

"Are you sure that's wise?" No Mr. Garrett anymore. He'd stopped being scared.

"No. I'm never sure of anything. Come on . . .
Damn his infantile soul. Look at that."

The Dead Man had turned loose. The bombers were
running like frightened mice.

Even in my anger I didn't really think he'd let go
out of spite. He's long on argument but he's also long
on sense. My guess was he'd hoped I could track them
to their hideout. Which meant he hadn't taken a close
enough look at me.

I couldn't fault the reasoning but I couldn't carry it
off, either. I didn't have any energy left. Too much
activity, not enough rest.

I shrugged. "The hell with them. I'll settle up with
them pretty soon, anyway." Garrett whistling in the
dark. "Ask Miss Craight to come to my office. Then
bring me a pitcher of beer. Then cook supper. Bring
it when it's ready. She knows what's going on. It's
time to squeeze a little blood out of that stone. Why
the hell do you keep shaking your head?"

"Jill left shortly after you did. She said to tell you
she was sorry for the trouble she'd caused you. She
hoped your retainer would make up for it. Before you
ask, yes, she sounded like she wouldn't be back. She
left a note. I put it on your desk."

"Beer and dinner, then, and I'll question the note."
Nothing was going to stay still long enough for me to
grab it.

I went to the office, planted myself, put my feet up,
and waited until I had beer before I opened Jill's note.

> *Garrett:*
> *I really did have a crush on you. But things hap-
> pened and that little girl's heart petrified. She is only
> a bittersweet memory, cold copper tears. But thank
> you for caring.*
>
> *Hester P.*

I leaned back, closed my eyes, and considered the snow queen.

The little girl wasn't dead yet. She was hiding, way back somewhere, afraid of the dark, letting Jill Craight take care of the business of staying alive. The little girl wrote that note. Jill Craight wouldn't have been able. I don't think she'd have thought of it.

With a few beers inside, then a decent supper stacked in on top, Garrett turns halfway human. I asked Dean to stay late again. Over more beer I told him the whole story, not because he needed to know but because I knew the Dead Man would be listening. If he wouldn't take my news direct he'd get it this way.

I'd try to talk to him in the morning, when I was rested and feeling civil and he'd had a chance to contemplate his sins.

I set a record falling asleep.

27

I didn't set any record staying asleep, though I did get in four hours of industrial-weight log-sawing before Dean interceded. "Hunh? Wha'zat? Go way." Other highly intellectual remarks followed. I don't wake easily.

"Mr. Dotes is here," Dean told me. "You'd better see him. It's important."

"It's always important. Whoever it is or whatever it is, it's always more important than whatever I want to do."

"If that's the way you feel, sir. Pleasant dreams."

Of course it was important if Morley had bestirred himself enough to come over personally. But that didn't touch off any fires of enthusiasm.

It just isn't good to ask me to do more than one thing at a time. And right then sleeping was the skill I was honing.

Dean came back after only a flirtation with retreat. "Get up you lazy slob!"

He knows how to get me started—just get me mad enough to want to brain him.

His technique is somewhat like the way I get the Dead Man started.

Rather than endure his harrassment I got me up and halfway dressed and headed downstairs.

Dean had Morley settled in the kitchen, where he was drinking tea and commiserating with the old man over the trouble he was having getting his gaggle of nieces decently—or even indecently—married and out of his house. Dean nattered on about how they were driving him crazy. I think he has some notion that someday I'll feel guilty enough to take one of them off his hands.

I suggested, "Why not sell them?"

"What?"

"They've got some good years on them yet. And they're all good cooks. I know a guy might give fifty marks apiece. He sells brides to the guys who hunt and trap up in thunder lizard country."

"Your sense of humor leaves something to be desired, Mr. Garrett." He used his admonitory "Mister."

"You're right. I'm not at my best lately. Not getting enough rest, I think."

"You can relax now," Morley told me. "Your nemesis, Jercé, got excited and lost his head a while ago."

The way he made a joke of it I suspected he'd had something to do with that.

It *is* his line and he's the best there is. And two thousand is enough to get his attention.

Maybe I should have been grateful. But grateful doesn't come easy for most people and my mood was too black to make me the rare exception. I kept it bottled up. I kept most of my sour in there with it, too, though. I didn't need to hand out more excuses for folks to get ticked off at Garrett. So I just hinted. "I wonder what he could have told me."

Morley scowled. "What difference does that make? He's a closeout. You can get on with your life without watching over your shoulder."

"Want to bet?"

He gave me an ugly look.

"Sorry. Bad choice of words. What I mean is, he wasn't the source. He was an agent of the source. Unless his getting killed is enough to scare them off, we'll both hear from them again. I don't have the faintest idea what they're up to, but they're serious about it and they're not worried about the costs or consequences."

Morley wanted to disagree but had no facts. He was wishful thinking and he knew it.

I asked, "What became of the guy who was following me?"

"I put Puddle, Wedge, and Slade on him. They followed him following you here. He tried to talk to some men who were part of the excitement. They decided to each take one and see what happened."

I know my Morley Dotes. He was stretching it out because he didn't want to get to the bad news. "So what happened?"

"Puddle and Wedge lost their men. Slade hasn't reported back yet."

So the big news was that there was no news. "Odd. Those guys strike me as amateurs."

Morley shrugged. "Even an amateur is hard to stay with one-on-one."

True. A decent tail job needs at least four men.

Somebody pounded on the front door. I told Dean, "I'd better," and wondered what it was now. I'd just started wondering how I could ease Morley out and now somebody else wanted in. Jill, I figured, after some thinking about being a walking target.

I peeked before I opened up.

There were no gorgeous blondes on Garrett's stoop this time, panting for protection. This was an ugly, little old Magister who was very unhappy.

I opened up and checked to make sure nobody would come speeding in behind him. "Come in. I'd given up on you." Actually, I'd forgotten he'd said he'd be coming.

He pushed inside. "Those morons! Those short-sighted fools! They force me—me!—to sneak out in the dark, like a thief, because they're too scared to let me out on my own."

What the hell? At least he wasn't mad at me. I guided him into my office, planted him in the good chair, got some lights burning, and asked, "Can I get you something to drink?"

"Brandy. In a jar. I haven't gotten blotted since I was in the seminary. If ever there was an appropriate time, it's now."

"I'll find something." I hustled into the kitchen. Dean and Morley had heard enough to keep them quiet.

Dean had drawn my pitcher and was digging for a bottle of brandy. Morley tried to look like he'd explode if I didn't whisper a name. I didn't. He stayed in one piece. I grabbed everything and headed for my office.

We got comfortable. Peridont poured himself some brandy, sipped, looked surprised. "Not bad."

"I thought you'd appreciate it." I wet my whistle. "I gather things aren't going well."

"To understate. My brothers in God are cowards. I presented my information and suspicions and instead of responding vigorously, with the full power of the Church, they've chosen to turn their backs and hope the whole thing fades. They've withdrawn permission for me to employ you. They've enjoined me from telling you anything. They've done their damnedest to sew me up, to tie my hands, to shut my mouth, knowing I can't possibly disregard canon law after having spent a career enforcing it."

"In other words you came over to tell me to forget it instead of to point me in the right direction."

He smiled. The nasty man of legend shone through. "Not quite. They overlooked a possibility. They didn't rape away my rights as a private person."

I tried my eyebrow trick. This time it worked.

"Mr. Garrett, they failed to overrule my right to, say, employ an investigator to look into the death of Wesley Pigotta. I give you that as your express brief. Whatever else you stir up, well, that's beyond my control."

I smiled back. "You think as sneaky as a lawyer. I like that. In this case." I put the smile away. "How blind do I have to fly?"

"Almost completely. They sewed me up on that. You already know enough to realize you have to be careful. You're well grounded in the basic information. You'll have to develop from that. Once you flush the villains we can put our heads together again. My brethren might be moved by an opportunity for a quick resolution."

I don't like that kind of game. But I smiled and pretended. I wanted to stay on good terms with him. He could be helpful even while playing mental chess to get around telling me anything. "All right. I'll play along." That had been my intention no matter what he wanted. "Is there anything you *can* give me?"

He took a long pull of brandy. He was serious about getting ripped. He grinned and tossed a bag of money my way. A big bag. "My own money. Not Church money." He sobered a little. "The only thing I can tell you is that the woman who occupied the apartment where Pigotta died was my mistress. I knew her as Donna Soldat. I think that was a false name. She was a difficult woman. Though I kept her in style she had other lovers. One of those men may have been why Pigotta went there that night."

I asked him some standard questions about his relationship with Jill and got some ordinary, sleazy answers. They embarrassed the hell out of him.

"I'm sure this is all more amusing than sordid to you, Mr. Garrett. I'm sure you see worse every day."

Right.

"For me it was a traumatic surrender to my sinful side." He took a long pull of brandy. He was drinking straight from the bottle now. "I've always suffered from a weakness for female flesh."

"Don't we all."

He scowled. "That wasn't a problem when I was younger. If I visited a prostitute and she found me out, she'd laugh. Priests are their best customers. But if I were found out now I could be destroyed."

I understood. It was not that it would make him a better or worse person, but it would be a tool that could be used to bludgeon him.

"I wrestle the demon within but in the end I always lose, so discreet women are a must. Donna was a godsend. Whatever her faults, she kept her mouth shut."

She did that. "Did she know who you were?"

"Yes."

"That's a lot of power to hand a working girl."

"It was accidental. And she never abused it."

Maybe. "How did you meet her?"

"She was an actress. Working in a playhouse on Old Shipway. I saw her. I wanted her. She led me on a long chase but persistence paid off."

For both of them. But I didn't say that.

"I moved her into that place barely three months ago. It was less dangerous to visit her there. Those were three happy months, Mr. Garrett. And now all this."

He finished the brandy. He looked the sort to become a maudlin drunk. I didn't need that. I had no time to feel sorry for anybody but me. It was time to start easing him toward the door. "How should I get in touch?"

"Don't try. I'll find a way to see you." Suddenly, he was as ready to leave as I was to have him go. The beer had me too sleepy to concentrate. He started toward the door. "Good luck, Mr. Garrett. And thank you for a fine brandy, though I cheapened it by swilling it like bottom-grade wine."

I got him out the front door, locked up, and hurried back to see how many marks could be stuffed into a bag a little bigger than my clenched fist.

Morley invited himself in as I got started. "What was that, Garrett? He was weird."

"A client who prefers to remain anonymous."

He didn't like that. Like everybody else, he thought I should make an exception and trust his discretion.

"I don't want to seem impolite, Morley. But I haven't been getting much sleep."

"I can take a hint, Garrett. Let me say good night to the old man."

"Go ahead."

A minute later, as I took the money to the Dead Man's room, I overheard him giving Dean advice about how to adjust my diet so I wouldn't be tired and cranky all the time.

Good old Morley, looking out for my well-being behind my back. If Dean started trying to feed me salads and bean curd, I'd strangle them both.

28

I closed the door behind Dotes, bolted up, leaned against the door frame and sighed. Now back to my dreams of blonde sugarplums. I'd stay with them a while. No need to be a fanatic about getting an early start.

Then I recalled that I hadn't tried to straighten things out with Tinnie. The longer I let that slide, the more difficult it would be. And I really needed to find Maya and apologize to her.

There are only so many hours.

The street was so quiet I heard the hollow, echoing clop-clop of horse approaching, the metallic rattle of iron rims on cobblestones. I listened. There isn't much vehicular tràffic after dark. It advertised the fact that here was somebody worth robbing.

The sound died.

My heart sank, though there was no obvious reason it should.

I went to the kitchen to see if Dean could use some help. Maybe I'm a little psychic and sensed there was no point in trudging upstairs.

Someone pounded on the door. The knock had a ring of determination, as though whoever was there had no intention of going away.

I employed my best put-upon sigh and went to see what it was.

It was the kingpin's man Crask, looking uglier and meaner than ever because he was trying to be friendly and courteous. "Chodo says he'd consider it a big favor if you'd come out to the house right away, Mr. Garrett. He said to give you his assurance that it's important and that you'll be compensated for your trouble.''

I was getting compensated by everybody in sight without having the slightest notion what was going on. I'd get rich if the mess never sorted itself out.

And the Dead Man thought I couldn't survive without him.

I didn't turn Crask down. Sooner or later I'd end up butting heads with his boss, but when that happened it would be over something more substantial than lost sleep.

''Let me finish getting dressed,'' I said. Damn, Crask gave me the creeps. I never met anybody who reeks of menace the way he does, except his sidekick Sadler, who has a soul struck from the same cold mold.

Five minutes later I clambered into Chodo Contague's personal coach. Chodo wasn't aboard. Morley Dotes was. I wasn't surprised. He looked as sour as I felt.

Not much was said during the trip. Crask is no conversationalist. His presence tends to put the damper on a party.

Chodo's estate is a few miles north of TunFaire's northernmost gate, in a manor that would do any duke proud. The grounds are extensive, manicured, and surrounded by a wall meant more to keep in than to keep out. Several hundred thunder lizards cruise the grounds and provide protection more certain than any moat or castle wall. I've heard that Chodo has survived assassination attempts he knows nothing about because his guardians ate everything but the assassins' names.

I looked out the window. ''Chodo's pets seem frisky tonight.'' It was cold out. The colder it gets the more sluggish thunder lizards become.

''He had them warmed up,'' Crask said. ''He thought there might be trouble.''

''That why we're here?''

''Maybe.''

There must be two guys living inside Crask's skin. One is the stiffly formal butler character that Chodo turns loose on diplomatic errands, and the other is the Crask who grew up on the waterfront, whose hobby is

biting the heads off cobras. I hope I never have to deal
with that Crask, though I expect it's inevitable. He's
a completely casual and remorseless killer and he's
smart. If he got the word to get me, he'd have me
before I knew he was coming.

The coach stopped at the foot of steps leading to
Chodo's front door. There was light enough to read
by, lanterns by the dozen burning, like Chodo was
throwing a party and we were the first to arrive. Crask
said, "Don't get out." Like Morley or I might be
dumb enough to step outside and pet the monsters snuf-
fling around the coach. He got out and went up the
steps. The beasts didn't bother him.

Morley employs profanity sparingly so when he spat,
"Shit!" I knew he was rattled. I looked around.

A thunder lizard with a head the size of a five-gallon
bucket and breath that would gag a maggot was peek-
ing in on Morley's side. It had about a thousand teeth,
every one like a four-inch knife. When it stood back
up to claw at the door with its silly little hands, it stood
about twelve feet tall. Its scales were a lovely shade
of putrescent gray-green. The coach driver whacked it
across the snout with the haft of his whip. It made a
noise like twenty jackasses singing and stomped away.

Morley said, "Reminds me of a woman I knew
once. Only this one had better breath."

"I always knew you'd plook anything that moved.
What did you do with her tail?"

"You got room to talk, don't you? I've seen the
woolly mammoths you go around with."

"They still have their own teeth."

"I noticed the other night. Snappy dresser, too, with
an amazing concept of what constitutes good grooming. You going to dump her when she loses her baby
teeth?"

I was saved having to defend Maya by Crask's return. He got into the coach. He handed us each a stone
pendant on an iron chain. "Wear these while you're
here. They'll keep the lizards off. Come on."

I put my gizmo on and got out behind him. A shoulder-
high lizard muzzled me but didn't nibble. I managed to
keep from drizzling down my leg.

The inside of Chodo's place is plush. The King himself should live so good. It was quieter than the last time I'd visited, though there were more hoods around. Last time the place had been overrun with naked women, part of the decor. There were no girls tonight.

Chodo awaited us beside the indoor lake of a pool where the cuties liked to congregate. I resisted an urge to chide him for disappointing me.

Chodo was a hairless, colorless, ugly lump confined to a wheelchair. People wonder how a cripple can be so feared. They haven't gotten close enough to look into Chodo's eyes. What Crask and Sadler have, Chodo has squared. And he has them to be his hands and legs. In some ways they have no independent existence. But they seem content.

Sadler was there behind Chodo's chair. So were several lesser lieutenants I didn't know by name. I stopped six feet from the old man, didn't offer to shake. He doesn't like to be touched.

"Mr. Garrett. Thank you for responding so promptly." His voice wasn't much more than a raspy wheeze.

"Crask said it was important. He implied some urgency."

Chodo smiled thinly. He knew the smell of crap. We understood one another, which was maybe more to his advantage than to mine.

"There's something strange afoot, Mr. Garrett." So much for the amenities. "Because of that, because I've striven to keep you alive, I've been drawn into it and have, perhaps, fallen deeper into your debt."

I opened my mouth to deny that. He lifted one white hand an inch off the drab brown blanket covering his lap. For Chodo that was an impassioned gesture. I kept silent.

"Earlier today I learned that the people chasing you had the temerity to invade a building owned by the organization. They killed a man there. I find this intolerable."

I didn't look at Morley, though he had to be Chodo's source. And he'd had the nerve to get indignant when I wouldn't give him Peridont's name.

"Still, I might have overlooked that, crediting it to youthful high spirits, had they not, tonight, offended me again in an inexcusable manner."

Now I saw it. He was hot. He was so angry smoke should have been pouring out his ears.

"Sadler. Tell Mr. Garrett." The old man wanted to gather his energy.

Sadler had a voice like winter. "Shortly after sunset three men, representing someone they called the Master, came to the gate. Their manners were so offensive that Chodo asked to see them himself."

The kingpin's indignation bubbled over. "In fine, Mr. Garrett, this Master has *ordered* me to stop interfering in his business. He *threatened* me."

I call that a stupid move. Not even the King dares make a direct threat against the prince of the underworld. Whatever else he lacks, Chodo has an ego. It wouldn't let something like that slide. I pitied the guys who brought the message. They would've paid the first installment on the tribute Chodo was going to extract.

Sadler smiled thinly, divining my thoughts. "One survived to carry the heads of the others back to the fool who sent them."

I said, "These people are raving amateurs. They don't bother finding out what they're jumping into before they leap."

Chodo growled. "Nevertheless, their confidence may not be misplaced. They don't mind wasting men. Maybe they have them to throw away."

He paused to gather his strength again, signing that we were to wait.

Finally, he said, "I suggest we join forces, Mr. Garrett, to the extent that we have a common interest." He was a realist, that old thug. He knew I had no love for him or his. "You haven't the resources to battle an organization. It would take you an age to do the footwork. I have those kinds of resources. On the other hand, you have your network of friends and contacts, your knowledge in hand, your access in places where my men have no entrée." He ran out of energy again.

I surprised myself. "I wouldn't mind that. But I

don't have much to kick in. I don't have any idea what's going on. I *think* that way back in the shadows there's a nasty dragon waking up, that has religious overtones, and the guys involved don't have any qualms.''

"Why don't we pool what we know?" Sadler said. I'm sure Chodo fed him that line before I got there. He started talking.

He gave me everything they had, which wasn't diddly. For them, the thing had been a triviality until Chodo got his feelings bruised. There had been no special significance to the coins he'd sent me, for instance, except he'd thought they'd point me toward the temple that had put them out.

"They did," I said. "Only the outfit is supposed to have been out of business for two hundred years. Banned by Brian the Third." I told the story. In for a copper, in for a mark in gold. I gave them everything but the name of my connection inside the Church, and they got that soon enough.

Chodo said, "This would be a good moment for refreshments."

One of his lesser lieutenants took off. He was back in two minutes pushing a cart loaded with goodies. In the silence, while Chodo ruminated, we became aware of a nasty thunderstorm approaching from downriver.

There was beer for me. I went after it determined to make the trip worth the trouble. It had to be getting on toward dawn. By the time I got home it would be so late there would be no point hitting the sack.

Chodo said, "This churchman knows things. Maybe I should press him."

"That might not be wise." I named the name.

"Malevechea himself?" Chodo asked. He was impressed. There are powers whose indignation he won't risk needlessly.

"The very one." The kingpin's organization is powerful and deadly, but the Church is bigger and has heaven on its side and might not have much trouble recruiting the support of the state.

Thunder crashed as though to make a point.

"The woman will be the key, then. Mr. Garrett, I'll

deal with the Master. I'll haunt him and hunt him and hold his attention. I'll become his worst nightmare. You find that woman." Because I was the only one who knew what to look for, I presumed.

Life must be simple when you have no conscience and enough power to just say you want something and have people bust their butts to get it for you.

Morley spoke for the first time. "The gods must be holding a barn dance." The thunder had gotten unruly.

Chodo made a sign. Sadler took two sacks from beneath the kingpin's chair. He tossed me one and handed a bigger one to Morley. Morley's two thousand, I supposed. Sadler said, "You've been avoiding the waterbug races, I hear."

A thug came in and whispered to Crask. He looked excited.

Morley told Sadler, "I've been trying."

Sadler looked at the sack and smiled, confident Dotes couldn't resist betting now, confident that money would find its way home.

Crask said, "Sadler, problems. Out front." He took off. Everybody but Chodo and a bodyguard went with him.

Chodo said, "I'll keep in touch, Mr. Garrett. Let me know when you find the woman. Crask will take you home once he's dealt with whatever is brewing out there."

I nodded, turned away, dismissed.

He had such confidence in Sadler and Crask. But confidence was one of the attributes that took him to the pinnacle of TunFaire's underworld.

Morley didn't move. He'd received some sign that Chodo wanted to talk privately.

I headed to the front door, bemused. I'd made an alliance with the man I disliked most in this world.

I hoped I wouldn't regret it.

29

I stepped out of Chodo's house into weirdness like nothing I'd ever seen.

Crask, Sadler, a dozen goons and a herd of thunder lizards had gathered out front. They gawked at the heavens.

The storm kicking up the racket didn't cover more than a few acres of sky. And it was headed straight for Chodo's place. I'd never seen a storm so close to the ground.

Lights bobbed inside that thunderhead, three the color of candle flames, the fourth a malignant red. When the cloud arrived, the yellow lights dropped toward the crowd on the lawn. When they got closer I saw that they were three guys walking on air, all of them in old-time armor.

The mind works funny. I didn't boggle over them walking on air; I wondered what museum they'd robbed to get their iron suits.

A couple of thugs headed for the house. Their eyes were huge when they stampeded past me. Crask and Sadler decided their move made practical sense and ordered everybody inside. They weren't equipped to face men in armor, let alone guys who pranced on moonbeams.

They pushed by without a word. Inside, Crask and Sadler started yelling about crossbows and pikes and whatnot. If they had the weapons they'd know how to use them. They'd served their five in the Cantard, too.

Nobody invited me to the party.

My feelings weren't hurt.

The first floating guy touched down. The light

around him faded. He took a step toward me, raising a hand.

The thunder lizards hit him. They took him apart in two blinks of an eye. Lucky for him he was wearing plate. Without armor they would've killed him quick.

The other two changed their minds about coming down. I don't know what they'd thought they were headed into, but they weren't here to become monster snacks. They hung there trying to decide what to do. The lizards started snapping at their heels. The guys decided to go up a little.

They started whipping lightning bolts around. The thunder lizards were too dumb to hightail it but Garrett knows when he's overmatched.

As I turned away I noticed the red light was missing from the thunderhead.

I got a bad feeling.

Crask, Sadler, and the boys went racing outside, carrying enough deadly equipment to mount a siege. I hadn't seen any of the big wizardries during my war, but I'd seen enough little ones to realize those flying guys could be in trouble.

They couldn't do three things at once. If they protected themselves from missiles and kept flailing around with thunderbolts, they were going to have to come down. Bingo. Instant monster munchies.

It was not my worry. I was headed for the pool.

The whole manor shook.

I hit the doorway and skidded to a halt.

Something was tearing its way into the pool room through the roof, going at it like the place was made of paper. A big, shiny, ugly, purplish-black face like that of a fangy gorilla glared through the hole. Then it started ripping the hole bigger.

Damn, it was huge!

Chodo's bodyguard headed for it. I don't know what he thought he was going to do. Maybe he just wanted to show the boss how brave he was.

I arrived beside Morley and Chodo. "Might be smart to get him out of here. That thing don't look sociable."

It dropped through the hole, and landed at the far

end of the pool, fifty feet away. It was twelve feet tall, had six arms, and might have been the thing on those temple coins. It wavered as though I was seeing it through an intense heat shimmer. Or as though it didn't know if it wanted to be a six-armed gorilla or something even uglier.

Chodo's bodyguard stopped charging. I guess he had suffered a fit of sense.

Morley said, "I think you're right."

The thing jumped Chodo's man before he could turn around. Their struggle was a one-second contest. Pieces of thug flew. The ape thing munched on a leg and eyed the rest of us.

Chodo cursed. Morley got his chair moving. I dipped a hand into a pocket. This seemed like the time.

The thing roared and charged. I let fly with the ruby bottle Peridont had given me. It splattered on the monster's chest. I spun to race Morley and the king-pin.

The monster skidded to a halt, scratched itself, and woofed puzzledly before it let out a howl. I reached the doorway and turned.

Flesh dribbled down the thing's chest like wax on a candle. And it was evaporating, shedding a red mist. It screamed and clawed itself and threw gelatinous gobbets of itself that splattered on the marble floor, evaporated, left pitted stains. It went into convulsions, tumbled into the pool, thrashed the water into a scarlet lather.

Morley said, "I'd hate to be the one who has to clean that up."

Chodo croaked, "Now it's a life I owe you, Mr. Garrett."

And Morley said, "Garrett, I grow ever more fearful that someday I'll be with you and you won't have a trick up your sleeve."

"Me too, Morley. Me too."

"What the hell was that thing?"

"Tell me and we'll both know."

"Never mind," Chodo growled. "Talk later. Take me to the front door."

He was right. We weren't out of anything yet. There was a brawl out front.

We arrived as it broke up. Most of the thunder lizards and half the thugs were out of action. But the effort put out by the airborne guys cost them, too. An athletic lizard caught one with a flying leap and dragged him down. The other, with about twenty missiles stuck in his armor, shot off like a comet going the wrong way.

Crask and Sadler noticed their boss. They came over as fast as they could limp.

Chodo told them, "Gentlemen, I'm angry." He didn't sound it. He's one of those guys who is at his nastiest when he seems his coolest. "There will be no more surprises."

The house and grounds shuddered. A scarlet fog belched through the spine of the house and dispersed in the breeze.

A diminished thunderhead went off with the last skywalker. And the sun peeked over the horizon, checking to see if it was safe to come out.

Chodo told his boys, "Find those people. Kill them." What a sweetheart. He looked at me and Morley. "Have someone drive these men home." He seemed blind to the fact that Crask and Sadler had been knocked around like shuttlecocks. "Here come Cage and Fletcher. Get their reports. Then move."

Two thugs were coming up the drive, their chins dragging on the ground.

30

I dropped out of the coach in front of my place and thought I'd keep dropping. "Getting too old for this," I muttered. This thing had become too deadly. I barely had time for a cleanup and maybe an hour nap before I started tracking Jill down.

If I could decide where to start.

I was sure she hadn't gone back to her apartment, though I'd check. She'd have more savvy.

Dean let me in. He fed me. I told him what had happened so my useless boarder could listen in. Dean was properly appalled, though he thought I'd exaggerated an incident into a whopper. Afterwards I went upstairs, stretched out, and continued to worry the problem I'd badgered all the way home.

Was I becoming identified with the kingpin?

People were getting killed and people were trying to kill me and all I could think about was the chance that my reputation for independence might be sullied.

That rat Dean let me snore for four hours. I yelled at him. He just smiled. I didn't yell too much. Chances are his reasoning was sounder than mine. Rested I was less likely to do something stupidly fatal.

I jumped up, did a quick change and cleanup, a quicker meal, and hit the street. My first stop was Jill's apartment. I had no problem getting inside. At first glance nothing had changed. But I felt a change. I looked around until I caught it.

The coin drawer was empty. Anybody could have gotten to that. But a battered old rag doll had disappeared too. I was willing to bet nobody but Hester Podegill would bother taking that.

So she'd risked coming back, if only for a moment. Just to grab a doll and some change? I didn't think so, not the ice maiden. It felt like a by-product of a more desperate mission. So I tossed the place again. And I didn't find another thing added or taken away.

I wasn't pleased as I slipped out. There should have been something . . . I eyeballed the doorway across the hall.

Why not look?

The door swung quietly as I pushed it inward. Nobody stampeded over me. I went inside. And there it was, lying in plain sight on a small writing table.

> *Darling:*
> *The key is safe. I have to disappear. They are getting desperate. Be careful. Love.*
>
> *Marigold*

Marigold? The handwriting matched that in a note written to me by one Hester Podegill. Did she have a different name for every person she knew? That would make her hard to find. No one would know who I was talking about.

She was an actress. Suppose she *became* a different person each time she donned a different name? She'd really be hard to find then.

I had to get to know who Jill had been before I looked for the Jill who existed now. That was a technique Pokey had used when he was after someone who was voluntarily missing. He talked to relatives, friends, enemies, neighbors, acquaintances, seducing them into talking however he had to, until he knew the missing person better than anyone else alive—until he was able to think like his quarry.

But that took time, and time was at a premium.

My best bet was Maya and the Doom. They were handy. And I owed Maya that apology.

I hit the street, troubled by a vague certainty that I'd overlooked something critical. But what? Nothing came. I moved slowly, checked my surroundings. Yep. The boys were out there.

They'd picked me up as I'd left my place. I'd spotted three of them coming over. They weren't getting close. They didn't seem inclined to get in the way. Nor did they work real hard at staying out of sight. I couldn't get a close look but they didn't have the lean, impoverished look I'd seen in my recent enemies.

If they were going to keep their distance I'd worry about them when the time came.

I was a block from the Doom's lair when I realized those guys weren't the only folks stalking me. The Sisters of Doom were on me, too.

People don't pay enough attention to kids, especially youngish girls not showing colors. I didn't get it until I realized I'd seen the same faces several times. Then I paid enough attention to pick out a couple I'd seen before.

Now what?

They closed in as I neared their hideout. I must have hurt Maya's feelings more than I'd thought.

She always was touchy and unpredictable.

If there was a confrontation it would come off better in the open, where I'd have some choice about which way I'd run.

I sat down on a tenement stoop.

That threw them, which was the plan. I expected them to get Maya and she'd come explain what a horse's ass I am.

It didn't work that way.

After a few minutes the girls understood that I was calling. They moved in. Some electric sense of trouble flooded the street. Everybody who wasn't part of it disappeared, though nobody ran and nobody hollered. The girls edged toward me with the group confidence of pack animals. I slid a hand into a pocket and toyed with one of Peridont's gifts.

I picked a sixteen-year-old I recognized, looked her in the eye and said, "Maya is overreacting, Tey. Tell her to get her tail out here and talk before somebody gets hurt."

The girls looked at each other, confused. But the one I'd spoken to didn't let an antique baffle her with bullshit. "Where is she, Garrett? What did you do with her?"

The gang was in close now, feeling nastier. And those guys that I'd noticed before were moving in behind the girls. There were five of them and I knew two, Saucerhead Tharpe and a slugger named Coltrain.

I got it.

Chodo was sure he'd need Jill's knowledge before he could settle with the Master. He was just as sure that I'd be the guy to find her. So he'd gotten Morley to lay on a loose cover to make sure I stayed healthy and to keep him posted.

Morley is a friend, sort of. He's a lot better friend when you keep an eye on him. He works these deals with his conscience.

I watched those five drift in behind the girls. I chuckled.

"You think it's funny, Garrett? You want to find out what we do with comedians? You want to see if you can laugh with your balls down your throat? What did you do with Maya?"

"I didn't do anything with her, Tey. I haven't seen her. That's why I came here. I want to talk to her."

"Don't feed us a ration of shit, Garrett. The last time anybody saw Maya she was hanging out with you, with moon eyes as big as a cow."

One of the little ones noticed my guardian angels. "Tey. We got company." The girls all looked around. The level of hostility dropped dramatically. Five guys like those five guys are enough to dampen anybody's belligerence.

"So," I said, grinning. "Tey. Why don't you sit down and we'll talk like civilized people." I patted the step.

Tey looked around. So did her friends. Those guys didn't look like their consciences would bother them much if they stomped a bunch of girls. They looked like they ate kids for snacks.

Tey was one of Maya's lieutenants. She fancied herself Maya's successor. She was a nasty little thing, uglier than a boiled turnip, with manners that made Maya seem genteel. But she had brains. She understood talk as an alternative to more popular methods of resolving disputes. She sat. I said, "I get the impression you guys have misplaced Maya."

"She never came home. Things she said made it sound like she had plans."

"She was with me," I admitted. "We wandered around trying to get a lead on some guys who killed a buddy of mine." I outlined our evening. The mob listened like they wanted to catch me in a lie.

Tey said, "You don't know Maya the way you think. You've got to take her seriously. She don't say it unless she means it. You know what she's done, don't you?"

"She tried to follow those guys so she could show me what she could do on her own," I said.

"Yeah. She gets dumb stubborn sometimes. What're we going to do?"

"I'll find her, Tey."

"She belongs to the Doom, Garrett."

"These guys play rough. This isn't a turf rumble, bang a few heads and it's over. These guys tried to hit Chodo Contague. They used sorcery."

She didn't bat an eye. "Sorcerer bleeds same as anybody else."

I looked at her hard. She wasn't whistling in the dark.

"You recall a blonde gal used to belong to the Doom, used a lot of made-up names, told a lot of lies about herself to make herself look important?"

"Hester Podegill?"

"That's one name she's used. She may be a little crazy."

"More than a little, Garrett. Sure, I remember her. Hester was her real name. She *wanted* to be crazy. She said when you're crazy the truth is whatever you want it to be. She wanted what she remembered not to be true."

I gave her the hard eye again. "You were close?"

"I was her only friend because I was the only one who listened. I was the only one who understood. I was the only one who knew what she had to forget."

Sometimes you cross the river so fast you don't get your toes wet getting to the other side. I flashed on all those lamps in Jill's apartment. "She started the fire that killed her family."

Tey nodded. "She dumped a gallon of oil on her stepfather when he was passed out drunk. She didn't think what the fire could do. She just wanted to hurt him."

If I'd killed my whole family I'd want to be somebody else, too. I'd want to be crazy. I might even want to be dead like them.

"What about her?" Tey asked.

"She's the key in the mess Maya and I were snooping around." I gave her more background. "She might be able to tell us something." I spoke softly, not wanting word to get around that Garrett wasn't the only one who might get a line on Jill Craight. For my sake and the Doom's.

Like I said, Tey had a brain. I'd told her enough for her to put a lot more together. "You're a snake, Garrett. A slick-talking snake. We're going to turn you loose. But next time you see me I just might be Maya's maid of honor."

I didn't handle that well. She laughed at me. It wasn't a pleasant laugh. She said, "I have some ideas where to look for Hester. I'll let you know."

I wanted to argue but it was too late. My convoy had decided I was safe and had faded. If I pressed I'd get the hostility perking again. So I sat quietly while the girls went off to do the hunting themselves.

I could think of nothing better to do so I went home, where Dean told me there had been no message and no visitors. I told him Maya might be in trouble. That upset him. He blamed me without saying a word. I asked if the Dead Man's temper had improved. He told me the old sack of lard had gone back to sleep.

"Fine. If that's the way he wants it, we'll just leave him out of our lives. We won't even bother him with the latest about Glory Mooncalled."

I was bitter. I blamed me for Maya's predicament, too. I had to take something out on somebody. The Dead Man could handle it.

31

I took a bath, changed again, ate, then for lack of any brilliant plan, walked up to the Tate family compound and had a big row with Tinnie. Then we made up.

Making up was so much fun we decided to do it twice.

It was getting dark by the time we finished making up for the third time and I started having trouble keeping my mind off business, so we had another little row to give us an excuse to make up again later. Then I headed out.

On the way I bumped into Tinnie's uncle Willard and he kind of obliquely wondered when Tinnie and I would be setting the date. He had the same problem Dean had.

It was going to start with him, too?

How come there are so many people trying to get other people hitched? Maybe if they backed off and didn't keep reminding a guy, he might drift into it before he sensed his danger.

Why was I so sour?

Because it had been such a nice afternoon. Because while I was playing, the bad guys were hard at work. Because a troubled kid that I liked was in it up to her ears and I hadn't lifted a finger to do anything about it.

"Oh, boy. Here we go again." I knew the signs. Out comes the squeaky old armor and the rusty old sword. Garrett was going to get all noble.

At least this time somebody would pay me for my trouble—though I wouldn't exactly be doing what they were paying me to do.

But I never quite do what they want done. I do what

I think needs doing. That is why not all of my former clients give me favorable references.

Not having any better idea what to do, I headed for the Old Shipway theater district. Who knew? I might stumble onto something blonde.

My convoy went with me. The faces changed periodically but there were never fewer than four men hovering around. It's nice to know you're loved.

I wondered why the Master's gang hadn't tried to pick me up again. Those I'd seen already had been too unskilled to notice I was travelling with protection.

I talked to everybody I knew in theater. They knew gorgeous blondes by the cartload, but none they could connect with any of the names I could tie to Jill. Since there was nothing about her that wasn't shared by a platoon of others, my sources couldn't help much. They were reduced to showing me the crop of blondes (some of them *very*) available, all of them squeezably lovely, and none of them Jill Craight.

Some of those lovelies were pleased to speculate on other lovelies not present, usually in less than flattering language, but that didn't help. Some just purred and begged to be petted.

It's a hard life.

Had I been in another mood it might have been a marvelous little treasure hunt. I made a mental note to cook a similar story someday and come wander through wonderland again, taking time to smell the flowers.

Where did they all come from? Where were they on my better days?

Sometime toward the end what was old news to everybody else caught up with me when I overheard a conversation among City Watch officers and their wives.

What the Watch is most famous for is its invisibility. TunFaire has one thousand men employed in the interest of public safety, but over the past century the Watch has become a place to hide freeloading nephews and other embarrassing relatives without recourse to the familial purse. These days ninety percent of those guys do their damnedest to stay out of harm's way and not interfere with the disorderly progress of life. When they do try something, it's invariably the wrong thing and they screw it up anyway.

The officers get to wear pretty uniforms and they like to show them off. The theater is a good place.

This bunch was grumbling about a crime so monstrous that popular outrage might get their butts kicked until they had to go out into the streets and *do* something. The consensus among the wives was that the Army ought to evict all the lower classes and nonhumans.

I wondered who they thought would cook for them and garden and do their laundry and make their cute little shoes and lovely gowns.

"What the hell was that all about?" I asked the guy who was squiring me from blonde to blonde at the Stratos.

"You haven't heard?"

"Not yet."

"Biggest mass murder in years, Garrett. A real massacre. It's all over town. You had your head under a rock?"

"A sheet. Cut the editorializing. What happened?"

"In broad daylight this afternoon a bunch of gangsters busted into a Wharf Street flophouse down in the South End and killed everybody. Smallest number I've heard is twenty-two dead and half a dozen dragged away as prisoners. They're saying Chodo Contague did it. Looks like we're in for a gang war."

I muttered, "When Chodo gets mad you don't have any trouble understanding his message." I wondered what Crask and Sadler were getting out of their prisoners. I'd hate to think they were ahead of me because they were less restrained in their methods.

What could I do? The one angle I had was Jill Craight. And that was turning up a big dead end.

Hell. Might as well go home, get in eight hours, and make an early start in the morning.

32

As Dean let me in he whispered, "There's a young woman here who wants to talk to you about Maya." His wrinkled nose told me what he thought of the visitor. And gave me a good idea who she was.

"Tey Koto?"

"She didn't offer a name."

Tey had gotten into the beer while Dean was away. "You got it whipped, you know that, Garrett?" She tried to pour beer down like she'd been drinking for twenty years, got some down the wrong pipe. She coughed foam all over the kitchen. Dean wasn't pleased. I pounded her on the back.

And as though he'd been waiting for me to get home, someone started pounding on the front door.

"Damn it! Now what?" I stomped up the hall, took a peek. It wasn't anybody I knew. He did have the rangy, weathered, impoverished look I associated with the Master's gang. So Chodo hadn't gotten them all.

I gave a look around to make sure he wasn't part of a tribe, then eyeballed him to get an estimate of what he might do himself. He kept pounding away.

"Guess I'd better talk to you before Saucerhead eats you up." Having a flight of guardian angels occasionally gets in the way.

I yanked the door open, grabbed him by the jacket, jerked him inside, and slammed him against the wall. He was astonished. "What?" I demanded.

He gobbled air and stammered.

I slammed him against the wall a couple more times. "Talk to me."

"The Master . . . The Master . . ." He had a set

speech to make. My welcome had put him off his pace.
He'd lost his lines.

Slam! "I can't play all night, low grade. You got
something to say, spit it out. I'm ticked off at you guys
already. Try my patience and I'll hurt you."

In a semi-coherent babble he let me know that the
Master felt the same about me and was going to allow
me one chance to get out of his way and start minding
my own business. Or else.

"Or else he'll put a bug down my shirt? Come on.
The creep has more nerve than brains. He's dead meat.
He's got about as long as it takes Chodo Contague to
find him. If you and your buddies have the sense of a
goose you'll dump him and run back where you came
from." I started muscling him out the door. "Tell your
harebrained boss he *is* my business and I intend to
mind it real close."

"Wait!"

The "or else" came. It wasn't the personal threat I
expected. I've been threatened plenty so I don't pay
much attention anymore. But this guy told me, "The
Master said to tell you he has your friend Maya Stump
and it will be she who pays if—"

Wham! Back against the wall. "And I have you, old
buddy."

"I am nothing. I am a finger on his hand. Cut me
off and another will grow in my place."

"You really believe that crap?" He did. What our
commanders in the Cantard wouldn't give for a few
thousand guys who didn't mind being expendable.
"Tey! Come in here."

She came. She'd been eavesdropping, anyway.
"What?"

"This guy says his boss has got Maya and they're
going to do nasty things to her. He doesn't care what
we do to him."

She sneered. "He'd care before *I* got through with
him." Oh, the easy cruelty of the young.

"He would. But his boss wouldn't have sent him if
he knew anything. So I think I'll just bruise him a little
and throw him out with the trash."

Like I said, she was a smart kid. She figured out

what to do. "Well, if I can't have him, the hell with you." She pranced back to the kitchen. And out the back door to talk to the Sisters she would've left around the neighborhood.

I banged the guy off the wall again. "You tell your boss if he messes with Maya he better pray Chodo finds him first. All Chodo wants to do is kill him.

"There. We've threatened each other and pounded our chests and acted like jerks. Get out before I lose my temper."

He looked at me like he thought it was a trick. Then he edged toward the door. When he was almost there I jumped at him. He yelped and took off.

I settled on the stoop and watched him go.

All that bullying hadn't accomplished a thing. I hadn't gotten any pleasure out of it. It didn't make me feel good now. I couldn't even convince myself there had been purpose in it.

33

Tey came out of the dark. I asked, "You got some-body tailing him?"

"Yeah."

"So that's taken care of. Why did you come? Dean said it was about Maya."

"Yeah. I think we've got a lead."

I gave her my raised eyebrow. It went to waste in that light, so I said, "How's that?"

"You hear about that mess on Wharf Street? Where Chodo's boys offed a whole mob? That sounded like some of what you told me about. We went down there and talked to kids who live there. Some of them saw the whole thing. Chodo's guys didn't kill everybody. A bunch got away out the back. They dragged a couple people with them. One of them sounded like Maya."

Well, well. "Very interesting. Where did they go?"

"We couldn't find out. They jumped into boats and headed down the river. But they didn't go far. The kids told us what the boats looked like. We found one of them a half mile away. And we know they didn't leave Tun-Faire because that one just came here to threaten you."

I sure as hell didn't feel like taking a walk but I said, "Suppose we go nose around?"

I told Dean what I'd be doing. I expected some backchat, because he'd had to stay away from home a lot. But he didn't say a word. I bet he would've said a few if I hadn't been looking for Maya.

It was several miles to the Wharf Street massacre site. Tey's boats had gone south from there, a goodly hike. After a while we started talking, mostly Tey making herself shine bright in the Doom. I asked her about Maya. She wouldn't tell me anything I didn't already know. From time to time a messenger came to tell her about the man being followed. He was headed the same direction we were. Tey told the messengers our anticipated route so she could be found again.

My angels were out there, too, shadowing me.

We had a parade going.

"I tried looking for Hester tonight," I said at one point. "I looked at every blonde who works Old Shipway. None of them were her."

Tey laughed. "Old Shipway? You're precious, Garrett."

"Eh?" *Precious*?

"You *believed* that actress stuff?"

Well, yes, I'd bought it after Peridont validated it.

"Garrett, the only acting she ever did was the kind where the other actors are donkeys or guys that should have been born donkeys or ogres or trolls. You know what I mean?"

I grunted. I knew. I was disgusted, not so much because of what Jill might be doing as because of a failure of my vaunted eyesight. I'd let myself see only what I'd expected to see. I'd swallowed it whole when Peridont had fed me a whopper about the provenance of his mistress. I'd forgotten the first rule: everybody lies about sex, and the client *always* lies about it.

I felt pretty dumb.

Tey said, "She's back in the Tenderloin. I had a couple kids go down there. They saw her but she disappeared before they got close enough to find out anything."

I wondered if I ought to buy that. Jill had come up with the Doom. They didn't have much reason to turn her up for me.

This was an odd one, all intangibles. In a case where a pot of money is the stake, you know where the axis is. You watch the money and soon enough everything becomes clear—even when some of the players aren't motivated primarily by greed. For them the pot becomes an excuse, a lever.

So far I hadn't caught a whiff of a pot, excepting maybe the Relics Peridont had mentioned the first time we talked, or whatever it was the boys had been so sure they could steal from Jill. That seemed to have been forgotten in the fusing and feuding since.

I'm a guy who doesn't understand intangible stakes. I know some would argue that I have a set of values I take pretty seriously, but if I can't eat it or spend it or make it go purr in the night, I don't know what to do with it. It's a weakness, a blind spot. Sometimes I forget there are guys willing to get killed over ideas. I just go bulling ahead looking for the pot of gold.

We got onto Wharf Street. The guy who had dropped by my place was still ahead of us. My angels were out there in the dark, probably cussing me for my thoughtlessness in running them all over the city. Didn't I ever sleep?

Guys, I was cussing me, too. For the exact same reason.

"There's the place where it happened."

Wharf Street, the waterfront, the whole commercial and industrial strip down there facing the river, is a whole lot like me. It never goes to sleep. When the day people move out, the night workers come in and the economy keeps rolling along.

Forty or fifty goblins and ogres and whatnot were standing around gossiping while a group of city ratmen got set to load the bodies on wagons for delivery to crematoria. Moving with its customary lightning efficiency the city was just now getting around to cleaning up.

The operation was proceeding in the usual fire-drill state of confusion.

The ratmen moved at a velocity barely perceptible. I said, "I'm going to go nose around."

"Won't they stop you?"

"Maybe. But any human who turns up this time of night looking officious they'll figure belongs."

I was right. I got some dark looks but they were the kind reserved for bosses in general, for being bosses. Nobody said a word.

I didn't expect to find much and I was right again. The scavengers and sightseers and souvenir hunters had picked the bones clean. They'd even stripped the stiffs. The ratmen were bitching because there wasn't anything left.

If they want the cream, they ought to get there in time to skim it.

I did notice one thing right off. Those sopranos had

taken over the whole building and had been there long enough to turn it into a weird residential temple. One wall in every room had been replastered and painted with murals depicting creatures with eight limbs, no two the same. I saw a spider, a crab, an especially ugly octopus, and a lot of things that don't come with eight limbs, including a ringer for the thing that had visited Chodo. One double-ugly was human except that it had a skull for a face and something disgusting in every hand. Above him was the same motto as on the temple coins, "He Shall Reign Triumphant."

I said, "I don't think I'd like that."

"Ugly mother, ain't he?" a ratman remarked.

"He is. Any idea who he's supposed to be?"

"You got me, chief. Looks like something somebody dreamed up while he was doing weed to get him through a withdrawal fit."

"Yeah. Not your average boy next door."

There wasn't anything else. I hit the street. We headed south. I didn't have much to say. I was thinking that if I ever stopped chasing around long enough I'd have to spend some time researching these guys and their devil god.

We walked another mile. I started mumbling about only now realizing how damned big TunFaire is. One of the Sisters told us the guy we were following had gone into a warehouse half a mile ahead, fifty yards from where the one getaway boat had been abandoned.

The girls had the place scouted when we got there. There were two doors, front and back, and no windows at ground level, just some high up to let out the heat during the summer. The main door was big enough to roll wagons in and out. The girls had the back covered. They had no idea who or what was inside. They didn't want to find out.

I looked at the place. What did I have here? An army of kids, nasty but not real fighters. My angels, who had no interest in launching a raid. And a big unknown.

"I'm going in there," I said.

"You're crazy, Garrett." Tey shook her head slowly.

"Sometimes you have to make things happen."

34

The man-sized door in the wagon door wasn't locked. I stepped inside. The place was as dark as a tax man's heart. I listened. I heard nothing but what might have been mice scurrying, then what sounded like a door slamming at the far end of the place.

I eased forward, sliding my feet, feeling the air with my left hand. Far away, I glimpsed a flicker of light above head level. I kept moving cautiously, wishing I had owl's eyes.

I didn't get that wish but I did get light.

A bunch of guys jumped out of nowhere, opening the shutters of lanterns they'd kept well hidden. I counted nine. A tenth, from behind the others, said, "Mr. Garrett. We'd begun to fear you hadn't taken the bait."

"Sorry I'm late. Had trouble with tardiness all my life."

Weapons appeared. My sense of humor wasn't going to play with this crowd.

"If I'd known it was that kind of party I'd have dressed."

I had no idea how I'd be affected myself, but I let loose with my green bottle.

I reacted the same as everyone else. In three seconds I not only didn't know where I was or why I was there, but I wasn't too sure who I was. I couldn't move in a straight line. I tried—and hung a left and walked into a stack of crates. They were empty. I kept going. The whole pile came down on top of me.

That was one to brag to the grandkids about.

I tried to fight the crates, but they were too quick. So I just gave up and let them have their way with me.

I would have taken a nap except a bunch of people kept yelling at some guy called Garrett and I couldn't get to sleep for all the racket.

Somebody dug me out of the pile. Two of my angels stood me up while another popped me in the face. That didn't help a whole lot.

The other two started tying guys up. There were girls all over the place, looking for something portable and valuable. I got my tongue untangled. "Maya."

Kids started running around yelling, "Maya!"

Guys yakked about getting hold of some guy named Chodo, they could sell him their prisoners for a fortune. I seemed to remember them as angels. They didn't sound very angelic.

My head began to clear. "I'm all right now, guys. You don't need to hold me up."

Wedge snapped, "What the hell kind of stunt was that, Garrett? Walking into a trap you knew was there."

"Had to make something happen." I wasn't going to admit the ambush had been a surprise to me, too. Anyway, I figured it would not be smart to brag that I'd wanted to make them come in the warehouse after me. They might not appreciate that.

They grumbled and let me go. I picked up a lantern and tottered back into the warehouse, following shouting girls.

Maya was in a loft office all the way back, above another double-ugly homemade temple. She was tied up enough for four kids. She looked a little shopworn, with bruises and abrasions that said she hadn't been a cooperative prisoner.

I didn't find her. The girls got there first. They were slicing her out of her cocoon when I arrived. But I got the credit. "Garrett! I knew you'd come."

"Had to, Maya. When somebody does something to a guy's partner, a guy is supposed to do something about it."

She squealed and stumbled at me.

Some females can't tell a wisecrack from a marriage proposal. "I don't want to hurt your feelings, kid, but maybe you ought to stand downwind till we get you next to some soap and water.''

"We can throw her in the river, Garrett," Tey suggested.

Maya glared green death. Tey glared back. There was no love lost between those two. I asked, "How many got away?"

"None." Tey snapped it. "They were all waiting for you except one. They have him out back."

"Good. Can you walk, Maya? We can't hang around. These guys have friends who'll check up on them. Not to mention the Doom is way off its turf."

"You're not going to ask those guys questions?"

"If I was to set an ambush I wouldn't use guys that could tell anybody if they blew it. And these guys are making a career of screwing up. You think any of them can tell me anything you didn't pick up while you were their guest?"

She admitted it was unlikely. "They were a bunch of farmers before they came to TunFaire. They don't know spit from dog doo. They're just trying to do what their wacko god wants." But she wanted to get back at somebody.

"Kick somebody in the ribs on the way. Come on. We've got to go. Thank Tey for helping find you. She didn't have to."

Maya did, but not very graciously. She must have felt threatened. When you're a chuko, you have to prove yourself everyday.

There wasn't anyone for her to kick. Wedge had decided reinforcements were likely to arrive so he and his buddies had made sure they'd collect whatever bounties Chodo had put on those guys.

Maya looked bad when we hit the street. I said, "I told you Wedge wasn't nice people."

"Yeah." After we walked a while, she said, "Men like that Wedge, they're a whole different kind of bad, aren't they? People like my stepfather . . . He was cruel, but I don't think he could've killed a dog. That Wedge did it like it was nothing."

Chukos put a lot of value on being tough. And a lot of them are hard, nasty little critters—especially in front of an audience. Some are dead losses at thirteen. But some still have the kid in there somewhere behind the defenses, and that kid wants to believe there's some point to living. Maya still contained that hidden child. And it wanted some reassurance.

"Who do you think does the most real harm?" I asked, thinking maybe anybody else was better qualified for this. "The emotional cripple who tries to cripple people who can't protect themselves? Or the emotionally dead killer like Wedge who basically doesn't bother anybody but them that asked for it?"

That wasn't saying what I wanted to say the best way. Maybe there were big holes in it, but there was plenty of truth, too. The hurt a creep like her old man did lasts a lifetime. It gets passed on to the next generation. Wedge's kind of hurt is flashy but it doesn't last. And it doesn't eat up kids who can't fight back.

I didn't like Wedge. I didn't like what he was. He probably didn't have much use for me but I'd bet he'd agree.

Anyway, I knew what I was saying. And Maya seemed to get the message. "Garrett . . ."

"Never mind. We'll talk when we get home. The bad time is over."

Sure it was. You smooth talker, Garrett. Now try and convince yourself.

Dean fussed over Maya like he was her mother. I didn't get a chance to talk to her. The sun was coming up, so I said the hell with it and went to bed.

35

My own body turned traitor. I woke up at noon and couldn't get back to sleep. I should have been smug, the hero who had gone out to save the damsel and had succeeded, but I didn't feel smug or heroic. I felt confused, angry, put upon, frustrated. Most of all I felt out of control.

I'm not used to getting knocked around without at least some idea of what's happening and why. In this one I was starting to suspect that maybe nobody knew and everybody was too busy bobbing and weaving to figure out why we were in the ring.

Well, hell! I'm a thug for hire. I get paid. Do I have to think, too?

I want to know, for my own peace of mind. I'm no Morley Dotes, for whom the money is the only morality.

I went downstairs to stoke the body's fires.

Dean had heard me knocking around and had gotten a meal started. Hot tea was on the table. Rewarmed muffins landed beside it as I entered the kitchen. There was butter and blueberry preserves and apple juice, and sausages were popping in the pan while eggs boiled.

The place was crowded. "You having a party?" Two women were there with Dean.

He gave me one of his looks.

I recognized one of his more determined nieces, Bess, but the other woman, whose hair Bess was plaiting . . . "Maya?"

"Do I look too awful?"

No. "Stand up. Turn around. Let me look at you." She didn't look awful at all. They'd drum her out of the Doom if they saw her like this. "I just ran out of excuses for not taking you out. Except for maybe there'd be riots." She looked good. I'd guessed that. But I hadn't guessed just how good.

Bess said, "Down, boy."

Dean said, "Mr. Garrett!" He used his protective father tone.

"Phoo! I don't mess with children."

"I'm not a child," Maya protested. And when you thought about it, she wasn't. "I'm eighteen. If it wasn't for the war I'd be married and have a couple of kids."

It was true. In prewar times they'd married them off at thirteen or fourteen and had given up hope of getting rid of them by the time they were fifteen.

"She's got a point," I told Dean.

"You want these eggs the way you like them?"

How typical of him to drag in extraneous issues. "You won't hear another word from me."

"Grown men," Maya told Bess, who nodded in contempt. That nearly sent Dean off on one of those tirades that bust out of him every time one of his nieces opens her mouth.

It occurred to me that Bess was barely three months older than Maya. Dean had no trouble picturing Bess married to me.

People seldom see any need to be consistent.

The key word there, though—of course—is "married."

I said, "Let's forget it. Maya. Tell me what you learned while those people had you." I went to work eating.

Maya sat down. Bess started on her hair again. "There isn't much to tell. They didn't try to entertain or convert me."

"You always pick up more than you think, Maya. Try."

She said, "All right. I got the bright idea I could show you something if I followed those guys. All I showed you was a fat chance to tell me you told me so."

"I told you so."

"Smartass. They grabbed me and dragged me off and kept me in a place they used for a temple. A weird, grungy place they'd made over by painting the walls with ugly pictures."

"I saw it."

"I sat through their religious services. Three times a day I sat through them. Those guys don't do anything but work and eat and pray for the end of the world. I think. Mostly they didn't use Karentine in their services."

"They sound like a fun bunch."

Maya snatched a buttered muffin off my plate and smiled brightly. She was moving right in. "Get used to it, Garrett. Yeah. They were fun. Like an abscessed tooth."

I chewed sausage and waited.

"They're really negative, Garrett. In the Doom I know people who are negative, but those guys could give lessons. I mean it. They were praying for the end of the world."

"You're telling me things I didn't know. Keep going."

That was praise enough to light her up. It takes so little sometimes. I had a feeling she'd turn out all right, given encouragement. "Tell me more."

She said, "They call themselves the Sons of Hammon. I think Hammon must have been some kind of prophet, about the same time as Terrell."

Dean said, "He was one of Terrell's original six Companions. And the first to desert him. A bitter parting over a woman."

I looked at him in surprise.

He continued, "Later dogma says Hammon betrayed Terrell's hiding place to the Emperor Cedric—if you find him mentioned at all. But in the Apocrypha, written that same century and kept intact in secret since, it's the other way around and Hammon died two years before Terrell was turned in by his own wife. Known to us as Saint Medwa."

"What?" I gave the old man the long look now. He'd never shown much interest in religion or its special folklore. "What is this? Where'd you get all this? When did you become an expert? I've never heard of this Hammon character and my mother dragged me to church until I was ten.''

"Council of Ai, Mr. Garrett. Five Twenty-One, Imperial Age. Two hundred years before the Great Schism. All the bishops and presters and preators attended, along with a host of imperial delegates. In those days every diocese spawned its own heresy. And every heretic was a fanatic. The emperor wanted to end a century of fighting. In Five Eighteen in Costain, in one day of rioting, forty-eight thousand had been killed. The emperor was a confirmed Terrillite and he had the swords. He ordered the Council to expunge the memory of Hammon, so the proto-Church and Orthodox sects wrote him out of their histories. I know because my father taught me. He was a Cynic seminarian for three years and a lay deacon all his life.''

You never know everything about somebody, do you?

You can't argue with an expert. Besides, the ''facts'' I'd been taught had never made sense. The histories of Terrell's time, outside the religious community, didn't jibe with what the priests wanted us to believe.

We had been told that Terrell had been martyred for his witnessing to the masses. But the way the secular histories go, the religion business was wide open in those days. Every street corner in the cities and every hamlet in the country had its prophet. They could rave all they wanted. Moreover, Terrell had been a prophet of Hano, who had had more followers then than he does now.

"Then why did Cedric kill him?''

"Because he started in on the imperial household and establishment. He got political. And he didn't have sense enough to shut his mouth when they told him to stick to putting words into the mouth of Hano, who can look out for himself.''

I always figured that. Why would Hano need henchmen down here to knock the heads of unbelievers when he's the Great Head-knocker himself? "So who are these Sons of Hammon?''

"I don't know. I've never heard of them.''

Maya said, "They're devil-worshippers, Garrett. They won't even speak their god's name. They just call him the Devastator and beg him to bring on the end of the world."

"Crazies."

"He answers them, Garrett." She started shaking. "That was the bad part. I heard him. Inside my head. He promises them the end of the world before the turn of the century if they carry out his commands faithfully. Many will die in the struggle but the martyrs will be rewarded. They will be drawn to his bosom in peace and ecstasy forever."

I exchanged looks with Dean. Maya's eyes had glazed and she was babbling like something had taken possession of her. "Hey! Maya! Come back." I clapped my hands in front of her nose.

She jumped and looked bewildered. "Sorry. I got carried away, didn't I? But it got pretty intense when those guys got a service going and their god talked to them. Hell. It was really bad the night before last. He showed up in person."

"Yes?" Did I want to know about this? "A thing like an ape, six arms, twelve feet tall?"

"That was the shape he assumed. Uglier than a barrel of horned toads. How did you know?"

"I met him. Out at Chodo's. He didn't make good company. But he seemed kind of puny for a god."

"That wasn't really the god, Garrett. I'm not sure what they meant but the thing was something like what the real god dreamed. Only he had control of the dream, like you do sometimes. You know?"

The more she talked the more nervous she got. I wondered if they'd done something to her that she either wouldn't talk about or couldn't remember. "Is this upsetting you?"

"Some. Things like that don't happen to people like me."

"Maya, things like that don't happen to people like me, either. Or anybody else. I've had some weird cases but I've never gone up against a god. Nobody these days has to deal with gods who really show up."

I glanced around. Dean was troubled. Maya was

troubled. Even Bess, who didn't have a notion what we were talking about, bless her vacant head, was worried. I thought back on what I'd said.

A god who really shows up.

That's nightmare stuff. Who expects the gods to take an active role these days? Not even guys like Peridont. The gods haven't busybodied since antiquity.

What Maya had to tell was interesting, but useful only in a cautionary sense. I still had to get my hands on Jill Craight and maybe squeeze her. Something had started all this excitement bubbling.

I recalled the note Jill had left in that apartment. I had made maybe the biggest screwup of a career checkered with goofs.

I should have sat on that sucker for as long as it took. Somebody was going to come and get it—somebody who might be at the root of this whole damned business.

Maybe I hadn't needed Jill at all. If only I had waited there until he came . . . But then I wouldn't have gotten Maya loose . . .

Maybe it wasn't too late. "I have to go out."

36

It was too late. The note was gone. I cussed my blindness. I tore that apartment to shreds looking for something, anything, and found exactly what I deserved to find. Nothing.

So it would be the hard way after all, hunt Jill Craight until something shook loose.

I hoped I wouldn't be hearing from the Sons of Hammon for a while. The way they'd taken it on the chin, I couldn't see them doing anything but backing off to regroup. I just hoped the bastards were as confused as the rest of us.

I got out of there and headed to the area where Tey Koto claimed Jill was likely to be found.

There are pimples and pockets of Hell and Purgatory all over TunFaire. People wouldn't want their daughters hanging out there. The kingpin probably has a finger in all of them. The worst, the biggest, where Chodo's presence is heavier than that of a king, is the Tenderloin, sometimes called the Street of the Damned. If you want it, someone there will sell it. And the kingpin will get his cut.

It's Hell on earth for those who survive that way, used and abused and discarded the instant they lose their marketability. For those who haven't been to the underside and haven't lived with the ticks on society's underbelly, it's difficult to believe people will use each other so badly.

Believe me, there are people out there who'll destroy a hundred lives for pocket change and never know a moment's remorse. Who wouldn't, in fact, understand if you told them they'd done something

wrong by addicting a twelve-year-old so she'd cooperate as a thirty-a-day flat-backer.

They understand "against the laws of Man" but not
"against the law of humanity." Right is whatever you
make it, for as long as you can make it last.

They're out there. And they're the real bogeymen.

And through those mean streets walks a lonely man,
a solitary knight-errant, the last honorable man, bent
but not broken by the lowering storm . . .

Boy! Pile it on like that and I might have a future
as a street-corner prophet—complete with all the kicks
in the teeth that implies.

People don't want to be told to do right. They don't
really *want* to do right. They want to do whatever they
want—and whine that it's not fair, it's not their fault,
when it comes time to pay the piper.

There are times when I don't care much for my
brothers and sisters, when I'd gladly see half of them
buried alive.

I don't go into my high holy mode too often, but a
trip to the Tenderloin gets me every time.

So much that goes on there is unnecessary. In many
cases neither the exploiters nor the exploited need to
be doing what they do to survive. TunFaire is a pros-
perous city. Because of the war with the Venageti and
Karenta's successes in it, there's work for anyone who
wants it. And honest jobs go begging until nonhuman
migrants come to the city to fill them.

A century ago nonhumans were curiosities, seldom
seen, more the stuff of legend than real. Now they
make up half the population and the bloods are becoming inextricably mixed. For real excitement wait until
the war is over and the armies disband and all the war-
related jobs dry up.

I'll step down off my box with the observation that,
hell though the Tenderloin is, and as vile, vicious, or
degraded as its habitués may be, most have some
choice about being there.

"Garrett."

I think I jumped about four feet high because my
sense of survival had gone into hibernation. I came

down so ready for trouble I had the shakes. "Maya! What the hell are you doing here?"

"Waiting for you. I figured you'd come this way."

Was the little witch turning into a mind reader? "You didn't say why." I knew why, though.

"We're partners, remember? We're looking for somebody. And there's some places a man isn't going to get into no matter what he tries."

"You get hiking right back home. I'm going into the Tenderloin. That's no place for—"

"Garrett, shut your mouth and look at me. Am I nine years old and fresh out of a convent?"

She was right. But that didn't make me like it, or incline me to change my mind. It's weird how the symptoms of fatherhood had set in. But damn it, Maya out of her sleazeball duds and chuko colors wasn't anybody's little girl. She was a woman and it was obvious.

And that was maybe two-thirds of my problem. "All right. You want to stick your neck out, come on."

She joined me, wearing a smug smile filled with good teeth.

I said, "You snuck up on me, you know. You grew up. I can't help remembering the filthy brat I found beat to hell all those years ago."

She grinned and slipped her arm through mine. "I didn't sneak, Garrett. I took my time and did it right. I knew you'd wait for me."

Whoa! Who was talking shit to who here?

Maya laughed. "If we're going to do it, let's go."

37

To understand the Tenderloin—to even picture it if you've never been there—you have to get in touch with the seamiest side of yourself. Pick a fantasy, one you wouldn't tell anyone about. One that makes you uncomfortable or embarrassed when you think about it. In the Tenderloin there's somebody who'll do it with you, for you, or to you, or somebody who'll let you watch if that's your need.

Let your imagination run away. You can't think of anything somebody hasn't thought and done already. Hell, somebody's thought of something even more disgusting. And it's all available there in Wonderland. And not just sex, though that's the first thing that jumps to mind.

At that time of day, late afternoon, most of the Tenderloin was just waking up. The district worked around the clock, but the majority of its patrons were like insects who shun the light. The district wouldn't get white-hot until after sunset.

I asked Maya, "You been down here before?"

"Never with a gentleman." She laughed.

I tried to scowl but her constant good humor was catching. I smiled.

"Sure," she said. "One of our favorite games. Come down here and watch the freaks. Maybe roll a drunk or kick the shit out of a pimp. We got up to lots of stuff. Most of the people who come here don't dare complain."

"You know how dangerous that is?" The people of the Tenderloin are solicitous of their customers.

She gave me the look the young save for old farts who say dumb things. "What did we have to lose?"

Only their lives. But kids are immortal and invulnerable. Just ask them.

It wasn't yet dark but we had plenty of company on the outer fringe, where the offerings are relatively tame. Gentlemen were window shopping, barkers were barking, my angels were lurking, and a dozen prepubescent boys were trying to mooch copper. When I turned one down he took a big pinch of Maya's bottom and ran off. I roared in outrage, as I was suppose to do, and took a step after the brat, then the humor hit me. "You're on the other side now, sweetheart. You're one of the grown-ups."

"It hurts, Garrett."

I laughed.

"You bastard! Why don't you kiss it better?"

There in the tamer parts the houses display their wares in big bay windows. I couldn't help admiring what I saw.

"You're drooling, you old goat."

I probably was but I denied it.

"What's she got that I don't?" she demanded half a minute later. And I couldn't answer that one. The delicacy in question was younger than she and no prettier, but provocative as hell.

I needed blinders. My weakness was getting me into deep shit.

"There she is."

"Huh? Who? Where?"

Maya gave me a nasty look. "What do you mean, who? Who the hell are we looking for?"

"Take it easy. Where did you see her?" Grow up a little, Garrett. You got somebody's feelings to consider.

"Right up ahead. About a block."

Her eyes were better than mine if she could pick somebody out of the crowd at that distance.

I caught a glimpse of blonde hair in a familiar style. "Come on!"

We hurried. I tried to keep that hair in sight. It vanished, reappeared, vanished, reappeared. We gained ground. The hair disappeared in the swirl near the en-

trance to a "theater" just opening for the first show.
And it didn't reappear.

I was as sure as Maya that we'd spotted Jill.

I tried asking questions of the theater's barker. He
was a lean whippet of a man, hide tanned from expo-
sure to the weather. He didn't look like a nice guy.
He looked at me and saw something he didn't like,
either. The promise of five marks silver got me a look
of contempt. This guy not only didn't know anything
about any blonde, he'd forgotten how to talk.

Maya pulled me away before I tried to squeeze
something out of him. One must be careful putting the
arm on the help in the Tenderloin. They hang together
like grapes, them against the world. "Next time how
about I do the talking?" she said. "Even these jaded
apes will listen to me."

They would, just to spite me. "All right. Let's go
across the street and sit and give this a think." The
Tenderloin does boast a few amenities absent from the
rest of the city, like street-side loos and public
benches. Anywhere else benches would get busted up
for firewood and loos kicked down for the hell of it.
Here the busters themselves would get broken up for
kindling before they got done with their fun.

The organization has no patience with people who
cost it money.

We went across. We sat. I considered the area and
my options while Maya turned away offers by explain-
ing that she was engaged. "Although," she told one
would-be swain, "I might be able to shake this old
guy later."

"Maya!"

"What do you care, Garrett? You're not interested.
He looked like he might know how to have a good
time."

Damn them all! I swear, before they let them go into
puberty, they make them sign a contract in blood saying they'll cause us all the aggravation they can. "Give
me a break, Maya. At least give me a chance to get
used to the idea of you being a woman."

That put a smug look on her face. She chalked up
six points for Maya on her secret scoreboard.

The majority of nearby businesses catered to spectators rather than participants. My stomach did a little growl and knot at the thought of Jill Craight starring in one of those shows.

Nothing is impossible, of course. I just didn't like it.

I didn't have much trouble believing it. The woman obviously had mental problems. I could see her making the kinds of connections that would convince her she was fit for nothing else. The human mind does weird things.

What amazes me is that we manage to cope as well as we do, that the race not only survives but manages to make the occasional stumbling advance. Maybe there is a force greater than ourselves, an engine driving us toward greatness.

It would be comforting to know my species is destined for something that will outshine its past and present. The Church, the Orthodox sects, all the Hanite cults and factions and denominations, offer that hope, but they've surrounded it with so much bullshit and in so many cases have given in to worldly temptations which act against the hope, that they've forfeited any right to guide us toward the brighter day.

Maya snuggled a little closer, as though the evening breeze had begun to bite. "What're you brooding about, Garrett?"

"The Sons of Hammon as a committed entropic force, convinced that our proper destiny is oblivion."

She leaned back and looked me in the eye. "You trying to shit me? Or are you just talking dirty?"

"No." I started to explain. After a minute she snuggled up again, got hold of my hands, and rested her cheek on my shoulder. She grunted in the right places to show she was listening. I'm sure we made a touching picture.

After a bit I said, "We got to get our minds back on business." I had to anyway. The little witch was getting to me. "You know anything about this area?"

"There's a lot of freaks."

I didn't need to be told that. I have pretty fair eyesight.

Six of the nearer buildings hosted live shows. Several more were havens for those who provided special services. A few seemed to be genuine residential hotels. And there was one place I couldn't pin down at all.

It had no barker. It had no sign. It had no heavy traffic, but in the time we'd been sitting, five men and a woman had entered the place. Four had come out. Only one had shown the furtiveness which characterizes a move toward an act considered perverse. Those who had come out had looked pleased and relaxed, relieved, but not in the way the sexually sated do.

"What about that place?" I pointed. "Know it?"

"No."

Curiosity had ahold of me. A lamplighter was working his way toward us, pushing his cartload of scented oils from post to post, topping things up and lighting the parti-colored lights that lend Tenderloin evenings a sleazy mask of carnival. When he stopped at the lamppost at the end of the bench I opened my mouth to ask about the place that intrigued me.

Maya elbowed me in the ribs. "My turn, remember?"

She got up.

It must be something they get in their mother's milk. I've never seen a woman yet who couldn't turn on the heat when she wanted. She whispered. The lamplighter's eyes took fire without help from his match. He nodded. She touched him over the heart and let her fingertips slide over a half foot of his jacket. He grinned and looked at the place that caught my eye. Then he saw the deaf barker looking daggers his way.

He ran out of words before he spoke. He turned stupider than an ox. I told Maya, "I'm getting irritated. Let's go."

I got up, took her hand, headed for the entrance to the curious place.

The barker saw my intent and abandoned his post. He hustled up the street, planted himself in my path. I told him, "Friend, you're getting on my nerves. In about two seconds I'm going to break your leg."

He grinned like he hoped I'd try. Maya said, "Garrett, be careful."

I looked around. Half a dozen natives were closing in. They looked like they'd been deprived of the pleasure of stomping somebody for a long time. But my angels were moving in behind them, and Saucerhead was leading the pack. He could handle this bunch by himself. I told the barker, "Move it or lose it, Bruno."

"You asked for it. Take him."

Saucerhead smacked a couple of heads together. Wedge cracked a couple more with a club. The barker's eyes got big. I asked, "You ready to move?"

Saucerhead said, "Garrett, you got to quit this crap. You're going to start a riot."

The barker's eyes popped. He had a nasty suspicion. "You the Garrett that works for Chodo?" He stepped out of the way. "Why didn't you say so?"

Saucerhead rumbled. "Yeah, Garrett. Why didn't you say so?"

"Because I don't care what Chodo claims, I *don't* work for him. I work for me." I had to keep that point clear for my own peace of mind.

The barker said, "You understand, I didn't know you was working for Chodo. We get all kinds down here. I wouldn't of give you no shit if you'd told me."

It was going to be a long fight, shaking loose from that tie. "Look, all I want to do is go in there and see what goes on."

The barker said, "You was asking about some blonde bitch. What you want to know? If I can help . . ."

And Saucerhead, at the same time, said, "I come down here to tell you Morley needs to see you. Says he got some news for you."

"Good for Morley. If you'll all excuse me?" I pushed past the barker and headed inside. Maya stuck close and kept her mouth shut. Good for her, too.

38

The door to the place was unlocked. Maybe it couldn't be locked. It sagged in its frame. Inside there was a scrawny old guy in a rickety chair shoving sticks into a stove. It was hot enough to broil steaks but he was grumbling about the cold. He was one giant liver spot. "Drop it on the counter," he said, not bothering to look up.

"What?"

He looked, then. At me, then at Maya. His brushy white eyebrows wormed around. "You together?"

"Yes."

"Well, whatever. Have to charge you. Six marks silver. First time? Take any box where the curtain is open. You don't like what you get, you can move once on the house. You still ain't satisfied, it's another mark every move until you light."

I put the money down. He went back to feeding the fire. Maya gave me a puzzled look. I shrugged and stepped up to a curtained doorway.

It opened to reveal a long hallway. A half-dozen curtained alcoves opened to either side. Four had their curtains drawn. We walked down the hall and back. I heard soft voices behind the drawn curtains. Where the curtains were open there was nothing but a chair and a table pushed against a wall of glass. There was nothing behind the glass but darkness.

"What is this place, Garrett?"

"I guess if you have to ask you don't belong here." I led her into the nearest open room and drew the curtain. The place was five feet deep by six wide and very dark with the curtain closed. I felt for what looked like a pull cord and gave it a tug. Bells tinkled somewhere overhead, muted. A light appeared high on the other side of the glass.

A well-dressed and impossibly beautiful woman came down a spiral staircase into an eight by twelve room that might have been a lady's bedroom transported from the Hill. It was a set, obviously, but just as obviously perfect in every detail.

"Garrett," Maya whispered, "that woman isn't human. She's pure high elf."

I saw it but I didn't believe it. Who ever heard of an elvish whore? But Maya had it right. She was elvish, and so damned beautiful she hurt my eyes.

She began to undress as though unaware that she was being observed, pulled a chair up to a table facing the glass from the far side, then sat in her underthings. She began removing makeup slowly. The glass must be a mirror on her side.

Maya pinched me. "Stop panting. You'll fog the glass."

The elvish woman heard something. She cocked her head quizically. She asked, "Is someone there?"

That was a voice men could kill for. I didn't know her from dog food. I like to think I'm as hard-nosed a cynic as they make, but I had no problem imagining that silver-bells whisper on my pillow, sending me whooping through the teeth of Hell.

She stood up and slipped out of another layer of clothing.

Maya said, "I'm not going to ask what this one has that I don't." She sounded awed.

I was petrified.

"Is someone there?" she asked again.

I reached out and touched the glass. A sound-permeable glass that could be seen through from one side only? Someone had invested heavily in some very specialized designer sorcery. And I could see the touch of genius in it. This mundane bit of voyeurism and pretense was a hundred times as erotic as any crude stage coupling of women with one another, nonhumans, apes, or zebras. And the main reason was the natural talent of the woman behind the glass. She turned every move into something ripped out of a blazing fantasy.

She touched the glass where my fingertips rested. ''That's all right. You don't have to talk if you don't want.'' It felt like my fingers were pressed to a grill.

I wanted. I wanted desperately. I was in love. And I was as tongue-tied as a twelve-year-old with designs on someone Maya's age.

I yanked my hand away.

I didn't know what to do.

Maya stepped in. ''Who are you?''

''I'm whoever you want me to be.'' She registered no surprise at a woman's voice. ''I'll be whatever you want. I'm your fantasy.''

Yes. Oh, yes.

She started on the last layer of clothing.

I turned around. I couldn't handle it, not with Maya there.

I wondered if there was some drug in the air, or maybe a subtle sorcery that enhanced the normal magic of a beautiful woman disrobing.

I *knew* what kind of acting Jill did. She'd be a natural here. She had the looks, she had the style, and she had the heat when she wanted. Put her in one of those rooms, and she could be bewitching.

I rested my hand on Maya's shoulder, whispered, ''I'm going to check the other boxes.''

She nodded.

When I stepped out only two sets of curtains were drawn. A man was just leaving. I went up and down the hall quickly. Four of the empties had signs up indicating there would be no response if you rang. I guessed the place was a twenty-four-hour operation and only one woman used a setup. Most would be on duty now because the Tenderloin was headed into its busy hours.

I rang a bell and conjured a redhead who reminded me of Tinnie but wasn't Jill Craight. I got out before she worked a spell on me.

The old man was in the hall. He looked at me quizzically. I dropped coins into his hand. ''I'm going to take the tour.''

"Suit yourself." An old veteran of the Tenderloin. No surprises. None of his business what I did as long as I paid.

Each woman was as marvelous as the last but none were Jill. I even waited out the occupants of the two busy boxes. One of the ladies wasn't Jill and the other put out her sign and refused to answer her bell.

Twelve possibilities whittled down to five. I considered working on the old man, discarded the idea. Unless I wanted to sit on him he'd warn Jill that somebody was asking questions. I knew where to look now. All I needed to do was come back until I'd seen them all.

I went back to box one. Maya and the elvish woman were chattering like sisters. The woman had her clothes on. Just as well. There are limits to what a man can take.

Maya glanced back to make sure it was me. "I'm almost done. Time's up anyway."

They exchanged a few pleasantries in a way that made me suspect I'd interrupted some girl talk. Maya got up and leaned close, whispered, "You have to leave a tip. That's the way they make their money. The old man keeps what he takes."

Except for the kingpin's cut, of course. Which would come out of the tips, too.

"Where?"

Maya showed me a slot in the tabletop which was the only way to pass objects from one side of the glass to the other. I filled it with a generous sprinkle of silver. I wasn't out much. It had come from the kingpin to begin and some of it might have gone to him from here.

Maya squeezed my arm. She was pleased with me. I figured the woman had run a good game on her. I led her out of there.

A man was coming in the front door as I parted the hall curtains for Maya. I caught only a glimpse of a little dink with a shiny head and an epic schnoz. He froze. Maya froze. I walked into her. We tangled. When we untangled he was gone. "What the hell?"

"That was him, Garrett. He recognized me."

"That was who?"

''The guy that was in that apartment. The one that ran me over.''

The old man fed his fire. He saw nothing. He heard nothing.

That runt had some eye if he'd recognized *this* Maya as the filthy girl who'd been in that apartment.

I plunged into the street and saw a lot of what the old man saw inside. The dink was a magician. Or maybe he was just so short he couldn't be spotted in the crowd.

It's carnival every night down there. I have to admit it's not all whoring and sleaze. There are tamer entertainments. Hell, two doors from where I stood there was a bingo hall with the vanguard of its regiment of old ladies just arriving. But sleaze is the axis of the Tenderloin and the misery there outweighs the innocuous entertainments.

I asked my angels if they'd seen the little guy. They didn't know what I was talking about. I asked the barker. He hadn't seen a thing and was too busy to chat. Irked, I told him, ''I'll be back tomorrow. We'll talk when you're not so pressed.''

''Yeah. Sure. Nobody's going to say I don't cooperate with the organization.''

Exasperated, I collected Maya and headed home.

39

We didn't say much for a while. Then I recalled something and changed course abruptly.

"What're you doing now?"

"Almost forgot I have to see Morley."

"Oh. Mr. Charm."

"He gets a look at you tonight you might have to fight him off with a stick."

She gave me a look. "Thanks for the compliment. I think."

Half a block later she told me, "I was going to seduce you tonight. But now I can't."

"Hunh?" Investigators are fast on their feet and quick with a comeback.

"If I did, it wouldn't be me you were with. You'd be thinking about her."

"Who her?" Look at that footwork. The boy is so fast you can't see him move.

"Polly. The elvish girl."

"Her? I'd forgotten her already," I lied.

"And the moon is made of green cheese."

"That's what the experts say. But as long as you bring her up, what'd she have to say?"

"I couldn't get specific because I didn't want her to know what we were up to. She might tell Hester. I think you're right. One of the girls sounds like her. Polly doesn't like her. Polly is kind of a prude."

"A what?" I laughed.

"It's all look-and-don't-touch on the premises there, Garrett. Polly says her regulars just want to talk to somebody who's easy on the eyes. Somebody who can listen and talk back, and who isn't any kind of threat. She never actually sees any of them. She says some of them must be important men but she doesn't know who they are. She never sees them outside. Some of the other girls do. Polly claims she's a virgin.''

Maya found that hard to swallow. I didn't want to think about it.

It was a strange setup but I could see how it could be a gold mine—without extortion. The one thing the movers and shakers lack is somebody they can relax with and talk to without risking betrayal.

That was the essence of the racket. Polly harvested enough in tips to satisfy herself. But some of her co-workers wanted more.

''It's because she's elvish,'' Maya guessed. ''She doesn't have to hurry. She can trade on her looks for a long time. Human women only get a few years.'' Hint, hint. Nudge, nudge. The girl had her own talent for distraction. Had to be inborn. How would she learn it running with a street gang?

We got to Morley's place. Maya reaped a harvest of appreciative looks. Nobody paid any attention to me. So that was the secret of getting in without the gauntlet of hostile stares—bring a woman to distract them.

Slade was behind the counter. He lifted the speaking tube and pointed upstairs. We took the hint. I knocked on the office door. Morley let us in.

''Your taste has improved, Garrett.'' He ogled Maya.

I slipped my arm around her waist. ''Didn't have time to get her into the disguise we use to protect her from characters like you.''

His eyes popped. ''You're the lady he was with the other night?''

She just smiled mysteriously.

''Miracles do happen,'' he said. And whined, ''But they never happen to me.''

At which point a gorgeous half-caste brunette stepped out of his back room and draped herself on his shoulder.

''I hope your luck turns, Morley. Saucerhead said you had some news for me.''

''Yes. Remember the man whose name you mentioned to the kingpin? The one who visited you the night you got into your mess?''

I presumed he was being cagey about naming Peridont. ''That religious character?''

''The very one.''

''What about him?''

''Somebody sent him to his reward. Put a poisoned quarrel in his back. About four blocks from your place. I figure he was going to see you. He wouldn't have any other reason to be around there dressed like somebody's gardener.''

Maybe. ''Damn! Who did it?''

Morley spread his hands wide and gave a blank look. ''I suppose one of the same fun-loving bunch. It went down in broad daylight, in front of fifty witnesses. Farmer-looking guy just steps out of a doorway behind him and lets him have it.''

''Being a wizard ain't everything.'' I'd developed an itch between my shoulder blades. That could happen to anybody at any time. If somebody wants you bad enough, they'll get you. ''I don't know if I wanted to know that.''

''We'll tighten up around you, Garrett. We'll make them work for it.''

''That's a comfort, Morley.'' Peridont getting it bothered me bad. I had this feeling I'd lost my last best ally.

''You think I want to go tell Chodo I blew it?''

I knew what he wanted to say, but he was saying it so clumsily it was worse than if he hadn't said anything. For Morley, the actual expression of concern or friendship is next to impossible.

''Never mind,'' I told him. ''Quit while you're ahead. Was there anything else?'' His friend was tickling his neck with a fingernail. He wouldn't keep his mind on business long.

''No. Go home and stay there. We won't have to pick up pieces of Garrett if you keep your head down.''

''Right. I'll think about it.''

''Don't think. Do.''

''Come on, Maya. Let's go home.''

Morley and I both knew I wouldn't give it a thought.

40

It started when we were two blocks from my house, a roaring and grumbling hurrying up from the south. Lightning zigged around it. I pulled Maya into a doorway.

"What is it?"

"Something we don't want to notice us." A big, red nasty bobbed in the middle of the cloud.

People stuck their heads out windows, got a look, and decided they didn't want to know.

The microstorm headed straight for my place.

Wouldn't you know it?

This time there was no roof busting. A nasty red spider strutted down out of the night—and something swatted it right back.

"Old Chuckles is going to pay his rent tonight," I muttered.

"You're shaking."

I was, worse than if I'd been in the thick of it. Yet my mind wasn't working right. I didn't think about Dean or the Dead Man. All I could think about was what might happen to my house. It was all I had in the world. I'd gone through hell to get the money to pay for it. I was getting too long in the tooth to start over.

The storm whooped and hollered. The spider headed in again, scarlet swords of fire leaping from its eyes. Bam! They hit an invisible wall. The spider bounced back.

"I didn't know he had it in him."

The Dead Man had a lot more than I'd suspected. He never tried to hurt the spider, but he turned every assault. The more its efforts were stymied, the more ferocious the monster became. It didn't worry about damaging the neighborhood.

This was going to make me popular with my neighbors.

You can only stay keyed up so long. When I began to settle down I had a thought. "This doesn't make sense. I may have been a pain in the ass to those guys, but not this big a pain. There's something else going on."

The flash and fury distressed Maya less than it did me. Maybe it was her lack of experience with sorcery. "Analyze it, Garrett. This is the second time your place has been attacked. You weren't home either time. Maybe it doesn't matter if you are. Maybe it's the house."

"Or something in it."

"Or something in it. Or someone."

"Besides me? Nobody . . ." The Dead Man? But he'd been dead too long to have enemies left. "Know what I think? I got started on the wrong foot at the beginning. I've been trying to get it to make sense."

Maya looked at me weird. "What the hell are you yapping about?"

"I'm trying to make sense of something that isn't rational. I knew from the beginning that religion was involved. Several religions, maybe. You can try from now until the end of the world and you're not going to make sense out of that. I shouldn't be attacking it that way. I should be going with it, going after who's doing what to who and not trying to figure out why."

Her look got weirder. "Did you get hit on the head? You're raving."

Maybe I was. And maybe somewhere in my nonsense there was a kernel of wisdom. That business down the street looked like a good argument for reassessing my place in the excitement. "Ever been to Leifmold, kid?"

"What?"

"I'm starting to think the smart thing would be to get out of town. Let this thing take care of itself."

She didn't believe me for a moment. And she was right. Maybe it's a lack of common sense. Maybe I just have a feeble survival instinct. I'd hang in until the end.

I mean, what kind of reputation would I get if I backed off just because that was the safe thing to do? Somebody hires you, he wants you to stick. You want to work, you got to do that—at least until moral revulsion forces you out. You don't let a little thing like fear slow you down.

The thing with eight limbs was on the ground now, stomping around the house, making the earth shake, roaring, grabbing up cobblestones and throwing them. I told Maya, "Every living city flunky will be around to pester me now." I didn't look forward to that. I'm not at my best with those people.

One of my angels darted through the shifting witch light. I recognized Wedge.

"Remind me I don't want to get into your line of work, Garrett." He looked up the street. "What the hell is going on?"

"You got me. I'm not sure I want to know."

The eight-limbed thing tore chunks out of a couple of houses, and flung them at my place. They bounced back. The Dead Man was showing unnecessary patience. The monster jumped up and down like an angry child. It looked to me like he and the Dead Man had a standoff. I was amazed. I couldn't picture my boarder holding his own against the avatar of a god.

"I didn't sign on for this, Garrett," Wedge told me. "I ain't no chickenshit, but saving your ass from demons is a little too much."

I could empathize with that. "Saving my ass from demons is a little too much for me, too, Wedge. You want to do a fade you won't hear me cry. I didn't beg Morley for any guardian angels."

"You didn't. Chodo did. If you did he'd have told you to go tongue-kiss a ghoul. Bye, Garrett. Good luck."

"Yeah." Candyass. When the going gets tough, the smart get going and the stupid keep heading toward trouble. Garrett didn't have enough sense to follow Wedge's example. He hung on where he was.

Maya asked, "We going to do something?"

"Find a tavern and hang out till it's over."

She knew a wisecrack when she heard one. "We hang around here and the Watch will scoop us up. They must be awake by now."

She had a point. Something this loud would force those guys to come out so their asses would be covered when questions were asked later. In that way having the spider get held off was worse than having the house get smashed. This was a hurrah that couldn't be ignored.

"Hell!" I spat. "Enough is enough." I stepped out of the doorway, trotted up the street, stopped a hundred-fifty feet from home, eyeballed the spider, wound up and let my last bottle fly like it was a flat rock. It didn't hit the spider but it did smash between the monster's legs. Whatever was inside splashed.

The thing jumped about forty feet high and shrieked like the world's biggest stuck hog. It turned in the air. It picked me out of the crowd, which wasn't all that tough. It started its charge before it hit the ground.

Now what, genius?

I shoved Maya into a breezeway and scooted in after her. The spider smashed into the buildings as though trying to bull right through. It let out a big bass whoop of frustration, then started ripping materials out of its way. One hairy leg kept reaching for me.

There were greenish spots on the leg where Peridont's stuff had splattered it. Every little bit it paused to scratch those. In five minutes it was scratching more than it was trying to get us.

The breezeway was a dead end. We were caught good. I didn't waste the five minutes it took the spider to become preoccupied with itself. I tested two doors and attacked the weakest. I got it open just as the spider started spending most of its time scratching.

"Come on." I pushed into the darkened interior, part of someone's home. Maya stumbled around behind me. When I paused I heard rapid, frightened breathing. There were people in there, trying to keep quiet and not be noticed.

We got through without killing ourselves on unseen

furniture, found a window in back, got it open and slithered through.

"Slick, Garrett," Maya said. "You'd better hope they didn't recognize you."

"Yeah." I already had enough trouble getting along with my neighbors.

"What now?"

We took half a block along an alleyway, toward home, to where I could check on the spider.

For a god it wasn't very bright. It was still trying to tear its way into that breezeway, when it wasn't scratching. Doing a fair job, too. "When I say go, we head for the front door. And pray Dean lets us in before that thing catches up."

"I think maybe going to Leifmold was a better idea."

"Maybe. Ready?"

"Yes."

"Go."

That damned spider wasn't as fixated as I hoped. It spotted us and began bouncing in our direction before we'd gone ten steps.

We wouldn't make it in time.

41

Maya pounded the door with both fists. I bellowed at Dean. The spider galloped toward us. I spotted a human skull-type face where the thing's head was, sort of like it had been painted over the usual spider face. Spreading mandibles made that skull look like it was grinning.

Chains and bolts rattled on the other side of the door. We had gotten Dean's attention.

But it was too late. The spider was on us—

It hit something. Or something hit it. There was a sound like crunching gravel. The monster went tumbling back the way it had come, trailing another of its bellows of frustration. "The Dead Man is still on the job," I gasped at Maya. "Come on, Dean!"

The monster was charging again before the old man got the door open. We plunged inside, trampling him, then tumbled over one another trying to bolt up. Though a fat lot of good bolts and bars would do against that thing.

"What's going on, Mr. Garrett?" Dean was pale and rattled.

"I don't know. I was just going to call it a night when that thing dropped out of the sky."

"Like the thing you saw at the kingpin's place?"

"Same kind of thing in a different shape."

"I don't think I want to be involved anymore, Mr. Garrett. Things like this don't happen in your regular cases. I think I want to go home until it's over."

"I don't blame you. But first we have to get that thing to go away." I peeked out. It had quieted down. I thought it might be getting ready to try something nasty.

It was standing in the street, balanced on three legs. It scratched itself with the other five. The green spots on its legs had grown and now shed a phosphorescent light. The more it dug at those the more they irritated it.

Good. Maybe it would forget us altogether.

It pounced at my place like it meant to take us by surprise. Off it went with a howl, slapped away. It stood up unsteadily, scratched vigorously. I told Maya, "I'm going to have a chat with my dead buddy. Why don't you help Dean in the kitchen?" Hint, hint.

It took the old boy a while. But he got it after I told him to bring me a pitcher.

The house shook again. Storms of rage played around outside. I went into the Dead Man's room, settled into the chair we kept there for me, and considered the old mountain of blubber. Despite the excitement he looked no more animated than usual. You couldn't tell if he was asleep or awake if it wasn't for a sort of electric radiation bleeding off him. "Whenever you have a minute or two," I told him.

He wasn't himself. *Go ahead, Garrett.* He was saving his irritation for the thing outside.

"Got any idea what that thing is?"

I have begun to develop a suspicion. I have not yet gathered evidence enough to establish a certainty. I do not like the suspicion. If that thing is what I fear. . . .

He wasn't going to say, but then he never let anything out of the bag until he was sure he wouldn't contradict himself later. I knew what sort of answer I'd get, but I asked anyway. "And what's that?" Maybe he'd be distracted enough to let something slip.

Not yet.

"Can you at least get it to go away?"

I do not have that power, Garrett. You seem to have done what was needed to discourage it, though it is losing its determination very slowly.

Not sure what he meant, I took a peek outside. The spider was more involved in scratching itself and less interested in my place. I went back. "You going to contribute something now or are you just going back to sleep?"

Though I am certain you brought this upon yourself and deserve any villainies visited upon you, it seems—

"Don't get wise, Old Bones. That thing didn't come

to see me. Neither did those firebombers. I wasn't home either time. So you tell me—"

Quiet. I must reflect. You are correct. I have failed to see the obvious, that you are too small a mouse to interest this cat.

"I think you're special, too."

Quiet.

He reflected. He batted that spider away. I got tired of waiting. "You better not take forever. It won't be long before we're up to our hips in people who want to know what's going on. Hill-type people."

Correct. I have foreseen that. I do not have enough information. You must tell me all that has happened since you became involved. Spare me no detail.

I protested.

Hurry. The thing will accept defeat soon. The minions of the state will bestir themselves. It will be to your advantage to be absent when they arrive. You will not be absent if you do not hasten.

That was true, though maybe it wasn't his full concern. I played along, anyway. I started at the beginning and gave him everything to the moment I'd gotten in a step ahead of the spider. The telling took a while.

He took a while longer to digest everything. I was pretty antsy when Dean stuck his head in. "Mr. Garrett, that thing gave up."

I hurried to the front door and peeked out. Dean was right. It was staggering down the street, not even trying to walk on air, spending more energy scratching than going. I bounced back into the Dead Man's room. "It's headed out, Chuckles. We don't have much time." I leaned back into the hall. "Dean, tell Maya we've got to get out of here."

He scowled at me. He muttered and cursed and made it damned clear he thought I had no business putting Maya at risk.

The Dead Man said, *If I can have your attention?*

"You got it, Smiley."

Your sense of humor never rises above the juvenile. Pay attention. First, it is probable that you are correct. The attacks upon this house were not launched either to get you or because the place belongs to you. For a moment I

*considered it possible that I was their target. That seemed
reasonable under the assumption that this trouble springs
from the source I suspect. But that source should not be
aware of my presence, considering its prior indifference
to researching the nature of its adversaries. So its focus,
its interest, must be something within the house.*

Say what? He knew who was stirring all the com-
motion?

*Have you bothered to examine the guest room? You
did not mention having done so, yet I cannot imagine
any protegé of mine having been so lax as to have
overlooked the obvious.*

He was going to bounce right up on his high horse.
He loves it when he nails me.

Damn it, I'd thought about this before and I hadn't
bothered to see if Jill had left something.

Sometimes you get too busy to think.

Now, with him sitting there smirking, I began to
wonder if Jill hadn't set me up.

"Dean! Go upstairs and see if Jill left anything in the
guest room. Maya can help you look. If you don't find
anything, look wherever she could've gotten to while
she was here. If you still don't find anything, look where
she couldn't have gotten. There must be something."

Better late than never.

"Right. I'm sure the neighbors will agree when they
try to figure out why their houses got torn up."

He understood. If he'd gotten off his mental duff
back when, we might not have this mess now.

*Let us not fall to bickering, Garrett. Time has been
wasted. Let us waste no more.*

"Check. So let's get at it. You think you know
what's going on? Do you know anything about these
Sons of Hammon?"

*I recall them. A vicious and nihilistic cult. For them
all life is sorrow and misery and punishment and shall
continue to be till their Devourer has been unchained
to scour the world clean. The many shall be consumed
and the True Believers, the Faithful, who serve without cavil, who help release the Devourer and set the
Devastation in motion, shall be rewarded with perpet-
ual bliss. Their paradise resembles the adolescent par-*

adise of the Shades cults. Milk and honey, streets of gold, an inexhaustible supply of suppliant virgins.

"That part doesn't sound so bad."

To you it would not.

I waited for him to tell me more.

The cult's roots reach back to the time of your prophet Terrell. It was declared heretic and a persecution launched against it a thousand years ago. Till then it was just one of countless Hanite cults. The heretics fled into various nonhuman areas. A colony formed in Carathca, where its doctrines became polluted by dark elvish nihilism, then fell under the sway of devil-worshippers who brought it around to its present philosophical form three hundred years ago. About that time its high priests began claiming direct revelations from heaven, revelations the laity could feel themselves. The cult began acting politically, trying to hasten the Devastation.

They were persecuted, Garrett. First in the power games of empire and churches, then because the masters of Carathca grew afraid of them and wanted to drive them out.

The cult faded into the human population, which supported it because humans were not well treated in Carathca. It deployed all the instruments of terror. After two generations it mastered Carathca. The dark-elfin nobility survived only as puppets. The countryside for fifty miles around fell under cult sway. Fanatic assassins went out to silence the Devastator's enemies. The cult became so dangerous, so vicious, that the early Karentine Kings had no choice but war or submission. They chose war, as humans always do, determined to exterminate the cult. For a time it seemed they had succeeded. King Beran declared them extinct only to be assassinated by a branch which had established itself in TunFaire under another name. His son Brian continued the fight and, it appeared, succeeded in extinguishing the cult's last lights a century and a half ago. Do you follow?

"Well enough. I don't understand, but I don't have to understand to deal with them, do I?"

You need understand only that they are more dangerous than anyone you have ever battled, excepting

*perhaps vampires defending their nest. They do not just
believe, they* know. *Their devil god has spoken to each
of them directly and has given each of them a look into
a paradise where they will spend eternity. They will do
anything because they know there is no penalty to com-
pare with their coming reward. They fear nothing. They
are saved and will be born again, and concrete evidence has been given them for this. They need take the
word of no one but their god himself.*

I got a really creepy feeling. "Just wait up, Old Bones.
What the hell? I don't need this. I'm a nonbeliever. You
trying to tell me there's no side of the angels, that there
really is a god and he's really a devil and—"

Hold! Enough!

I calmed down a little, though I was still pretty
shaky. Think about stepping up face-to-face with possible proof that something you find completely repel-
lent is the law of the universe.

*We Loghyr have never found proof of the existence
of any gods. Neither have we disproved their existence, although logic militates against it. They are not
necessary to explain anything. Nature does not provide that which is not needed.*

He'd never spent half a year trying to survive in a
swamp infested with five-hundred parasitic species.
Were gods some sort of psychic or spiritual parasites?

*However, proof or lack thereof are unnecessary to
the mind that must believe. And that mind becomes
doubly narrow and doubly dangerous when it is given
what it perceives as proof. Then it can begin to create
that in which it believes.*

Hanging out with him wasn't all a dead waste. "You
mean somebody is running a game on the Sons of
Hammon, making like he's their god? Fooling them
into doing his dirty deeds?"

*Someone was back when the cult ruled Carathca and
its environs. We who brought about his downfall believed we had destroyed him. Perhaps we failed. Or
perhaps another has taken his place, though what
other there could be is a greater puzzle than how the
one we fought could have escaped to nurture his wickedness in secret.*

I was on a roll. "We're talking another dead Loghyr here, aren't we?" It didn't take much imagination to see how my old buddy here could kick ass if he wasn't so damned lazy.

We are. We are speaking of the only Loghyr ever to have gone mad. We are speaking of a true son of the Beast, if you will, who did great evils while he lived, in the guises of several of your history's bloodiest villains, and who strove to do greater evils still after the righteous slew him.

We chattered back and forth. He convinced me that not only could a live Loghyr pass for human, but that it had been done countless times—and some of the worst men of olden times and a couple of *saints* hadn't been human at all. But he couldn't make me understand why, even though we humans are notorious meddlers. Loghyr are supposed to stand outside and observe and look down their noses.

"Interesting as hell. I'm learning things about Loghyr I never suspected. We'll have to have a long chat someday. But we don't have time right now. We have to make moves and make them fast, or all the machineries of the state will have us under siege and we won't be able to do a thing."

You may be right.

"You figure there's a Loghyr out there somewhere who's revived the old cult? I'll buy that. But why the hell are they tearing up TunFaire?"

I must confess, that has me baffled. It is my guess that Magister Peridont could have told us. The Craight woman might know. She was trusted more than any rational man should trust a woman. Peridont may have revealed himself. Find her, Garrett. Bring her to me.

"Right. Like snapping my fingers."

Also find, or at least identify, the man who was in that apartment opposite hers. I have a hunch he is as important as the Craight woman. Perhaps more so.

A *hunch?* The Dead Man? That flabby lump of pure reason? It couldn't be.

Dean came in. "We couldn't find anything, Mr. Garrett."

"Keep looking. There's got to be something."

Not necessarily, Garrett. All there needs be is the perception that there is something.

I'd thought that myself but I didn't like it. "She set us up as a diversion?"

There is that possibility. It gains weight if we presume Magister Peridont told her something that would be of interest to those who are plaguing us.

"I just might break both her kneecaps next time I see her." I could see her siccing those guys on us in hopes they'd get into it with the Dead Man. It was the kind of stunt I might have tried if I wanted somebody off my back.

A troop of the Watch is coming, Garrett. You would be wise to absent yourself now. I will deal with them. Bring me that woman.

I ducked out the back way, leaving Dean to bolt up behind me, mumbling and grumbling and secretly pleased to be close to the heart of things.

Maya stuck with me again. There was no arguing her into going back to the Doom.

"At least let them know you're alive and healthy. I don't want Tey Koto ambushing me because she thinks I've trifled with you."

She burst out laughing. I guess I would have, too, if somebody had tossed "trifle" at me. "You're too much, Garrett. How can somebody in your business have so many little blind spots and naivetés?"

It was a question you would expect from someone beyond her age. But the young aren't stupid and sometimes they're more perceptive than us old cynics with our arsenals of preconceptions. I told her the truth.

"I nurture them. There are poetic truths as well as scientific truths. They maybe look silly to you, but I think they deserve to be sustained."

She laughed but there was no mockery in it, just pleasure. "Good for you, Garrett. Now you know why I love you. Inconsistencies and all."

The little witch sure knew how to rattle a guy.

42

Back about a thousand years ago the other evening, Morley had made a crack about how I might be better off if everybody thought I was dead. I didn't know how to make that look believable, but I figured I could do the next best thing and disappear. Wedge and my angels had taken off. Though the neighborhood was in a state of ferment, with what looked like the whole damned population of TunFaire in the streets wanting to know what had happened, I didn't think anybody else would be watching. It seemed the right time to get lost.

"Where can we go?" Maya asked.

"Good question." There had to be somewhere nobody would think to look, someplace we could get in and out of without anybody noticing. Someplace we could live a while without the regular business of life giving us away. I couldn't think of anywhere perfect, though I had a few morally indebted ex-clients who might put me up.

Maya asked, "How about that apartment across from Hester's? She's gone and everybody's sacked her place, so nobody ought to be interested in the building. And you know that squeenky little guy isn't going to come back."

"Squeenky?"

"Yeah. You know. Dorky and creepy at the same time."

She was right. The place was as decent a hideout as we were likely to find. We headed over there. We had no more trouble getting inside than we'd had before. It must be nice having the kingpin holding an umbrella over your head.

Sometimes. Hadn't done me that much good, had it?

We barely got inside before Maya started grumbling. "I'm hungry."

"I saw some stuff in the kitchen when I tossed the place."

The apartment hadn't been set up for living. The stores consisted mostly of stuff that couldn't be put together into a decent meal. As we did our best, I asked, "Why didn't you have Dean feed you before you left?"

"Why didn't you?"

"Point. I had too much on my mind." I stirred some goop and wondered why Dean hadn't been able to find anything Jill had left. The note she had left here indicated that what the Sons of Hammon wanted was safe. There would be no safer place than with the Dead Man, so I couldn't see her taking it out of the house.

I wondered how she'd planned to collect it later if that had been her plan. I wondered what the hell it was. The missing Terrell Relics Peridont had wanted me to find? Possibly. But it didn't seem likely the Relics would get a heretical cult so excited they'd risk destruction to glom them.

Once again I was back to a need for research. Thanks to Dean and the Dead Man I knew what the cult was and what it wanted, but that information was pretty spare. I had to know more about what they believed and why they believed it. A lot more.

Though if I could lay hands on Jill, that might not be necessary.

"Look. I found some wine," Maya said. She seemed pleased, so I was pleased for her, but the discovery didn't excite me.

"Good. Put it on the table." I went on thinking, about the kingpin. His people had been quiet for a while; probably lying low until the outrage died down. It would. It always does in TunFaire. Who could stay exercised about the deaths of a bunch of weird strangers?

The wine wasn't bad as wines go. Whoever laid in the stock had expensive tastes. It helped the rest of an absurd meal go down with less difficulty.

I said, "Dean's gotten me spoiled. I'm getting so I expect decent food all the time."

"We could eat out."

I gave her a sharp look. She was teasing. But she added, "You promised."

I did? That's not the way I remembered it. "Maybe after this is over. If you can stand getting fixed up." It had been a while since Dean's niece had worked her over. She'd begun to look a little ragged. But hadn't I, too? "I'm shot. I've got to get some sleep. We'll hit the Tenderloin again after breakfast."

I carried a lamp around to check the possibilities. I could make do in the parlor. I made sure the windows were covered so nobody would see a light moving around, then took my shoes off and started arranging a place to lie down. Suddenly I had about as much energy as a vampire at high noon.

Maya came in. "You take the bed, Garrett. I can sleep in here."

Old Noble said, "No. I'll be fine here."

"Garrett, you need the comfort more than I do."

Oh boy, here came the old-timer routine. "I don't play polite games, Maya. Somebody makes me an offer, I only give them one chance to back down, then I take them up on it."

"Don't get yourself in an uproar. I meant it. You're a lot more tired than I am. And I'm used to sleeping on floors and sidewalks. This is luxury for me." But there was the ghost of something like a twinkle in her eyes, like she was up to something.

"You asked for it, you got it." I headed for the bedroom. Maybe it was just because I was so damned tired, but I couldn't fathom what she had in mind.

I found out about six hours later.

I usually sleep in the raw. In deference to the fact that somebody might walk in, I sacked out wearing my underclothes. I lay there tossing and turning, worrying the case, for maybe seven seconds before I passed out. Next thing I knew I wasn't alone. And the someone with me was very warm, very naked, and very female. And very determined. And I sure don't have much will power.

There are limits to the nobility of even the best of us good guys. When she turned on the heat, Maya didn't have any trouble getting past mine.

It turned out to be one truly amazing morning.

43

I had Maya slicked down and spiffed up in some clothes
I'd swiped from Jill's apartment. I swear, the girl grew
more beautiful by the minute—the woman, I should say.
There was no doubt about that now. What she lacked
in experience she made up for in enthusiasm.

I helped her with her hair and with a touch of makeup. She was going to need grooming lessons. When
she got a hold on that she'd be deadly.

"I hate to do it, but I'm going to have to destroy the
whole effect," I told her after I showed her herself in
a mirror. "I can't take you outside looking like that."

"Why not?" She liked what she saw, too.

"Because you'd attract too damned much attention.
Come here." When I finished she didn't look like
Maya at all. "Pity we can't do as much for me."

"Do we *really* need to disguise ourselves?"

"Probably not. But there are people out there who
want to kill us. It can't hurt. And we can't be hurt if
nobody can find us." I didn't have the means to change
my own appearance much. I thought about Pokey Pigotta and some of the tricks he'd used, like putting a
rock in his shoe, walking stoop-shouldered, carrying
a couple different hats and changing them randomly,
and so forth. The hat trick I could do. There were
several in the walk-in here. And everybody who knew
me knew I'd wear a hat only when I had to to keep
from freezing my ears off.

I picked the most absurd topper, one people who
knew me knew I wouldn't wear at swordpoint. "How
do I look?"

"Like a buzzard nested on your head."

It did look a bit like a tricornered haystack. I'm glad

sartorial display is a vice confined to the better classes. I'd hate to try to keep up with fashion.

There were a few odds and ends of clothing, too, but all for a man so much shorter there was no using them for anything. So I had Maya use touches of lampblack to give my cheeks and eyes a hollow look, practiced a stoop and slight limp, asked, "You ready?"

"Whenever you are." She gave it a double meaning. The child seemed happier than ever I'd seen before.

You devil, Garrett. How do you get into these things?

You give in to yourself and you undertake a contract no matter how casual the collision. This was more than casual because this was somebody I cared about, independent of the body that had moved with mine . . . .

Damnit, sex *always* complicates things.

We hit the street looking like poor folks. Like almost everybody else out there. I did my limp and stoop to perfection, I thought, and invented a history to explain it if anybody asked. I had been wounded at Yellow Dog Mesa. Nobody asked what you did in the war. The fact that you'd gotten out alive was commentary enough.

I wondered what Glory Mooncalled was doing. There had been no talk for days. That meant nothing, of course. That's the way war works. Long periods of inaction sandwich brief, intense periods of combat. But I had a feeling something interesting would happen soon.

I wondered how the Dead Man was dealing with the bureaucratic siege. If he was as impatient with them as he was with me, they were going to regret bothering him.

We stopped at a third-rate place and ate, then ambled down to the Tenderloin. It was noon when we got there. The noon hour is one of the district's secondary peaks. Those who can't get away in the evening escape work for an hour to appease their hungers. Maya and I planted ourselves on the same bench we'd used before to watch the players parade. The day people were more furtive than those at night. Quite a few made some effort to disguise themselves. Once again I spent some time pondering the curiosities of human nature. What a species.

"I think we're some kind of practical joke on the part of the gods," I told Maya.

She laughed. She understood without me having to explain. I liked that. In fact, I was beginning to like a lot of things about her, in ways I hadn't when she'd been a charitable project.

She sensed that, too. She touched my hand and gave me a big "I told you so" smile.

Whoa! This wasn't going my way at all. I didn't even understand it. Garrett doesn't get involved. He makes friends and leaves them smiling. But he doesn't get caught up inside any commitment.

Damn it, this was a raggedy-ass kid I'd saved from abuse and exploitation. This was a project . . . .

I smiled at myself. You have to do that when you're wriggling on a hook of your own device.

I watched the barker across the way. "I think we have a small problem."

"What?"

"I need to talk to that guy. I can't without letting him know it's me. And that cancels out my disappearance."

"You must be getting senile, Garrett. You just tell him Chodo says forget he ever talked to you. He'll forget."

She was right. The man would chomp down on what he knew until somebody twisted him good. Nobody ought to have a reason. "You're right. I am getting senile."

"Or maybe you're just worn out. You did real good for an old guy."

I spat into the gutter. It's a wonder I didn't hit my mind. "You just aren't used to a real man."

"Maybe." There was a sort of soft purr in her voice. "You want me to go tell him you want to see him?"

"Sure."

I kept one eye on the place we'd visited last night. One old guy came out. Nobody went inside. I was surprised there wasn't more traffic. It seemed the kind of place that would appeal to the crowd that came down during the day. I still thought the guy who came up with the idea was a genius. We all need somebody to talk to. I did myself.

I sort of spread it out among Dean, the Dead Man,

Tinnie, and Playmate, maybe opening up more to Playmate than the others because I have no relationship with him other than friendship. And there are things I don't feel comfortable telling him because I value his good opinion.

Maya sat back down. "He'll be here in a minute. At first he didn't believe it was you."

"But you convinced him."

"I can be pretty convincing."

"No lie." I hadn't stood a chance once she went to work on me seriously. But that's my weak spot.

The barker settled beside me a few minutes later. He leaned forward to look into my face. "It is you."

"Last I looked. What's happening is, I've disappeared. Maybe run out of town. You aren't seeing me. You're seeing some guy who came down here to gawk."

He lifted an eyebrow. Damn, I hate it when people steal my tricks.

"It's getting tight. The organization is under pressure. Some of us are turning invisible till we make it ease up."

"What's going on, anyways? Tied up here, all I hear is crazy rumors."

"You haven't heard anything as crazy as the truth." I told him some of that, including a few details of the attack on Chodo's place. He didn't want to believe me, but the story was so outrageous he accepted it.

"That's weird," he said. "They must be really sick. I'm ready to help. We all are down here. But I don't see what I can do."

"Near as we can figure, there are two people who know what we need to put this mess away. One is the woman I was asking about. I can't give you a name because she uses about a hundred, but I'm pretty sure she's working that place over there."

He looked at it and sneered. "Doyle's wimp house. All that gorgeous pussy and half of them don't put out. You figure it, paying just to look."

"Takes all kinds to make a horserace. If people weren't strange, you and I wouldn't be in business."

"You got a point. What do you need to know?"

"Have you seen an outstanding blonde in and out of that place?"

"Several of them. You're going to have to be more specific."

I couldn't be. Jill Craight, for all her looks, had had a sort of nebulous quality, like she really was a whole gang of people, each one a little different from the others. "Forget her. I'll assume she's working that place. I'll get to her if she is. I'll just sit here till I spot her. How about that guy I came charging out after last night? When you didn't have time to talk?"

"What guy was that? I was pretty busy."

"Maya, you describe him. You got a better look."

"Not that good. He was short, kind of chunky, had a big nose that looked like it got broken once. His skin was kind of dark. He was bald but you couldn't tell that if he was wearing a hat. He was dressed in real dark clothes both times. Kind of sloppy, even though the clothes were good ones. Like he wasn't used to wearing them." And so on. And so on. I wished I had an eye as quick and sharp.

The barker said, "Come to think of it, I did see a guy like that before you came roaring up. Only reason I noticed was he was headed out like a demon was chewing his ass."

"So?"

"So that's all I can tell you. He lit out."

That was what I'd expected to hear. "Did you recognize him?"

"You mean, do I know who he is? No. But I've seen him around. Hits the Tenderloin every four, five days. Used to come in for the shows. He's mostly dropped that and the joyhouses since Doyle come up with his silly talk house."

"Don't seem so silly when you think about it."

"No. Guess not. The old fart is cleaning up. I tell you, I'll never understand the freaks that come down here."

I thought he understood them all too well, but I didn't say so. If guys like him didn't understand, they wouldn't be successful catering to people who needed the comforts of a Tenderloin.

I shrugged. "I guess that's that. I don't know what else I could ask."

The barker got up. "Always glad to help the king-pin. Hey. For what it's worth, the little bald gink with the big honker, I think he's some kind of high-powered priest."

Maybe I jumped. Maybe something below conscious level was excited. "You sure?"

"No. It's just the way he snuck around and at the same time acted like people ought to bend the knee. I seen other priests act that way. Don't want to be seen. But the bigger they are, the worse habit they have of expecting special treatment. Get what I mean?"

"Yeah. Thanks. I'll mention how you helped. Maybe a bonus will come tumbling down."

"I could use it."

"Couldn't we all?" I watched him cross to his post. "A priest," I muttered. "Another big-time priest, maybe. With a place in the same building where Jill was shacking up with Magister Peridont. That sound any alarms?"

Maya said, "It doesn't sound like a coincidence. You think it's important?"

I hadn't told her everything about Peridont. I decided to trust her now. I laid it out from the beginning.

She didn't speak for a while. When she did, she said, "I know what you're thinking. It's too outrageous."

"You're probably right. But . . . things tend to tie together. Even when they're outrageous. And the first time Peridont visited me, he wanted me to find Warden Agire and the Terrell Relics."

"Pure speculation, Garrett. Gossamer. Almost whimsy."

"Maybe. We could sink it quick with a description of the Warden that doesn't match that guy."

She nodded.

"Let me run with it. Tell me where the holes are."

"All right."

"Jill Craight works over there, listening to sad tales of woe. She's a little greedy so sometimes she meets her clients outside, when she's off duty. Maybe she's not completely honest and tries to find out who they are. Maybe it just comes to her by accident. But she finds out she has both the Grand Inquisitor and the Warden among her regulars. Maybe she gets an idea she can make a big hit. Maybe she gets idealistic.

"Whatever, she gets some kind of underground dialogue going. Maybe they're actually working something out. Then the Sons of Hammom hit town. They're after the Relics for some reason. Agire goes on the lam. He slips the Relics to Jill to take care of while he leads the baddies somewhere else. Peridont doesn't know what's going on, he only knows that Agire and the Relics have disappeared.

"Meantime, Peridont makes a connection with Jill and finds out what's up with Agire and the Relics. So he doesn't bother bringing that up anymore. Now he wants to find out more about the Sons, only he doesn't tell me that. Being a typical client, he knows what he gives me to work with will give away something about him, so he wants to send me out blind and let me thrash around till I kick up something he can use.

"After that, because he wants to cover his ass and because he's got Church politics to deal with things go from bad to worse. When he finally decides he's in so deep he's got to come clean (so I can dig him out), he gets ambushed as he's coming to see me. I'm not convinced the man who killed him was one of the Sons of Hammon."

It was about the longest continuous speech I've ever made, just sort of blurting out and not stopping. When I did turn myself off, Maya didn't say anything. Maybe she needed a little coaxing.

"Well? What do you think?"

"I think you're trying it out on the wrong person. I can't knock a hole in it. You should lay it out for the Dead Man. He'd tell you why it couldn't be that way."

"You don't think it was?"

"I don't want it to be. And don't ask me why. It's just an emotional thing. Actually, I'm scared you're right."

Why should that scare her? Because it might come out and give the scandal hunters a boost?

Intellectually I saw danger. The Sons of Hammon going public with an ascetic lifestyle and a god who really talked at a time when the two major Hanite denominations could be shown to be conniving and powerless and riddled with corruption . . .

No. The people of TunFaire wouldn't go for something as crazy as the Hammon cult right now.

They hadn't chosen their time well. They should have waited for the war's end. Come into the city with any kind of a crazy promise then and I'd bet money, marbles, or chalk dust you could win battalions of converts.

I thought about that for a long time. I conjured me a grim future, decided me and the Dead Man would have to have a serious discussion about how to make things easier on ourselves. Maybe I'd have to take up Weider's offer of a job as chief head-thumper at the brewery. The brewery business prospers in hard times.

Maya just snuggled up and purred. For all I could tell there was nothing going on inside her head. Time drifted away.

I had a thought, which happens occasionally. "Think Jill would recognize you if she passed you in the street?"

"No."

"I think we ought to spread out, then. I can't fool her. She sees me, she's going to hightail it."

"You really think so?"

"I think she'll panic. I think she's gotten so far into this changing names that she thinks all she has to do to disappear is call herself something else. If somebody turns up that knows her some other way, she'll lose her confidence and overreact. It won't matter who she spots."

Maya frowned and gave me a searching look. "I don't know. But you're more an expert on people than I am."

I snorted. Me an expert? I can't even figure me out, let alone the rest of the world.

44

Part of my job is to remain patient. I probably do more waiting than anybody but a soldier. It ought to be second nature after five years in the Marines and all those since in this investigation racket. But I never was very good at sitting still, especially in the cold.

I needed to get up and prowl. That would make me easier to spot but my aching butt and stiffening muscles wouldn't listen to common sense.

I told Maya, "I'm going to stroll around the block and see how many ways there are to get out of that building."

"What if she decides to come out when you're gone?"

"There isn't much chance of that. Won't take me three minutes."

"You're the expert."

The way she kept saying that made it sound like she had some doubts.

I walked away, forgetting my act for a dozen steps because I was conscious of her questioning look.

I didn't find out anything that I hadn't reasoned out sitting with Maya. There was a back way out, down an outside stair into an alley behind the place. That had to be there because we'd seen no access to the second floor while we'd been inside. Hell.

Well, I got the kinks out, anyway.

I headed for the bench and my girl.

What girl? Maya was gone.

I gaped like a cretin for maybe fifteen seconds, then looked around, jumping to see over the heads of the crowd. There was no sign of Maya. I scuttled over to my friend the lanky barker. "You see what happened to the gal I was with? Over on the bench?"

He sneered a sneer that questioned my competence. "Yeah, man. This time I caught the action. Your blonde fluff came galloping past right after you left. Your twitch took off after her. They went that way." He pointed uphill, which meant back toward the heart of the city, whence we had come, and whence most everyone else came, too.

"The blonde was in a hurry?"

"Running. My guess is, she'd made you and was waiting for a chance to run."

"Thanks." I took off, ignoring the curses of those I jostled. I wondered how Jill could have recognized us from over there. . . .

Damnation! How dumb can a guy be? She probably didn't recognize us at all. But she sure as hell could've recognized the clothes Maya had borrowed.

How come we never thought of that when we were being so clever about changing who we were?

I kicked up the pace as the people thinned out. Once I was out of the Tenderloin I couldn't do anything but guess which way Jill was headed.

I saw nothing.

I wondered why I bothered. I wondered if Maya would hang on. I wondered what Jill would do if she couldn't shake Maya. I wondered how Maya would get in touch if she did run Jill to ground.

I looked down cross streets as I passed them. I questioned street-side vendors. Some told me to get the hell away from them. Some just looked blank. Here, there, one gave me a straight answer. One of those actually had noticed Jill.

She was still headed toward the heart of town.

I wasn't going to get much cooperation just being Garrett. So I swallowed my pride and started alluding to Chodo Contague. That kicked the level of cooperation up a few notches. A man with a sausage cart on a corner needs the goodwill of the kingpin. Else somebody's liable to put him out of business.

That kept me on the trail until I got out of the area

where there was anyone to ask, by which time Jill's course had shifted southward.

I wished I knew more about her. Where could she run? But I'd had no time to research her. In any of her guises, let alone all of them. More than ever I felt that things were moving too fast.

I'm a plodder. I get to the end of the trail through sheer stubbornness, just keeping on until I get there, doing what I have to do. I hadn't had a minute to catch my breath since Jill first turned up on my doorstep.

When you're moving like that sometimes you don't have time to think. Your mind works on things out of sight and you come up with hunches. Three minutes after Jill's trail turned southward I had one.

She was headed for the Dream Quarter.

She did have that one resource. That little gink who used the apartment across from the one Peridont provided. If he was who I thought he was . . . But Warden Agire had disappeared. I'd heard nothing about him turning up again. But I'd been too busy to stay in touch with that situation.

"Bet the long odds," I told myself. I adjusted my course and increased my pace. Ten minutes later I got to Playmate's stable.

He was about to close his main gate. But he brightened like a rising sun when he saw me. He always does. He is the one grateful former client I can count on any time. "Garrett. Been wondering about you. Where've you been?"

"Working. I've got a real mind-twister going. You been keeping up with the scandals?"

"Not much to keep up with lately. Too much other excitement. That your place where the demon turned up last night?"

"Yes. Part of what I'm working on."

"You're playing with fire this time, then."

"The hottest. You don't know the half. I'll tell you about it sometime."

"In a hurry?"

"Aren't I always?"

"Usually. What do you need?"

"A horse so I can make up some time on somebody

I'm chasing. And some info. The horse shouldn't be one of your damned Lightnings or Firebrands, either. I want one that will run but won't play games.'' Horses and I don't get along. I don't know why but the whole damned tribe is out to get me. They think it's great fun making my life miserable.

"You always say that. I can't figure a guy your age being scared of horses. But since you are I picked up a nag so docile and stupid even you'll be satisfied.''

Grumble grumble. He led me into the stable. While we walked I asked, "You heard anything about Warden Agire and the Terrell Relics?''

"Funny you should ask. Agire turned up last night. Minus the Relics.''

"Ha!'' I'd guessed right, more or less. But there wasn't time to congratulate myself. I had to move. "I need the beast fast. I have to get to the Dream Quarter before somebody who's already way ahead of me.''

Playmate threw a saddle blanket on a monster that didn't look docile to me. There were moments when he surrendered to a nasty sense of humor. This was no time for that. I jumped him as he started cinching the saddle.

"No joke, Garrett. The animal is a pussycat.''

"Yeah?'' I didn't like the way it looked at me, like it had heard of me and was determined to make a liar out of Playmate.

I have that kind of trouble with women, too, and have never understood it.

"Here we go.''

"Thanks.'' I grabbed the horse by the bridle and looked it in the eye. "I got work to do. I don't got time to mess around. You want to play games, just remember that around here you're never more than a couple miles from the glue works.''

It just looked back at me. I went around and mounted up. In a moment I was pounding through the streets. People cussed me. Some threw things. What I was doing was against the law because it was so damned dangerous. But there was no one to stop me. I had several narrow misses. The horse slipped and slid on sections that were cobbled, and a couple times I thought we were going down. As we neared the Dream Quarter I began to feel foolish. I was ready to bet that I'd outguessed myself and was going to find nothing.

Wrong. They were there. I spotted Jill first, from three blocks away, passing Chattaree, blonde hair flying. She was in a sprint for the Orthodox complex. Maya was right behind her and looked like she'd decided to catch her. Jill glanced over her shoulder. She didn't see me.

I booted the horse into an all-out gallop.

A gallop wasn't good enough. Jill reached the gates. Ordinarily those were open and unguarded, but not today and not since the scandals had begun. Jill spoke to the guards, glanced at Maya, then spotted me.

Maya reached Jill when I was still a block away.

The guards grabbed both women, flung them inside, and closed up.

I reined in outside. Though I could make out no specific words I heard the women and a man arguing inside the gate house. The gate the women had gone through was a small pedestrian entrance now shut. I eyed those steel bars, then the coach gate beside it. A guard looked at me nervously. He was unarmed but determined. I didn't have to talk to him to know he wasn't going to let me in or, probably, even answer me.

I wasn't exactly heavily armed, either. I had a couple of knives and my head-knocker tucked away, but nothing I could intimidate anyone with while they were on that side of the gate and I was on the street side.

The coach gate wasn't quite five feet high in the middle.

Maya let out a squeal. Three men dragged her out of the gate house, headed toward the center of the grounds, which was concealed behind vegetation. Jill walked along with them. She glanced back, eyes huge, looking almost apologetic.

All right. That did it.

I backed my horse away, took him across the street, faced the gate and kicked him into a gallop. He ought to clear that gate easily.

Let's just say he wasn't a jumper.

He skidded to a stop. I yelled as I went over his head, crashed into the gate, and fell on my face. About ten guys lined up inside. They had no weapons but they weren't going to let me in without somebody getting hurt. I was hurt enough already—especially my pride.

I peeled myself off the cobblestone. Still on hands and knees, I looked at that damned horse. I tell you, he was grinning. He'd scored big for his tribe in its old war against Garrett. "You've had it, beast." I stumbled to my feet, limped toward him. He ambled away, moving just fast enough to stay ahead of me.

The guys behind the gate had a lot of fun at my expense.

They were going to be real unhappy because they'd done that.

A kindly passerby took pity and held the horse until I could take charge. I walked the son of a bitch back to Playmate's.

Playmate—my old buddy—took the damned horse's side. "Every animal has its limitations, Garrett. A jumper has to be trained. You don't just climb on a horse and tell it to take a leap."

"Damn it, I understand that. I placed my bet and took my chances. I lost. I accept that." Like hell. "What I'm griping about is the way he laughed at me afterward. He did it on purpose."

"Garrett, you got an obsession. You're always complaining about how horses are out to get you. They're just dumb beasts. They can't be out to get anybody."

Shows you how much he knew. "Don't tell me. Tell them." They sure had him fooled.

"What happened? Eh? You'd be laughing about the whole thing if something else hadn't gone wrong."

So I told him how Maya had gotten herself grabbed and the reason I tried the jump was that I wanted to get her loose.

"You going to try again?"

"Damned straight I am. And it's not going to be any nice guy going in after her, either. I'm out of patience with these superstition mongers."

He gave me a little of my own raised eyebrow. "Girl means enough to get you upset, eh? What about Tinnie?"

"Tinnie is Tinnie. Leave her out of it. She isn't part of this."

"If you say so. Need some help?"

He meant it. And if it came to a slugfest he might be handy, being nine feet tall and strong enough to lift the horses he tended. But he wasn't a fighter by nature. He'd get himself hurt because he was too damned kindly. "You stay out of it. You did enough, letting me use that four-legged snake. Sell the damned thing for dog food."

Playmate laughed. He gets a kick out of my feud with the equine species. "Sure you don't want some help?"

"No. You do what you do best. I need a hand I'll get somebody who does it for a living." I'd shot hell out of my disappearing act. "You really want to do something, go by the house and see how Dean and the Dead Man are doing. I'll get back with you in the morning." If I was alive in the morning.

"Sure, Garrett."

I knew what I was going to do next. I was going to make a lot of people unhappy. I'd be the unhappiest of all if I got caught.

45

Crask was staked out at a table in Morley's place, alone. He looked like he'd been there a long time. He didn't look happy. I didn't spot him until I was halfway to the serving counter. Then it was too late to duck out.

He summoned me with a gesture. I held my temper, joined him. From the corner of my eye I saw Slade talk into the speaking tube connecting with Morley's office. "What you need?"

"Chodo's getting impatient for results."

I gave him a blank look. "I missed something. The way I hear, he's getting results right and left. The city ratmen are working overtime picking up the bodies."

"Don't get wise, Garrett. He owes you but that don't mean he's gonna let you mess him around."

"Crask, I'm farther at sea every time you say something. How could I mess him around?"

"You were supposed to catch a broad for him. Where is she?"

I looked over my shoulder, back to Crask. "Me? Catch somebody for him? I don't remember it that way. What I heard was we were going to join forces, let each other know what we knew. And that's the way I'm playing it."

"Chodo Contague ain't a guy you want mad at you, Garrett."

I agreed. "You're right. He isn't. But he isn't a guy I want trying to run me, either. The deal I made is the only deal. Exactly the way it was worded. No hidden meanings. Understand?"

Crask rose. "I'll tell him. I don't think he's going to be pleased."

"I don't care if he's pleased. Far as I'm concerned I stuck to my half of the bargain."

He gave me an evil look. I knew what he was thinking. Someday he was going to pull my toes off one at a time.

"One more thing. Everywhere I go I get this load of crap from people who think I work for Chodo. I don't. I work for Garrett. If somebody is putting it out that I'm on the kingpin's payroll, tell them to stop. I don't work for him. And I won't."

He sneered, sort of, which is the most emotion I'd ever seen him show. He stalked out.

I headed for the bar. My hands were shaking. That damned Crask really put the hoodoo on me. He came on like a natural force, distilled menace and intimidation.

Slade said, "Morley says come straight up."

I went. Morley wasn't alone but both he and his guest had their clothes on, which was all I could ask, I guess. The woman was the same one I'd seen before—record setter. I'd never seen him with the same one twice. Maybe he was settling down.

"Had a run-in with Crask?"

"Sort of. Chodo's working on me. Trying to recruit me through the back door. Crask is irritated because I won't cooperate."

"Heard you had some excitement at your place last night."

"Some. The Dead Man took care of it."

"Remind me not to get on his bad side. What's up?"

"I need somebody to cover my back on a break-and-enter gig. Targets aren't going to be easy. People won't be understanding if we get caught."

He frowned. "Sensitive?"

"Like a ripe boil. One wrong word in the wrong place afterward could get a bunch of people killed."

"Right. I know the man to give you a hand. Wait downstairs. I'll take you to him myself."

Good. He had the idea. Don't let the woman know any more than she'd heard already.

Though I'd be the engineer on this, I'd still have to be careful. Morley would volunteer himself. Once he found out what I intended he'd get real nervous. If *he* was to pull a stunt like this he'd get rid of his backup man afterward, just to make sure nobody ever found out, even twenty years down the line. Though he tried to understand me he still didn't really believe, in his heart, that I didn't secretly think the way he did. He might get so jumpy we'd have a problem.

He came downstairs as I was draining a brandy Slade had slipped me. Slade was one employee of Morley's who wasn't devoted to the vegetable cause. He kept the real stuff hidden out handy. Morley pretended he didn't smell it. "Let's hit the street. Not so many ears out there."

We went out. Before he asked, I said, "I'm going into Chattaree. I want to break into Peridont's office."

Morley grunted. He was impressed. "You have a good reason?"

"Somebody grabbed Maya again. To have a shot at getting her loose I have to steal something from Peridont's office."

Providing the Church guys hadn't messed everything up there, now the Grand Inquisitor had gone to his guaranteed reward. I couldn't see that Sampson character not trying to move in.

Morley walked half a block with me before he said, "Tell me straight. Not with your heart. Can it be done?"

"I was in there the other day. There isn't any internal security. They flat don't expect anything. They don't think they have reason to expect anything. I'm not worried about doing the job." Liar. "I'm worried about pulling it without anybody finding out who did it. I don't want every member of the Church after me for the rest of my life."

"You're up to something."

"I told you that."

"No. I know you, Garrett. You're not just going to steal something. You're going to make it look like something it isn't."

If I could. I didn't deny that. I didn't agree, either. I had some ideas. Maybe they'd work out, maybe they wouldn't. The way my life was going they wouldn't. Morley didn't need to know what those ideas were.

"You play them too damned close to your chest, Garrett. What's the other target?"

I shook my head, which he couldn't see in the dark, so I said, "We don't worry about that till we've handled the first one. If I don't get what I need from Peridont's office, I can't make another move anyway."

"Too close to your chest, Garrett."

"Did you let me in on anything that time we ended up going after those vampires?"

"That was different."

"Sure it was. It was you moving me like a pawn without ever telling me you were doing it. You in or not?"

"Why not? You're a pretty dull guy yourself but interesting things happen where you're at. And I've never been inside Chattaree. They say it's magnificent."

He'd never been in because his kind were banned. According to Church doctrine he had no soul despite having human blood which was not a smart stance in a world where nonhuman races added up to half the total sentient population. And the Church didn't talk it up much here in TunFaire, where so many would be quick to take offense.

"Yeah," Morley said, evidently thinking about that. "I'd like to get into Chattaree for a while."

"Let's don't go grinding any axes."

"Right." We walked away, toward the Dream Quarter. Then he said, "You're taken with that Maya gal, aren't you?"

"She's a nice kid. She got herself in trouble because of hanging around with me. I owe her."

"Got you."

I glanced at him. He was grinning.

"She's just a kid I know, Morley."

The trouble with Morley is, he does understand.

46

I'd been hustling so much lately the weather had had little chance to gain my attention. Sitting in a deep shadow opposite Chattaree, watching, getting a feel for the night, it got plenty of opportunity.

"Damned cold," I muttered.

Morley glanced up. It was too dark to tell anything except that there were no stars out. "Might snow."

"That's all we need."

There'd been something going on at Chattaree when we arrived, just breaking up. It was a holy day but I couldn't remember which one. Morley didn't know. He didn't keep track of human superstitions.

I asked, "Think we've waited long enough?" We'd given them an hour to settle down inside.

"Give it a while yet." He wasn't comfortable with the adventure anymore. He was trying to recall if anyone had invaded the temple recently. I'd never heard of anybody trying. People in there ought to be lax. But Morley suspected safeguards that fixed it so invaders were not heard from again.

I said, "Any guy who can go into a vampire nest shouldn't have problems with this."

He snorted. "That was do or die."

We gave it fifteen minutes. Morley stared at Chattaree with obsessive concentration. I wondered if he was mongoose or cobra. His night vision was better than mine. If there was anything to see he'd see it.

"Give me the layout again," he said. I did. He said, "Let's do it."

It was a good time. There was no one in sight. But I found myself reluctant to go. I went anyway.

I was puffing when we reached the temple door.

Morley looked at me and shook his head. He raised an eyebrow, barely discernible in wan light from inside the temple. Ready? I nodded.

He walked through the doorway. I ducked out of sight.

"Hey! Where the hell you going?"

I peeked. Morley had darted past the guard, who *was* awake. I wondered if that was a common occurrence. Morley turned to face the man, who was as wide as he was tall.

I wound up two-handed and stepped into it, whacking him behind the ear with my stick. He went down.

I let out a big breath. "I didn't think I could put him down."

"I worried too, the way you've let yourself go."

"Let's get him put away."

We used materials at hand, bound and gagged the guy and tucked him out of sight inside his post. Hopefully anybody who came by would figure he'd gone AWOL.

I led the way. We'd chosen our time well. They'd closed up shop except for one sleeping priest at the main altar. Passing through in the far shadows we didn't disturb his slumber. Morley made less noise than a tiptoeing roach. I found the stairway descending into the catacombs.

"We have a problem," I whispered, halfway down. It was tomb-dark. We hadn't brought a light. I didn't think I could negotiate the maze without one.

"I'll go steal a candle, " Morley said.

He could be a ghost when he wanted. He went right up to the main altar and lifted a votive candle. The priest on duty never missed a snore.

He came back grinning. He'd been showing off. He hadn't had to snatch a light from disaster's jaws.

We descended into the catacombs. They seemed more claustrophobic than on my previous visit. A dwarf would have felt at home, but humans weren't made to inhabit mole holes. I worked up a bad case of the creeps.

Morley did, too. He didn't have anything to say, just tagged along quietly, so alert you could smell it.

The old memory was cooking. I made only one false turn and corrected that before I'd gone a step. I marched right up to Peridont's door.

"This place gives me the creeps," Morley whispered.

"Me too." It was as quiet as a grave in there. I would have been happier if there'd been some guy howling down the way. Thinking just made the creeps worse.

The door was locked but the lock was of ancient vintage. It didn't take me half a minute to open it. We stepped inside.

The room was unchanged, though there was more litter on the big table. I told Morley, "Light a couple of lamps."

"Hurry," he suggested.

"It shouldn't take long." I moved to the cabinet from which Peridont had taken the bottles he'd given me. Morley fired up a couple of lamps and posted himself beside the door.

The cabinet doors weren't latched, let alone locked. Sometimes you have to wonder about people. I mean, the stuff stored there was as dangerous as you could get, yet it was just sitting there waiting to be taken. Just because you don't want to think somebody would rob you doesn't mean you shouldn't take precautions.

I used the votive candle for light. I saw green and blue and red bottles (only one of the latter), plus lemon, orange, amber, indigo, turquoise, lime, and clear, and one that looked like bottled silver dust.

The temptation was to take the lot, a fortune in useful tricks. But I had no idea what would happen if an unfamiliar bottle was used. You don't mess with the unknown when you're dealing with sorcery. Not if you want to stay healthy.

I wasn't shy about grabbing all the green and blue bottles. I dithered over the red one, then recalled how effective it had been at Chodo's. I might run into that ape again. I pocketed the bottle, but this time with more respect. I padded it with cotton I found on the bottom shelf of the cabinet.

"What're you doing?" Morley asked.

The look in his eye said he had a damned good idea. And he'd love to lay hands on some of those bottles. "Putting tricks up my sleeve. I don't know what these others will do so I'm not taking them."

"You done? We ought to get while our luck's holding."

He was right. I checked the cabinet, closed it up. It wasn't obviously disturbed. Let them go crazy wondering why somebody bopped the guard. "Done. Let's . . ."

"Damn!" Morley jerked a thumb at the door.

He'd left it cracked so he could listen for footsteps. I heard nothing but that meant nothing. Someone was coming. Wavering light shown through the crack.

I jumped, extinguished the lamps, blew out the candle, and ducked under the table as the door swung inward.

It was that creepy Sampson. He held a lantern up and glared around. Morley stood behind the door, ready to cut him down if he came inside. Sampson sniffed, frowned, finally shrugged and backed out, shutting the door behind him.

I slithered through the darkness, listening but hearing nothing. The light leaking under the door weakened, presumably because Sampson was moving away. He'd pulled the door all the way shut but he hadn't locked it. I was surprised he hadn't been more suspicious, finding it unlocked and ajar.

I opened up slowly so I'd make no sound, then put my eye to the crack. Sampson was twenty feet away, his back to me, about to turn a corner. He scratched his head, a man who had a feeling something was wrong but who couldn't put his finger on it. He might any minute. "You ready?" I breathed at Morley.

He didn't reply.

Sampson shrugged again and moved on out of sight.

"Come on. Let's get while we can." I hoped I could manage without a light. I had no way to get the candle going again.

Again Morley didn't answer. I heard the faintest sound, like a fairy's wing beat. It didn't come from where Morley was, though in the dark sounds are confusing.

I spoke a little louder. "Let's go! He knows there's something wrong. He just hasn't figured it out yet."

"Right." He was there after all.

I opened the door, slipped out, extended my hand to the wall, walked slowly. "You behind me?"

"Yes."

"Close the door tight."

"I did."

That Sampson had to be an insomniac or something. We'd lucked out getting in without bumping into him. We almost ran into him twice before we reached the steps leading upward. We almost got lost, having to adjust our route to keep from colliding with him.

But get out of the catacombs we did, and exit we did, without incident—until we reached the guard station.

Four guys jumped me. They'd found the guard and had set an ambush. A fifth, inside, sounded an alarm.

I spun away from the rush. They didn't see Morley, who had lagged, eyeballing the treasures of the altar, probably figuring how much trouble it would be to get them out. I thumped a guy, my back against a wall. They had their hearts set on bloodshed. I thought I was dead. They kept me too busy to shove a hand into a pocket.

Morley just walked up, jumped in the air, and literally kicked the side of a man's head in. He ripped another's throat out with his bare hand. I whacked the same guy over the head with my club. The remaining attacker and the guy who had sounded the alarm got a case of the big eyes. One tried to run. Morley folded him up with a groin kick. I put the other one down with my stick.

"Let's go!" There was all kinds of racket in the depths of the temple. The gods knew who or what lived in those twisty ways beyond the main worship gallery. It sounded like we'd have a hundred men after us in a minute.

"We're not finished." Morley indicated the three men still alive. "They can identify us."

He was right. They would know what faces to look for and the Church was known for holding a grudge. Hell, they were still trying to get even for things that happened a thousand years ago. "I can't."

"You'll never learn."

He used a thin-bladed knife to still three hearts as quick as you could blink.

I've seen a lot of guys killed. I've had to do a few myself. I've never liked it and I've never gotten used to it. I almost puked. But I didn't stop thinking. I got out the coin I'd taken from Jill's place a thousand years ago and stuffed it under a body. When Morley was past me I smashed a couple blue bottles in the entryway, hoping their contents would slow the pursuit.

We ran like hell until we were a block away, hidden in shadows.

"Now what?" Morley asked.

"Now we go after the real target." And I told him how Maya and Jill had disappeared into the Orthodox compound.

47

Men with lanterns poured from Chattaree. It looked like they'd dragged out every damned priest in the place. Morley said, "Better move out. You have a plan?"

"I told you the plan."

"Get the women out? That's a plan?"

"It's the one I've got."

We were across the street from the gate where the women had entered the Orthodox compound. A group of Church priests were set to head our way. I dashed across the street. Morley stayed at my heels. "Even if they saw us I don't think they'd come in after us," I whispered.

"Shit. You're such a goddamned genius."

I vaulted the coach gate. Morley followed. He had more difficulty because he was shorter. I'd barely landed when a couple of guys came out of the gate house. They weren't armed but they were looking for trouble. I gave it to one with my stick. The other dove for an alarm bell. Morley landed on his back.

We'd barely gotten them inside when the Church bunch roared up. I stepped outside. "What's going on?"

"Thieves. Murderers. Invaded the temple." They all wore priestly garb. I, as an Orthodox employee, should have no trouble knowing what temple they were from. "See anybody go by here?"

"No. But I heard somebody run past a minute ago. Going like crazy. That's why I came out."

"Thanks, brother." Off the gang went.

"Good thinking, Garrett," Morley said when I stepped back inside. I didn't look for the guards. Mor-

ley was nothing if not certain about covering his ass.
Those guys weren't going to come to, get themselves
loose, and raise an alarm. "You ever been here before? Know your way around?"

"Once when I was a kid. They used to let you wander around the grounds."

"You're a wonder. Don't you ever plan anything?"

In the circumstances it was hard to argue with him.
I didn't waste my breath. "You can back out any
time."

"I wouldn't miss it. Let's go."

Needless risk-taking isn't like Morley Dotes. He
wouldn't do this sort of thing unless he had an angle
somewhere.

No skin off my nose. If somebody looted the temple
or this place, I'd have my suspicions but I wouldn't
be heartbroken. Morley would just look at me blankly,
baffled, if I suggested he'd had anything to do with it.

We found a whole complex of buildings behind the
first stand of trees. The biggest was the main Orthodox
basilica in TunFaire. It was as grand as Chattaree but
had no name except something generic like All Saints.
Morley and I slipped into some shrubbery and re-
viewed everything we'd heard about the compound,
which wasn't much. We could identify only three of
the cluster of seven buildings, the basilica itself and
two structures housing monks and nuns. Those had
featured prominently in the scandals.

"Isn't there suppose to be an orphanage and a seminary?" Morley asked.

"Yeah. I think so." That would identify two more
buildings. But which two?

"Logic would suggest a building with kitchens and
whatnot to feed all the people."

"Unless each has its own."

"Yeah."

"How's this sound? If you grabbed a couple women
wouldn't you maybe stash them in the nunnery?"

"Maybe. Unless they have jail cells or something."

"Yeah. But I've never heard a rumor like that."

Short of searching the complex, building by building,

I had no idea what to do. I hadn't thought this part out. Like Morley said, I tend to jump without looking.

"Hey."

Somebody was doing a sneak from shadow to shadow. It was too dark to tell much but he came close enough to identify as a monk. Morley suggested, "Let's follow him."

That seemed as good an idea as any.

I let Morley lead since he could see better and walk more softly. In a minute he reached back and stopped me. "He's checking to see if anybody's watching."

I froze. After a minute Morley tugged at my sleeve. We didn't go twenty steps before Morley stopped again and urged me into some shrubbery.

The man had climbed steps to a side door of the building I thought was the nunnery—which explained his sneaking.

He tapped a code. The door opened. He embraced somebody, then slipped inside. The door closed.

"Think that would work for us?" Morley asked.

"If we had somebody waiting."

"Let's check that door."

It took only a second to discover that it was barred inside. It took only a few minutes to learn that all the building's four entrances were barred. The ground floor windows were masked by steel lattices.

Morley muttered, "See what happens when you bull ahead with no research? We don't have the equipment we need."

I didn't argue. I went around to that one side door and tapped the code the visitor had used earlier. Nothing happened. Morley and I got into a brisk discussion about my tendency to act without thinking. I didn't put up much of a defense. As Morley was getting irked enough to walk, I tapped the door again.

And to our astonishment it opened.

We gaped. The woman said, "You're early . . ." then started to yell when she saw we weren't who she was expecting. We jumped her, and managed to keep her quiet. We dragged her into the little hall behind the door, which was about six feet long and four wide and lighted by a single candle on a tiny stand. Morley yanked the door shut behind us. I let him take the woman, then I darted to the end of the hallway and looked both ways, but saw nothing.

I turned. "Let's make it quick."

Morley grunted.

I told the nun, "Two women came in today. A blonde, middle twenties, and a brunette, eighteen, both attractive. Where are they?"

She didn't want to play.

Morley placed a knife at her throat. "We want to know. We aren't worried about the sin of murder."

Now she couldn't answer because she was too scared. I said, "Cooperate and you'll be all right. We don't *want* to hurt anybody. But we won't mind if we have to. Do you know the women we want?"

Morley pricked her throat. She nodded.

I asked, "Do you know where they are?"

Another nod.

"Good. Take us there."

"Mimphl murkle mibble" came from behind Morley's hand.

"Let her talk, " I said. "Kill her if she tries to yell."

We were convincing because Morley would have done it. She said, "They put the blonde woman in the guest house. They put the other one in the dining-hall wine cellar. It was the only place they could lock her up."

"That's fine," I said.

"Dandy," Morley agreed. "You're doing wonderfully. Now take us to them. Which one first?" That to me.

"The brunette."

"Right. Show us this wine cellar."

Somebody knocked on the door, just a gentle tippy-tap. Morley whispered, "How long before he gives up."

She shrugged. "I don't know. I've never not shown up."

"Been late?"

"No."

I suggested, "We could use another door. Which building do you use for a dining hall?"

She was reasonably calm now, and pliant. She explained. Morley said, "Let's go. And quietly."

"I have no wish to die. Why are you doing this? The Holy Fathers won't tolerate it. They'll have you hunted down."

"The Holy Fathers won't have time. We approach the Hour of Destruction. We have entered the Time of the Devastator. The heretic will be devoured." I couldn't get much passion into it because it sounded so silly but I doubted she was calm enough to hear that. "Show us the way."

She balked. Morley pricked her. I said, "We *will* have those women, with or without you. You have only one chance to see the sun rise. Move."

She moved.

We went out another secondary door. The dining hall proved to be a one-story affair between the nunnery and monk's quarters and behind the main temple. A seminary, occupied by yet another bunch of people, stood behind the dining hall. Maximum convenience. I asked about the other buildings in the complex. Stables and storage, she told us. The guest house, orphanage, and a few other buildings, like homes for several of the Holy Fathers (four of Karenta's twelve lived in TunFaire), were scattered around the grounds, in semi-seclusion. I thought it must really gall the Church to be stuck with one oversized block while the Orthodox maintained a whole city estate. But that's the way it goes when you're number two.

We reached the dining hall without incident. It wasn't locked. Morley muttered something about moving too slow, that sooner or later there was going to be a change of guard at the gate and an alarm would sound.

I tried to hurry the nun.

48

The nun seemed a little old for clandestine assignations. I guessed she had fifteen years on me. But maybe we never get tired of the great game.

"There'll be a guard," Morley whispered. "Let me go first."

I didn't argue. He was better at that sort of thing. "Don't cut him if you don't have to."

"Right." He went down the stair like a ghost. It wasn't a minute before he called up, "Clear." I herded the nun down. Morley waited at the bottom. "I'll watch her. Get the girl."

Thoughtful of him.

The guard slumped on a stool in front of a massive oak door strapped with iron, hung on huge hinges. There was no opening in it. It was secured by a wooden peg through a hasp. Effective enough, I guessed.

I touched the guard's throat. His pulse was ragged but it was there. Good for Morley. I opened the door, and saw nothing but darkness. I used the guard's lamp to give me light.

I found Maya curled in a corner on burlap sacks, asleep, filthy. The dirt on her face had been streaked by tears. I dropped to my knees, placed a hand over her mouth, and shook her. "Wake up."

She started violently, almost broke loose. "Don't say a word till we get home. Especially don't name any names. Understand?"

She nodded.

"Promise?"

She nodded again.

"All right. We're going out. We'll collect Jill, then

run like hell. We don't want these people to know who we are.''

"I got it, Garrett. Don't pound it in with a hammer."

"You think somebody just heard you? Maybe somebody we forced to show us where you were? Somebody we'd have to kill so they won't repeat it?''

She got a little pale. Good. "Come on.''

I stepped out and told Morley, "I got her. Watch her while I put this guy away." The nun didn't look like she'd heard anything.

I dragged the guard inside, stepped out and shoved the peg home, then told the nun, "Lead on to the guest house."

She led on. Maya kept her mouth shut. Some notion of the stakes had gotten through.

There were lights on the second floor of the guest house, a cozy two-story limestone cottage of about eight rooms. Morley checked for guards. I watched the women. "Just a few minutes more," I promised the nun.

She shook. She thought her minutes were numbered. I kept on with the dialectic of nihilism, filling her with arrows pointing at the Sons of Hammon. I wouldn't let Morley do what he'd want to do after we used her up. I wanted one live, primed witness left behind. I wanted the Orthodox Holy Fathers to foam at the mouth when they thought of the Sons.

The trouble was, there would be some right to Morley's argument. The nun had had too many chances to get a good look at us.

Maya caught on. She put on a damned good act, pretending to be terrified. She kept whispering tales about her previous stay with the Sons of Hammon.

Maya knew most everything I did. She was able to lay it on thick.

Morley came back. "Guards front and back. One for each door."

"Any problem?''

"Not anymore. They weren't very alert.''

I grunted. "Let's go," I told the women. "Sister, behave for a couple more minutes and you're free."

We'd gone maybe fifty feet toward the house when Morley said, "There it is."

"It" was the alarm we'd anticipated.

Bells rang and horns blew. Signal lights and balls of fire arced through the night. "They do get excited, don't they?" I grabbed the nun's habit to make sure she didn't stray.

We stepped over a guard. The door he'd watched was locked but the top half was a leaded glass window, Terrell with a halo. I bashed it in and lifted the inner bar. We shoved inside. I said, "Put her to sleep." Morley slugged the nun behind the ear. He understood what I was doing.

Someone shouted a question downstairs. A man. I started up. Morley was right behind me. Maya was behind him, armed with a knife she'd taken off the guard as soon as the nun went down.

The hurrah outside got louder.

The stairs took a right angle turn at a landing twelve steps up. A man in a nightshirt met me there. He made a noise that sounded like, "Gork!"

"Not me, brother."

He was the guy I'd seen at the talk-talk place, the little gink with the nose. I grabbed him by the back of the nightshirt before he could run for it. I softened him up with my stick and shoved him at Morley. "Bonus prize."

Morley grabbed him. I went on. Maya followed me.

That Jill was a quick mover. When I charged in she had a window open and was shoving a leg through. It wasn't wide enough for a fast exit. I got to her while she was still trying to scrunch up small enough to fit. I grabbed an arm and pulled. She popped out like a cork. "Anybody'd think you weren't thrilled to see me. After all the trouble I've gone through to rescue you."

She regained her balance and dignity, then gave me a lethal look. "You've got no right."

I grinned. "Maybe not. But here I am. And there you are. And here we go. You've got one minute to get dressed. You're not ready then, you take it through the streets like that.''

The proverbial jaybird wore more than she had on. I couldn't help admiring the landscape. Maya said, ''Put your eyes back in, Garrett. You'll have me suspecting you of immoral thoughts.''

''The gods forfend. Jill?''

Maya moved between Jill and the window. I gave her an approving smile and retreated to the door to check Morley and the bald gink. ''We've got her. She's got to get dressed.''

''Don't waste time. The whole place is awake.''

''Speaking of. See if you can wake him up. He's going with us.''

Morley scowled.

''If anybody knows the answers, he does.''

''If you say so. Find something we can put on him. Can't drag him around like this.''

I looked around. The little man's clothes were on a chair, neatly folded. Jill was almost ready. She hadn't bothered with underwear. Maya was giving her some song and dance about us telling the nun that she'd been sent ahead to soften up the little guy for the grabbing. I raised an eyebrow, then winked. The girl could think on her feet.

I said, ''Jill, carry your friend's clothes. He's going with us.''

''I'm sorry I ever came to you.''

''So am I, sweetheart. Let's go.''

We stepped out of the room, me first, Maya last and brandishing her knife. She was having fun.

Morley had the little guy organized enough to stumble along. They were halfway down the stair. We caught up at the bottom. Morley said, ''We'd better head for the nearest fence.''

''Right.'' Though that would put us on the side of the Dream Quarter farthest from where I wanted to be.

We went out the door we'd entered. It faced the center of the grounds. There was all kinds of excitement over there. Some was moving our way fast.

Morley came up with a piece of cord. He slipped a loop around the little man's neck. ''One peep and I choke you. We didn't come after you so we won't be brokenhearted if we kill you. Got me?''

The little man nodded.

Morley headed due south. Maya and I followed with Jill between us. Maya threatened to stab Jill in the behind if she didn't move faster.

She *was* having a good time.

I'd like to turn the whole thing into high drama with harrowing near misses, ferocious battles with fanatic priests, and a skin-of-the-teeth getaway when all seemed lost, but it didn't work that way. We never came close to getting caught. A dozen priests with torches thundered up to the house as we fled, but they didn't see us. We were at the enclosure wall, with Morley and Maya and Jill and the little gink perched on top and me reaching for Morley's hand, before the gang charged out of the house again. We were gone before they found a trail.

We got ourselves lost in the alleys of the industrial district south of the Dream Quarter and made the little guy get dressed. He didn't have much to say. No threats, no bluster. Once he'd taken stock he remained calm, silent, and cooperative.

We spent the rest of the night working around the Dream Quarter the long way, out to the western parts of the city, beyond the Hill, then back down to my place. I was damned tired when home hove into view.

I was pleased with myself, too. I'd pulled off a grand stunt and it'd proven easier than I'd expected. The raid on Chattaree hadn't been necessary. I still had all my little bottles in my pockets.

49

There was a problem. The Watch had the house surrounded. And it was light out. There'd be no sneaking past them.

We hadn't talked much but I'd mentioned my notion of getting Jill and Warden Agire together with the Dead Man. The little guy had proven to be exactly whom I'd suspected. I'd gotten that from Jill, not him. She'd been the one to try bluster, dropping his name. It hadn't done her any good.

Morley said, "What now, genius? Want to hide them out at my place?"

"We'll get in. We just need a distraction."

"Better come up with it quick. Five of us hanging around is going to catch somebody's eye."

"Right. Maya. Could I buy a little help from the Doom?"

She was surprised. "What kind?"

"Like maybe have Tey run to the door and tell Dean to tell the Dead Man we're out here. Better, have her send one of the young ones. They wouldn't do anything to a kid."

"All right." She sounded doubtful but she trotted off.

Those Watchmen were on their best behavior. TunFaire is a funny city some ways. One way is a popular determination to protect the common-law sanctity of the home. Our worst tyrants haven't dared overstep people's rights within their homes. An invasion of a home without a lot of legal due process will stir up a riot quick. People will put up with almost anything else but will shed blood in an instant over their right to retreat into and remain inviolate within their castles. It's odd.

Those Watchmen would be under close scrutiny and they would be intensely aware of it. The whole neighborhood might come boiling out if they made a wrong move.

So there was a good chance an unknown could stroll right to my door without interference. They might try a grab once they saw where the messenger was headed but I was sure Dean would be alert. Once the messenger got inside there'd be nothing the Watch could do.

Maya wasn't gone long. She looked bleak when she came back.

"What's the matter?" I asked.

"I had to pay a price."

She was upset. I took her hand without knowing why. She squeezed hard. "Tell me about it."

"You got what you need. They're sending a girl. But she made me pay."

Oh-oh. I had a feeling Maya had given more than she should have. "What?"

"I had to step out. Leave the Doom. Give her warchief."

"Maya! We could've worked something else out."

"It's all right. You said it. I'm getting too old. It's time I grew up."

It was all true, but I felt guilty because she'd done it for me, not for her.

They sent the ragamuffin in a gunnysack who let me in that time I visited Maya. Tey would make a deadly warchief. That kid was perfect. Every one of those Watchmen stared and thought filthy, shameful thoughts, and not one considered interfering until she pounded on the door. By the time somebody reacted she was making her pitch to Dean.

Dean let her in.

Morley muttered, "That kid is a witch." He'd felt it, too.

I said, "Some are at that age. Even when they don't know what they're doing."

"She knows," Maya said. "She *is* a witch. She'll own the Doom before she's sixteen."

The Watchmen snapped to attention. I felt the lightest touch from the Dead Man as they presented arms. "Time to go, kids."

Jill and Agire balked.

Agire refused to move. Morley cured that with a quick kick to the foundation of his dignity. Jill wanted to yell. Maya laid a roundhouse on her nose. "That's for the way Garrett looked at you."

"Take it easy." I knew she was spending her disappointment.

"Sorry." She didn't mean it and apologized to me instead of Jill. I let it slide. Jill had decided to cooperate.

We walked over to the house. Near as I could tell the Watchmen didn't see us. Dean let us in, croggled by the numbers. I told him, "Breakfast for all. In with his nibs."

"Not me," Morley said. "I did my part. You have it under control. I have to see if there's anything left of my place."

I thought he was in an awful hurry but I didn't argue. He'd done his share and hadn't tried to hit me with an inflated fee. He had something on his mind. I didn't want to interrupt.

Dean let him out after I had Jill and Agire installed with the Dead Man. Jill was frightened. Agire was terrified. He clung to self-control by concentrating on offenses to his dignity.

I trust there is some significance to the presence of these people, the Dead Man thought at me.

"Yep. How'd it go with the civil servants?"

They kept losing track of what they were doing and wandered off to drink beer or indulge other vices.

"What about those Watchmen? They going to call down the wrath of the Hill?"

They believe one of the stormwardens just went past. Once Mr. Dotes is out of sight they will return to their duties unaware that anyone has come or gone.

The little witch from the Doom was gone, too. I hadn't seen her go. Dean must have planted her in the front parlor, then hustled her out behind me.

These two? the Dead Man reminded me.

I made the introductions and suggested we might tie things up if he'd help out for a few minutes. He could, after all, plunder their minds if he wanted.

He astounded me by agreeing without being bullied. He went after Agire first. The Warden let out a squeal of panic. He yelled, "You have no right! What's going on is none of your business."

"Wrong. I have two paying clients and a personal interest. A friend of mine got caught in your game. It killed him. One of my clients died, too. Magister Peridont. Heard of him? His death doesn't end the commitment. And my other client is too damned nasty to walk out on. His name is Chodo Contague. He took offense at the Sons of Hammon. He's after scalps. If you know anything about him, you know you don't want to get on his bad side."

Agire knew something. He got rockier.

I said, "We don't have to be enemies. But my friend and I want to know what's going on so we can get ourselves out of a bind and maybe put the crazies out of their misery."

That is enough, Garrett. Say nothing more. He is considering his position and options and the probability that you are telling the truth. You are?

"The whole and nothing but." I glanced at Jill. Gone was the cool. She had a bad case of the fidgets. Her eyes wouldn't stay still. She might have tried to run if Maya hadn't been between her and the door.

We waited on Agire. Agire waited on divine inspiration.

Dean brought a small side table from the kitchen. "I'll set up a buffet," he said.

"Fine. As long as there's plenty of it." I was hungry and tired and impatient with my guests.

The Dead Man cautioned, *They are thinking, Garrett. That is enough.*

"Anything interesting?"

A great deal. We now know, for example, why Dean and your young friend could not locate what the woman concealed here. She is trying too hard not to think of it.

"What?"

My backchat disturbed my guests. I told myself to can it. I helped Dean when he brought a tray of goodies. I wasn't polite. I helped myself immediately. "Breakfast," I told the others.

After a pause calculated to have me panting with suspense, the Dead Man said, *She hid it here while I was sleeping.*

"I know." I went to the case on the short wall where we keep our maps and references, searched the shelf that kept drawing Jill's eye, and found a big copper key. It looked like it had been lying around turning green for a couple hundred years.

The Dead Man was irked. I had stolen his thunder. Jill looked like she was going to cry. Agire couldn't take his eye off the key.

It was six inches long and the heaviest key I'd ever hefted. It excited Agire but I knew there was no key among the Terrell Relics. It was squared off flat on the sides. There was an inscription under the verdigris. I scraped at it.

"My, my." It was the very slogan on those old temple coins. I chunked it under the Dead Man's chair, collected my plate, and started stuffing myself. Maya followed my lead. My guests were too nervous to partake. If they didn't get busy, I'd get their share.

50

Patience paid. Agire cracked.

"The Hammon cult has been making war on us. Its object is recovery of that key, which can unlock the Tomb of Karak, where legend has the Devourer imprisoned. The cult can't free him any other way. It's only been a few months since they found out who had the key, although they've known for decades that it was in TunFaire.

"For three decades they've slipped men into the priesthoods here. Sometime this year one of them reached a level of trust where he could find out the key is kept with the Terrell Relics.

"The cult's leaders brought men to TunFaire. Using sources inside my church, they began a whisper campaign meant to rip us apart, They might've succeeded, but a minor player defected. He told me what he knew. I tried to take steps but learned that the hierarchy was riddled with traitors.

"I shared some of this with my friend." He indicated Jill. "I didn't realize she knew who I was, nor that she had a relationship with Magister Peridont. Nor, for that matter, was I aware that my peccadillo was known to my enemies.

"I mentioned my informant in front of the wrong man, resulting in an attempt on my life and an effort to steal the Relics. By Orthodox monks. I fled to the one person I could trust." He indicated Jill again. "But I chose a bad time. She was entertaining her friend from the Church."

Pain shown for a moment. "I should have known she couldn't afford a place like that." Another pause. "Later she arranged for me to hide in the apartment opposite hers. She urged me to take Magister Peridont into my confidence. The threat to the Orthodox church was a threat to all Hanites. I was stubborn. She says she dropped hints to Peridont. Those set him moving along the course you know. I didn't yield to her till too late. I gave her permission to speak to Peridont after she saw you that first time, hoping you could protect her from men watching her in hopes of tracing me. When she tried to tell Peridont he was too rushed to get the full story and didn't understand that she could bring us together. He tried to hire you to find me.

"Then he made the mistake I did—talking in front of someone who had infiltrated the Church. The enemy immediately suspected that she knew where the Relics were."

He seemed to think that explained everything. Maybe it did, in some ways. But it ignored why I'd received so much attention. I asked.

Jill confessed. "I set you up, sort of. You have a reputation for stumbling around turning over rocks and getting away with it. You scared them. They tried to get rid of you without being connected to it. You got the best of the kids they hired. They panicked. Everything just escalated."

Really? It made a crazy sense. Maybe perfect sense to somebody in the religion business.

"You telling me there really is a Devastator? And that this character can destroy the world but can't bust himself out of a tomb? Come on. You might as well stuff him in a bag made of cobwebs."

Agire looked at me like I was a mental defective. Make that spiritually handicapped.

"I know you priests believe six impossible things everyday before breakfast," I said. "Some of you, anyway. I think most of you are parasites who live off the gullible, the ignorant and the desperate. I don't think any of you who get ahead believe what you preach. You sure never practice it. Convince me you're an honest man and a believer, Warden."

Garrett.

I thought he was going to caution me about pushing the man.

True, the man does find some dogma a useful fiction. He manipulates the laity cynically and he is devoted to improving his place in the hierarchy. But he believes in his god and his prophet.

"That's absurd. He's an intelligent man. How can he buy something so full of contradictions and revisions of history?"

Agire smiled sadly, as though he had overheard the Dead Man and pitied me my blindness. I hate it when priests do that. Like their pity is all the proof they need.

You believe in sorcery.

My brain was in better shape than it should have been, tired as I was. I got his argument.

"I see sorcery at work every day. It's absurd but I see concrete results."

Agire said, "Mr. Garrett, you appear to be the sort who needs to be cut to believe in swords. I understand that mentality better than you think. Do you comprehend the idea of symbol? You say you accept sorcery. The very root of sorcery is manipulation of symbol in a way that affects referent. And that's the root of religion, too.

"Say there never was a Terrell. Or that Terrell was the villain portrayed by some. In the context of symbol and faith the Terrell who lived is irrelevant. The Terrell of faith is a symbol that must exist to fulfill the needs of a large portion of mankind. Likewise the creator.

"Hano must be because we need him to be. He was before we were. He will be after we're gone. Hano may not fulfill your prescription for such a being. So call him Prime Mover or just the force that set time and matter in motion.

"He must be because we need him to be. And he must be *what* we need him to be. It is a philosophical argument difficult to grasp for we who live among obdurately hard surfaces and sharp edges that ignore our wishes, but the observer invariably affects the phenomenon. In this context, God—by whatever name—

is, and is constrained to be, whatever we believe him to be. The Hano of Terrell's time isn't the Hano of today. The Hano of the Orthodox denominations isn't the Hano of the Sons of Hammon. But he exists. He was what he was and he is what he's believed to be now. Do you follow? Hano is even what you believe him to be, in that infinitesimal fraction of himself that is yours alone."

I understood that they always have an argument. "You're saying we rule and create God as much as God creates and rules us."

"Ultimately. And that's how we get a fragment of God called the Devourer that can be locked in a tomb even though he can destroy the world. He can't get out because nobody believes he can get out—except by unlocking the door from outside. In fact, you might be able to argue that *nobody* wants him out—not even his followers—so the tomb becomes a total constraint."

"Too spooky for me. I'll keep thinking you're a bunch of crooks." I punctuated with a grin, telling him I knew what he'd say next.

"And the vast majority of people would as soon keep thinking in the symbols to which they're accustomed."

"All of which doesn't get us a step closer to cleaning this mess up before those guys turn TunFaire into a battleground. Symbols haven't been getting killed."

"The crux. Always the crux. The practicalities of everyday life. The early kings did what they had to when they exterminated an insidious and vicious enemy. Only a handful survived to rebuild. That solution is impractical today because we couldn't convince the agencies of the state that a threat exists. Symbolism again. A threat must be perceived to exist before the Crown will act. We have bodies all over the city? So the lower orders are slaughtering each other again. So what?"

I glanced at the Dead Man. He seemed amused. "Old Bones, you were going on about a rogue Loghyr the other day. This guy hasn't said anything about that."

He does not know, Garrett. The possibility of a true, cynical manipulation of men and their beliefs has not occurred to him, except in his own feeble way.

Ah! There is no contradiction, as you are about to protest. I am aware that I mentioned a great evil being created because some people needed it to exist. That is what the Warden has been saying. The rogue created a god in order to manipulate men. Men then created that god with their belief. Agire is right. There is a thing in a tomb. It can be released. It could destroy the world. It is a product of the imagination that has taken on life. Now it rules the rogue who imagined it. It has sent him to find the key.

"But . . ."

To end this you must find the rogue. You must destroy him.

"Oh boy." I glanced at Agire and Jill. The Dead Man had let them listen in. Jill seemed lost, Agire just frightened. "And how do we pull that off? How do you put an end to a Loghyr when even death doesn't slow him down?"

We will discuss that later. You are too tired to act, let alone think. I will consider means while you sleep.

Just dandy.

51

The Dead Man must not have let Dean rest while I was sawing logs. When I went downstairs the place was a zoo. The most exotic animals in TunFaire were there. They included Chodo Contague (who never leaves his estate) and his top two lifetakers, Morley, a man I didn't know who was obviously off the Hill, several species of priest old enough to have gray hair or no hair, and—wonder of all wonders—that character Sampson who'd been Peridont's assistant. At least fifteen people united in a conspiracy to exhaust my food and potables.

Were they talking about how to get shut of the Sons of Hammon? No. All they had on their minds was Glory Mooncalled, whose latest stunt had come earlier than expected and had people reeling everywhere. He had won his biggest victory yet, his slickest, and his most treacherous.

He let himself be discovered by the last Warlords of Venageta. He led their three armies a merry chase until they ran him to ground and he caught them. At the same time his agents guided even vaster Karentine armies into the same area. Those jumped right in figuring to end the war with a single day's bloodwork. They killed all three Warlords and most of their men. But the victory didn't turn out the way they hoped. Glory Mooncalled extricated himself early, engaged only to keep the Venageti from fleeing. The night after the battle he attacked the Karentine camp and killed all the officers, commanders, witches, warlocks, storm-wardens, firelords, and what have you. He sent surviving enlisted men to Full Harbor with word that the Cantard's nonhuman peoples had declared it an inde-

pendent state. Any Karentine or Venageti presence
would be considered an act of war.

The man's audacity was amazing.

The Dead Man had gotten the news.

"You don't seem as smug as you should be. What
did he do that you didn't predict?"

*He declared creation of an independent republic. I
had foreseen him turning on Karenta, as you know,
but never considered the possibility that he had such
lofty ambitions.*

"The way I read it he just wants to be the warlord
of the Cantard republic."

*A convenient fiction. He permits the creation of an
assembly representing the various sentient races of the
Cantard. But who owns the power? Who controls the
hearts of every veteran capable of wielding a weapon?
Today he is not just a king or emperor or even a dic-
tator. He is a demigod. If Karenta and Venageta continue to make claims to the Cantard, his power will
not wane while he lives.*

There was no "if" about what Karenta and Venageta would do. There were vast silver deposits in the
Cantard. They were what the war was about. Sorcerers
need silver to fuel their sorceries. Sorcerers are the
true, hidden masters of both kingdoms. The war would
continue with Karenta and Venageta as tacit allies until
Glory Mooncalled's republic collapsed.

So it goes.

"What's this hungry horde I have filling up every
nook and cranny? I've gained a few marks in this mess
but at the rate they're going they'll eat up the profits."

*Bring them in. I suggest you bring Mr. Sadler, Mr.
Crask, and Mr. Chodo first and place them near the
door, then bring the others, then come yourself with
Mr. Dotes and Miss Stump. There could be some excitement when those priests realize they are in the
presence of a Loghry. Caution Mr. Chodo and his as-
sociates.*

I didn't have any idea what he was up to. I decided
to humor him. It was pleasure enough to see him awake
and working without carping.

When Sadler heard my warning he asked what was

up. I told him I didn't know. He wasn't pleased, but what could I do? Chodo was more understanding—on the surface. He would await events before making judgments.

Morley and I stood to either side of the door as the others filed in. All I detected was a rising note of excitement. Then Sampson strode by. He looked at me like I was something with a hundred legs he'd discovered crawling in his breakfast.

He started violently when he saw the Dead Man. He turned, saw me and Morley blocking the doorway, and turned back again.

We went in, me frowning, looking at the Dead Man as though he might give me some physical clue. Maya closed the door behind us. She didn't look pretty today. She looked mean, like the street kid she'd been so long.

Garrett, ask Mr. Sampson to disrobe. Mr. Contague, would you lend us the aid of Mr. Crask and Mr. Sadler in the event Mr. Sampson is reluctant?

Everyone but Chodo looked at Sampson. Chodo looked at me and his henchmen, lifted a finger granting permission. I said, "Sampson?"

He headed for the door. Maya knocked him up side the head with a brass goblet. That slowed him down. Crask and Sadler held his arms while I hoisted the skirt of his habit and yanked down his pants. Morley leaned against the wall and made a crude remark about human perversion.

Mr. Sampson of the Church, heir to the Grand Inquisitor, had a bald crotch.

If you dress him in peasant garb and put him into a doorway I believe witnesses would swear he was the man who assassinated Magister Peridont. I believe he is the only one of his kind present.

"Good enough for me," I said. "Pity there's no one else from the Church here. It would save us the trip to turn him over."

We will keep him here. He knows who in each denomination is what you call a ringer.

Sampson went rigid as a stone post. I had Crask and Sadler set him to one side. I glanced at the Dead Man.

Did he have an ulterior motive for having invited Chodo? Like wanting him to see how much aggravation he could get if he ever decided to push us? That kind of thinking ahead wasn't beyond him.

Gentlemen. As you know, the death of a Loghyr stills the flesh only. Many centuries can pass before the spirit separates from the flesh. In some cases, where the spirit is unwilling, Passing can be delayed almost indefinitely. In the ancient days of your race, when mine was more numerous, many of your local gods and devils were the departed of my species. It was the fashion to while away the Passing protecting or plaguing the primitives. Most of those animistic spirits have faded from memory, as my race has faded from the world. That game has lost its jest, so that now most Loghyr prefer to go to Khatar Island for their Passing. But there is one ancient, malignant presence among you. He has been known by many names in many times. He always attaches himself to dark, nihilist cults. In recent ages he has shown himself less because the rest of us took an oath to end his torment. He is the motive force behind the Sons of Hammon. And he is in TunFaire now.

He made a mistake coming here. But he did not know of my presence. He did not discover his mistake until he attacked this house in an effort to obtain the key that will unlock the tomb of the Devastator. I had suspected his presence earlier, based on reports from Mr. Garrett. His attack confirmed it.

Gentlemen, this ancient wickedness is most vulnerable at this moment. It is never likely to be this exposed again. Its adventures lately have stripped it of all allies but a handful hidden inside the priesthoods. A dead Loghyr is not very mobile. Without cohorts to remove it to safety, it can do nothing but await its fate, be that rescue or despair at your hands.

Determine amongst you what course to pursue. Though we of this house have done our share already we will continue to lend our support.

Thanks a bunch, Old Bones. If there was no more profit in it I wasn't that excited about staying involved. Who wants to duke it out with a dead Loghyr who's had several thousand years to practice being nasty? My own pet devil was bad enough. He's only been at it a few centuries and claims he's a friend. He doesn't create eight-armed demons out of whole cloth or send them calling in their own private thunderstorms.

He sent a personal message. *These priests have the power to make thousands forget their temples were profaned.*

And there were stormwardens and firelords and whatnot on the Hill who could turn into real pests if we kept attracting their attention. The priests could dissuade them. Maybe there was a profit after all.

Two hours of politicized yak passed before Chodo Contague asked the critical question. He'd gotten fed up with their bickering over precedence.

"Do you know where this thing is?"

That was the key question. If you're going after rats it helps to know where the rathole is.

Yes.

"Then this chatter is pointless. Mr. Sadler and Mr. Crask will tend to the matter. Are there special needs they should be aware of before they start?"

The Dead Man was amused. Within seconds the arguments collapsed. Everybody wanted to be right behind the kingpin. It didn't seem like that bad a spot, either. Better still would be behind his boys and the whole religious bunch. Then there would be nobody to trip over when I made a run for it.

52

The target had picked a spot.

Copperhead Bar is a long, skinny island that starts where the river bends as it passes the southern city limit. It's a mile long and maybe seventy yards wide at its widest. It's covered with scrub growth that has anchored the sand and silt that make up the bar. Forty yards of channel separate it from the mainland. It's a hazard and an eyesore and the only reason it isn't dredged out of there is that it belongs to the Church, deeded over in early imperial times. Way back they tried to establish a monastery on it but the footings were too infirm and the floods too frequent. There's nothing left but a tumble of creeper-covered building stone.

The Dead Man said our target was hiding under that rockpile.

He might as well have been in another dimension.

We had a good crowd gathered just south of the city wall, in an area kept barren by an eccentric owner. Chodo had sent a dozen street soldiers to back Crask and Sadler. The various denominations had contributed several hundred vigorous young priests. The guy who had come off the Hill, whose name I never did get, had juice enough to borrow a company of the Watch. Morley and I kind of stood off by ourselves, with Maya, wondering what was going to happen.

An ecumenical delegation had gone to Chattaree in hopes of recruiting a Magister or two. We were waiting on the Church's reply.

The drop-off to the river was about twelve feet, a sort of miniature bluff. Morley and Maya and I were on a knoll fifty yards back. Everyone else was between us and the river but kind of hanging back, not wanting to get any closer than they had to. I wondered if the thing on the island was aware of us.

I wondered, too, if I had some score to settle with Jill Craight. She and her pal Agire were standing separate, thirty yards south of anyone else. I'd been keeping an eye on them. They weren't talking and didn't seem very friendly. Maybe Agire was having trouble coping with being seen in a whore's company. It was too late for him to make it look like anything but what it was.

Maya noted my interest. She was too nervous to tease me. "What're they doing here?" she asked.

"I don't know."

The only men who had dared the lip of the bluff were Crask and Sadler. Now they headed our way. I was excited about that.

Crask came up, said, "Garrett, you were the Marine. How do we get over there?"

"I don't think we do, you want the truth."

He scowled.

"Remember the thing that came to Chodo's place? That's what we're up against." That and a lot more. This Loghyr had been polishing his tricks for ages. He'd lived through these things before. In fact, the Dead Man said this particular Loghyr was supposed to have been scrubbed after the fall of Carathca. "An attack will just get us all killed."

Neither Crask nor Sadler were known for subtle solutions to problems. Sadler asked, "Then what're we doing out here?"

"We're here because the people who tell us what to do don't understand what we're up against."

"All right, smart guy," Crask said. "You live with one of these things. How would you take it out?"

I'd hoped that wouldn't come up. I didn't want to give anybody something he could use against me and the Dead Man.

"We should wear him down. First thing, set up a kind of siege."

"A line here, and somebody on the river, to keep its people from rescuing it. After that I'd just collect mice and rats and bugs and float them to the island on rafts. For as long as it took."

"What?" They both looked lost.

"All right. First thing you got to realize, this thing *is* dead. But its spirit is tied to its body. No body, the spirit has to go away." Or so the Dead Man claimed. "There's nothing on that island for vermin to eat except that Loghyr body. The Loghyr knows that, too. He'll be watching for bugs and stuff. But if there are a lot of them, it'll be hard for him to spot them all and take care of them. Also, a dead Loghyr has to spend a lot of time sleeping. That's when they develop the energy they use when they pull their stunts. This one is probably sleeping right now. When he's asleep he can't keep track of vermin. They could work him over good. He wouldn't feel them biting because he's dead."

Crask snorted, disgusted. But Sadler nodded, seeing it. "Take a while, though."

"It would. But I don't know of any more certain, less risky way to handle it."

"We'd have to check with Chodo. He wants results quick." Chodo had retired to his estate.

"He'll pay dear for that if he insists."

Crask jerked his head at Sadler. They went off to talk it over. Morley asked, "Why not ring in a firelord or two? They could burn it out there, couldn't they?"

"Maybe. But a sorcerer wouldn't be safer from it than you or me."

"Garrett," Maya said softly, scared, "I don't think it's asleep."

She had a flair for understatement.

I saw nothing but a glow from where we stood but something was happening on the island. Those nearer the edge began yammering and backing away.

Then a spot of black cloud formed above the island, maybe fifty feet high. It grew quickly, spinning like a whirlpool. Everybody watched it, which was a mistake.

Sudden as lightning three guys in antique armor jumped over the lip of the bluff. Glowing, they charged the crowd. They hurled spears of fire.

A six-armed woman formed inside the spinning cloud. She grew huge. She wore nothing, was a polished black, and had a skull for a face and teats like a dog.

Priests screamed. The Watch company decided they weren't getting paid enough to deal with this.

Crask and Sadler and their boys were willing to take on the armored guys but couldn't get to them through the panicky mob.

The armored guys went to work. Pieces of body flew.

"Damn!"

I glanced at Morley but kept most of my attention on the black thing. It seemed especially interested in Jill and Agire. Morley dipped into a pocket. I caught a glimpse of something lemon-colored. He threw it at the armored men.

Damn him, he'd managed to sneak himself some of Peridont's goodies while the lights were out that night.

The bottle broke on a man's breastplate. For a moment I thought nothing was happening. When it did start it wasn't what Morley had in mind.

The guy started laughing. In a minute he was laughing so hard he rested his sword tip on the ground and leaned on the weapon, having one hell of a good time.

"Shit," Morley grumbled. "That was a bust." He threw a couple more bottles, other colors, at the other two armored figures. Those had even less obvious effect.

The yellow bottle wasn't a complete bust. Crask forced his way through the crowd, took the sword away from the laughing villain, used it to carve him up. Then he got the giggles himself.

One down. But the other two were slaughtering everybody they could catch. And the thing in the air was after Agire and Jill.

I threw my red bottle.

I didn't want to do that. In the back of my mind I'd hoped to get to the island and use it on the dead Loghyr.

The results were the same as they'd been at Chodo's place. The monster melted and evaporated. But I didn't have time to watch. Two armored guys were headed my way and, except for Chodo's troops, everybody was opting for discretion.

One of Morley's bottles began to take effect. One of the attackers started having trouble keeping his balance.

He slipped, staggered, and as he got closer fell to his knees.

Neither was throwing sorceries anymore. Though maybe that was because the thing on the island was distracted by what was happening to its monster.

Crask got behind the staggering character, ran a spear through him. So then there was one. All of a sudden it was at the heart of a circle of unfriendlies including Morley and myself, Sadler and most of Chodo's boys, and maybe a dozen priests and Watchmen with more than average nerve. The guy was like a giant thunder lizard surrounded by little hunters. We couldn't hurt him head-on but his back was always turned to somebody.

He didn't last long.

When it was over I glanced at the thing that had been in the air. It lay on the ground twitching, half devoured by the stuff eating it, black fog boiling off. Sadler stepped over. "I get the point you were making, Garrett. That thing can hack away any time it wants."

Somebody pulled the helmet off a suit of armor and discovered that the man inside had been a corpse longer than a few seconds. He had drowned days ago. Fish and corruption had been working on him.

I nodded to Sadler. "It has to rest sometimes, but this's what we can expect, or maybe worse, if we try to go over there." I thought about how the Dead Man could make people forget, could make them do things they didn't want to do. This could get rough.

Actually, though, I was surprised by the level of violence. I'd figured the Loghyr wouldn't want to attract attention from the Hill. Sorcerers could get real interested in this kind of show.

Morley said, "We'd better take care of the dead and get the wounded to help."

Two kinds of guys had run from the excitement, those who were so ashamed that they never came back and those that did come back looking sheepish. They helped sort the mess out.

Maya hadn't run. I don't know why not. She couldn't have done anything but get hurt. Fifteen minutes into the cleanup she grabbed my arm. "Agire bought it. And Hester is gone."

For a moment I felt sorry for Jill. She deserved more of life . . . Then suspicion raised its snoot. "Where's Agire?"

"Over where they were."

I walked that way, keeping one eye on the smoldering black thing. Its flesh—if flesh it could be called—was almost consumed.

I found the Warden and knelt. Maya dropped to her knees opposite me. "Been hard on religious bigwigs lately," I said. And on littlewigs, too, as the cults and denominations stripped their priests and monks to see how well they were hung.

Blood had run from Agire's mouth. He was lying on his back. There was no wound visible. I rolled him over, grunted.

A minute later I told Sadler, "Far as I can see I've done my part here. You guys know how to handle it. I'm going home."

Morley stayed. Maya tagged along with me. She had nowhere else to go. We had to do some serious thinking about her future now. She said, "You've got something on your mind. What is it?"

"Jill."

"What upset you?"

"She killed Agire. While we were distracted she stuck a knife in his back. Couldn't have been anyone else because the excitement never got to them."

"But why?" She didn't claim Jill couldn't do a thing like that.

"The Terrell Relics, I think. Agire gave them to her to hide. He never said he got them back. The only thing she left at our house was that key. That could've gotten her killed if she'd kept it. Hell. Maybe she was out to snatch the Relics from the beginning."

"Why?"

"She's fond of money and nice things. How much would the Church pay for the Relics? How about some other cult?"

Maya just nodded. After we'd walked a few blocks, she said, "We should be headed for the Tenderloin."

Maybe. But I'd wanted to ask the Dead Man if it was really any of my business.

53

It *was* my business. I'd been hired by Peridont and I'd
made a point of claiming he was still my client, dead
or not.

Maya was pleased. I wasn't so sure I was. It had
started to snow earlier than I'd expected, heavier than
I'd anticipated. The wind was nippy. If I'd let it go
I'd be home, toasty warm, sipping a beer, wondering
how I could get Dean out of the house and the Dead
Man to go to sleep so Maya and I could . . .

We walked into a Tenderloin like a ghost town. The
first snowfall always has that effect on TunFaire. Everyone gets in out of it and stays. We went around the
side of the talk house, into the alley.

"Too late," Maya said. There were tracks in the
snow on the steps to the second floor, downward
bound.

"Maybe." I hustled upstairs, went inside, hurried
along a hallway not unlike the one downstairs. One
door stood open. I stuck my head in.

Jill's, all right. I recognized the clothing scattered
around. It included what she'd worn to the festivities
down south. I cursed and headed out.

Maybe I was a little loud. A door opened. The elvish woman Polly looked out. "What're you doing?"
she asked.

I fell in love all over again. I gulped. "I came to
tell you how much . . . I'd better go. I'm making a
fool of myself." Not bad for off the cuff, Garrett. I
got out.

I rejoined Maya. "She's gone. Let's get after her
before her tracks disappear."

As we moved out I glanced up. The elvish woman

was at the top of the steps looking down, wearing a puzzled smile.

Jill wasted no time but the snowfall betrayed her. We gained ground. Her tracks became fresher. The snowfall tapered off. Visibility improved. The street we were following entered a square. A figure shuffled across it ahead of us.

"That's an old woman," Maya said. "Look at her. She's old enough to be Hester's mother."

I could see that, just the way the woman moved. She wore a lot of black, the way old women do, and moved slowly. "Damn it!" How had I confused trails? I thought back.

I hadn't. This trail hadn't crossed any other. That woman was the one who had come out of the talk house. And she was carrying a bundle she hugged to her breast. "Come on." I began to trot.

The snow and wind muted our footsteps till we were a half-dozen yards from the woman.

She whirled.

No old woman moved like that.

"Hello, Jill."

She straightened up, stopped pretending. "Garrett."

Maya moved around to cut her off if she ran. I said, "I can't let you get away."

She sighed. "I know. That's the way you are." She shrugged. "I didn't think you'd catch on so quick."

"It was pure chance."

"Suppose I turned them over voluntarily? Would that be enough?"

"I don't think so. There's a saying. Any man's death diminishes me. You shouldn't have killed Agire. You didn't have to."

"I know. It was stupid. I did it without thinking. The opportunity was there and I grabbed it. I knew it was a mistake before he fell. But that's not something you can take back."

"Let's go." I believed her. Maya didn't. She stayed behind us throughout a walk all the way to the Dream Quarter. And as I walked beside Jill, in silence, shiv-

ering, I did a lot of reflecting, most of it on the fact
that, though none had by my own hand, seven men
had died the night we rescued Maya from the Orthodox complex. I could rationalize however I wanted but
I was the guy who had taken Morley along.

As we approached the gate I told Jill, "Just hand
them the casket. Don't say anything. Don't answer
any questions."

She looked at me oddly, her eyes as old as she was
dressed. And that's the way she did it. A guard came
to see what she wanted. She pushed the casket into his
hands and turned away, looked at me to see what next.

I said, "Good-bye," and walked into a quickening
snowfall, holding Maya's arm. We pushed into the
wind with our heads down and our cheeks biting cold,
saying nothing. Crystals of ice formed at the corners
of my eyes.

54

The Dead Man was pleased with himself. He was cocky as hell. Even mention of his miscalculation regarding Glory Mooncalled didn't let the wind out of his sails. While Maya watched him nervously, unsure where she stood in his bachelor household, he crowed at me and I tried to shut him out.

I emptied my pockets, putting little bottles onto the shelf where the dread key had been hidden. We would do the obvious with that. There were no protective spells on it, only charms meant to fit it to the lock it served. I would cut it up and scatter the pieces among several scrap dealers. It would be no problem once it was melted down. That should've been done in the old days.

I placed the coin from the Blue Bottle on a shelf with memorabilia from other cases. I wished I had the one from Jill's place instead. It would've meant more and would've reminded me more strongly of our fallibility. I wondered what she would do.

She'd survive. She was a survivor. In a way, I wished her well. I wished her free of the burden of her past.

As I lifted an iron chain and rock pendant from around my neck I hit the point where I'd had enough of the Dead Man. "You blew it on Jill, Old Bones. She sucked you up. You were so damned proud because you spotted that key that you never looked at what she was hiding behind her worry."

You can shut him out or hide your thoughts from him if you concentrate. Obviously, Jill had kept the whereabouts of the Relics from him by worrying about the key, which was of no value to her anyway.

That slowed him down. But instead of confessing a shortcoming he changed the subject. *Why have you been wearing that rock? Have you joined one of the cults?*

"Not hardly." I grinned. "Sadler gave me this little gizmo. It keeps the thunder lizards away. In all the excitement that night he forgot to take it back. I didn't remind him. It might come in handy someday."

He gave me a big dose of that mental noise which serves him as laughter. *It might at that. It might at that.* I got a hint that his thoughts had turned to Maya. He sent, *I have stretched myself unreasonably rescuing you from the consequences of your actions this time. I am going to take a nap.*

That was as close as he could get to saying he approved of a female friend of mine.

I went into the kitchen and told Dean he had his nights off to go home again, starting immediately, and hastened him out the door over his protests.

The city buzzed for days about the reappearance of the Terrell Relics. Once that became old news, though, it looked like we were in for a quiet winter.

Then somebody raided Chattaree, stealing a fortune in gold and silver and gems from the altars. No villains were identified. The Church suspected darko-breed street gangs because of profane graffiti left at the scene.

I stayed away from Morley's place. My contacts told me the Chattaree raiders had used a variety of nuisance spells to neutralize the priests who responded to the initial alarm. I didn't want to be in the place if a gang of unhappy Churchmen turned up. From what Saucerhead told me, though, I gathered Morley didn't change his life-style.

When Chodo Contague decides to do something he sticks with it till it gets done. For eight months he masterminded and underwrote the siege of Copperhead Bar, employing a full-time staff of temporary employees numbering as many as a hundred. By the end of that eighth month he'd thrown damned near every rat, mouse, and bug in TunFaire at the island. He'd foiled four rescue attempts by the Sons of Hammon. He'd survived several attacks by eight-limbed devils conjured by the dead Loghyr. A very stubborn man, Chodo Contague.

He had a purpose behind his purpose, of course. He wasn't just settling a score, he was making a high-profile effort to show the world what you were in for if you pissed him off. I didn't look forward to that inevitable day when our careers pushed along irreconcilable paths. But for the moment he owed me and would do most anything for me.

For me it was a quiet, lazy winter for about ten days.